reading I had to try not to turn the page. I was intrigued to know how the story would unwind.' Megan, 11

'Wow! Secret Breakers is an irresistible book that made me curious about what it would be like to be one of the characters breaking mysterious real-life codes!' Elly, 11

'It's an extremely intriguing book. Once you've read one bit it's like it superglues your eyes to the book! You just want to read it all!' AJ, 10

'The book's a real mystery. It's like a code itself! I can't wait to find out what the rest of the story brings! It's addictive!' Eden, 11

'Full of surprises. A journey of adventure. To stop reading is not an option!' Lauren, 10

'Real codes. Real adventure. When you start to read you never want to stop.' Clarisse, 11

'Really exciting! Like nothing I've ever read before!' Talia, 14

'It is so intriguing you can't pull yourself away!' Mia, 10

'An exciting story that keeps you constantly thinking.' Harry, 11

'A number one must read!' Amee-Lee, 11

Also by H. L. Dennis

SECRET BREAKERS

SECRET BREAKERS

THE PIRATE'S SWORD

H. L. Dennis

Illustrations by Meggie Dennis

Hodder Children's Books

A division of Hachette Children's Books

Copyright © 2014 H. L. Dennis

Logoneo illustrations © 2014 H. L. Dennis and Meggan Dennis

First published in Great Britain in 2014
by Hodder Children's Books

The right of H. L. Dennis to be identified as the Author
of the Work has been asserted by her in accordance with
the Copyright, Designs and Patents Act 1988.

A Catalogue record for this book is available from the British Library

ISBN 978 0 340 99965 3

Typeset in AGaramond Book by Avon DataSet Ltd,
Bidford-on-Avon, Warwickshire

Printed and bound in Great Britain by
Clays Ltd, St Ives plc

The paper and board used in this paperback by Hodder Children's Books
are natural recyclable products made from wood grown in
sustainable forests. The manufacturing processes conform to the
environmental regulations of the country of origin.

Hodder Children's Books
a division of Hachette Children's Books
338 Euston Road, London NW1 3BH
An Hachette UK company
www.hachette.co.uk

For Beverley Birch
who supported this adventure from the beginning;

For Naomi Greenwood
who helped it through to the end;

and for Dave Green and all our American family –
who shared this story overseas!

In every adult there lurks a child – an eternal child, something that is always becoming and is never completed.

Carl Jung

Perhaps true imagination, nothing to do with fantasy, consists of seeing everyday objects with the eyes of the earliest days.

Paz

1

The Enemy Closing In

The blades of the helicopter sliced the air. The engine throbbed. Kerrith Vernan leant against the window so she could see more clearly. Waves churned below as the ragged edge of the cliff-face drew closer. She was excited. Annoyed, but still excited.

The man beside her was looking down at the floor and groaning loudly. He was one of the reasons Kerrith was annoyed. 'Look at the view, Morgan. We're nearly there.'

He gulped and closed his eyes.

'Oh, for goodness' sake, man. What use will you be to me if you can't bear to look at things?'

Morgan opened one eye. His face was twitching and there was a bubble of spit on his top lip.

Kerrith wrinkled her nose. He'd better not be sick. That would just about finish her off.

The helicopter banked to the left and the cliff was so close Kerrith was sure that if she leant out of the window she'd be able to skim her hand along the ridge of white chalk.

'I'm sorry, ma'am. You were saying.'

'Friedman's mine. Of all of them, *I'm* the one to take him in. You understand me?' She was covering her tracks; making up for the disaster of a few weeks ago.

The helicopter dipped and Morgan put both hands up to his face.

This was ridiculous. Level Five of the government code-cracking Black Chamber had decided Kerrith needed an assistant. Probably because of what happened with Friedman. She knew now that Morgan Summerfield was going to be no good to her at all.

The beach was rushing up to meet them; the smallest pebbles and dust whipped into a swirling haze. Kerrith swung open the door and stepped out, ducking her head to avoid the churning of the rotary blades. She guessed Morgan was behind her. She didn't check. She had a job to do.

The landlord of the Birling Gap Hotel was having a bad week. A bird flu scare over Easter had pretty much driven away all his guests. Eleven residents was hardly what you called bumper holiday custom.

He was used to the sound of the helicopter. Search and rescue around the cliffs was common. He wasn't so used to the sound of thumping on the bar door.

'All right. I'm coming. I'm coming!' Maybe things were picking up at last.

The door was barely open before a woman had forced her way inside. Her sidekick in the suit tumbled in behind her looking almost as green as the wallpaper.

'This man,' said the woman, waving a photograph in her hand. 'He's here?'

The landlord took the photo. 'Friedman. Yeah—'

'And he's healthy?'

It was an odd question to ask but then lots of discussions at the moment centred around the epidemic so the landlord wasn't surprised. 'He hasn't got flu if that's what you mean?'

It was obvious from the woman's scowl this wasn't what she meant.

'He was injured,' added the landlord. 'Came here from hospital.'

The woman's eyes flickered. 'Alone?'

'No, no. There's a whole group of people. Friends of his, I think.'

Something about his answer seemed to excite the

woman. 'You know you're breaking at least seven of the recent epidemic quarantine regulations by letting them stay here together?'

The owner knew that. He also knew that if he didn't let paying guests stay when they wanted to, he'd be out of business.

'Who's with him? I need names from the register. Hurry!'

'Guest details are private. I couldn't possibly—'

The woman stepped closer to the desk. 'I think you'll find you could.'

The landlord reached for the register. He didn't want any trouble. 'A group of them. Booked in by some guy named Smithies.'

'He's in charge,' the woman snapped in the suited man's direction and he scrabbled in his briefcase and took out a notebook to write things down.

'Two other old guys. Mr Bray and Mr Ingham. One of them's got allergies but assured me it wasn't the flu. A woman – Miss Tandari. Smithies' secretary maybe. And the American guy with all the money – Fabyan. Settled everything in advance.'

'And children?'

The landlord looked down again. 'I'm not really happy about—'

The woman slapped her hand on the desk beside the

register. Her fingers splayed across the photo of Friedman's face.

'OK. Five kids. The oldest one – Kitty McCloud. Think she's injured a bit as well. Two boys, one of them quite a good musician, Sheldon Wentworth. And the joker, Hunter Jenkins. Two girls. Tusia something . . . can't pronounce it. She's Russian, I think. Plays a lot of chess. And the old man's granddaughter. Brodie Bray. She seems the most shook up by everything.' He looked up from the register.

'That's all of them!' snarled the woman. 'All of the has-beens and wannabes who hang out at Bletchley and won't leave MS 408 alone.'

The landlord had no idea what she was talking about.

'Friedman's room. I need you to—'

'Oh, no. I'm sorry. Like I say, guest privacy is something—'

The woman closed her hand on the photograph and tightened her fist like a claw. Crumpled edges of the photo leaked through her fingers.

The landlord put the register back behind the desk and reached for the keys. 'This is against policy. I really shouldn't—'

The woman followed him down the corridor, her breath hot against his shoulder. The suited man and the crew from the helicopter were close behind.

The landlord fumbled for the key and turned it in the lock.

The woman pushed past him into the room.

It was empty.

The only sign the room had recently been used was the screwed-up Easter egg wrapper discarded on the end of the bed.

Brodie saw the lighthouse clearly. The light was carving into the sky. And in the light a man was hanging and unless she reached him he was going to die. There was water all around her. She was fighting and struggling but instead of getting closer to the lighthouse she was getting further and further away. Like she did every night.

And then, like he did every night, the hanging man slipped free from the light and fell.

Brodie sat bolt upright in her bed. Her sheets had twisted round her in the struggle. She could barely move her arms.

Her head was thumping but the noise wasn't just inside her head. There was a banging on the window. And someone was calling to her just like the hanging man had called to her in the dream.

Brodie fought free of the bedclothes and stumbled to the door.

'Hunter, what you doing? It's the middle of the night.'

He didn't answer but pushed inside the room.

Tusia had jumped up from her own bed and was fumbling her way into a dressing-gown.

'You OK, B? You look terrible.'

'It's just . . .'

Hunter rested his hand on her arm. 'I know,' he said quietly. She'd told him about the dreams. 'And I'm sorry and everything. But Smithies sent me to get you both. He needs us all in the mansion.'

'What? Why?'

'We need to leave Station X,' he said. 'Now!'

It took Team Veritas less than five minutes to assemble in the ballroom.

'I'm sorry,' Smithies said. He was holding a newspaper in his hand. 'It's the only way.'

Mr Bray took the newspaper article and read the headline aloud. 'SEASIDE HOTELIER ARRESTED FOR ALLOWING GROUP TO STAY IN EPIDEMIC HOTSPOT.'

'I don't understand,' Miss Tandari said. 'They sent Robbie back to us and now they're closing in again?'

Brodie looked across the room. Robbie Friedman was standing by the window. The man who fell from the lighthouse every night in her dreams had his back to the room, his shoulders hunched, his bandaged hands hanging awkwardly at his side. 'They're playing a game with us,' Friedman mumbled. 'I suppose they thought I'd die where they left me. They never reckoned my daughter would rescue me.'

He turned and Brodie smiled awkwardly. It still felt so new to know that Friedman was her dad.

'They hoped that little game at the lighthouse would finish us all off. Put out the fire of wanting to know the truth about MS 408.'

'Yeah, well. They were wrong,' said Sheldon.

'But it means they're back on our case,' said Ingham, flapping the newspaper again. 'They didn't expect us to keep going and they'll be wanting revenge.'

'That's why we need to leave,' said Smithies. 'For America.'

'The States?' said Friedman. 'You're sure?'

Brodie wasn't convinced that Smithies was sure . . . but he was determined. There was no doubting that. 'We've got to track down the lost Knights of Neustria ring. That's our best lead.'

Friedman held his bandaged hand up and winced from the pain. 'Hold on. Knights of Neustria. Lost rings. I can't keep up with all this.'

Brodie thought that was probably an understatement. Since he'd been missing from the team and held captive by Level Five, the secret breakers had discovered so much. The most shocking news was that Friedman was Brodie's dad and that he hadn't betrayed the team or her mum when she was dying, even though they'd all believed he had. But there'd been other stuff. About MS 408, the coded book they were trying to read and that Level Five was so keen they left alone. There were so many gaps to fill in, Brodie wasn't sure how Smithies could begin to explain.

'Start with the Knights,' offered Tusia.

Smithies blew out a breath. 'OK. We think now that the five-hundred-year-old manuscript MS 408 was written by members of a secret society called the Knights of Neustria.' He pointed to a chart where each of the knights they'd learnt about was listed under one of three symbols: a griffin, a phoenix or a branch. 'The Knights wrote in code and left messages in all sorts of things like poems and pictures and songs.'

'And we think the messages were about the place called Avalon,' continued Tusia. 'And we don't think it's a made-up place any more. We found a monument to a girl called Renata and it said she'd been there.'

'And these rings you mentioned?' asked Friedman.

RECAP

500 year old manuscript

↓

MS 408

TOP SECRET

↓

written by members of a Secret Society

↓

The Knights of Neustria

↓

Messages in code: poems, pictures + songs

About Avalon

↓

Shugborough Hall → Shepherds Monument → showed Renata had been there

3 rings for the original Knights of Neustria

His mother was Lucia
↓
had a servant called Beale

1 was owned by an American called Astor
↓
he drowned on the Titanic

'Belonged to the Knights of Neustria. We think there were three, like there were three original Knights, and we know that one of the rings was inherited by an American called Astor whose dad died on the *Titanic*.'

'And you think we should find this ring?'

'I think we should leave this country,' said Smithies, taking the newspaper and folding it precisely. 'Level Five are obviously not happy you survived. We need to get as far away from them as we can. Tracking the ring makes perfect sense. It might have another message from the Knights on it.'

'And it could lead us to a map of Avalon,' said Tusia.

'Now, hold on,' warned Smithies. 'We don't know there'll be a map. All we can do is keep hoping that if all the clues really lead to Avalon, like we think they do, then one day soon we'll find some way of working out where it is.'

Brodie was used to Smithies making his 'cautious teacher' speech. The adults on Team Veritas were always trying to make sure they took nothing for granted. They were making connections but nothing could be totally certain.

'Hold the ketchup,' said Hunter. 'I know the ring's the thing we need to find. But you're forgetting our other lead. We've got to track down a man named Beale.'

Bedivere	Amren (Bedivere's son)	Eneuvac (daughter of Bedivere)
Hans of Aachen (Orphan of the Flames)	Sir Nicholas Bacon (father of Sir Francis)	The Clay family of Piercefield
Hans' father Henry (jailor to Thomas Malory)		Mr Willer (the sweep at Piercefield)
Elgar (writer of the Dorabella Cipher)	Sir Francis Bacon (writer of New Atlantis)	
Van der Essen (writer of the Firebird Code)	Lord Anson (2 beast crest making him fit into the Griffin line)	Samuel Taylor Coleridge
		Tennyson (member of the Cambridge Apostles)
Sir Thomas Malory (writer of Morte D'Arthur)		Thomas Elliot (grave in Westminster Abbey)

'Beale?' said Fabyan. 'What's he got to do with anything?'

'He was a servant. Worked in Shugborough Hall where we found that monument to Renata. After she died, he left England with Renata's mother, Lucia.'

Fabyan narrowed his eyes in concentration. The American businessman hadn't been with them when they'd worked out those details about the servant. 'Beale, you say?'

'Yep. When Lucia went back to Italy, the Anson family sent Thomas with her.'

Fabyan looked even more confused. 'Thomas? I thought you said his name was Beale?'

'Well, yeah. Thomas Beale. His full name was Thomas Jefferson Beale.'

Fabyan's eyes widened. His eyebrows lifted. '*What* was his name?'

'Thomas Jefferson Beale. Why?'

'Have you gone totally mad?' Smithies had his glasses balanced precariously on the end of his nose as he stared at Fabyan, who was darting for the door, his arms raised above his head, his lips twitching. 'I've just explained we need to get out of here. Level Five will want revenge and we need to be gone.'

'So we need to hurry, then,' the billionaire urged,

his red leather boots clipping against the floor. 'There's something we can't go anywhere without!'

He led the way out of the mansion, across the gravelled drive and past the stable block where the zebras were sleeping, to the Ice House. The small hexagonal building was being used as a storeroom for all of Fabyan's belongings which had been shipped over from America. 'Come on,' he called, rushing inside and then returning with a hammer swinging madly from his hand. 'We've got to take this with us!'

Brodie's head was still throbbing from the dream and she was pretty sure they didn't need to take a hammer with them, wherever it was they were going.

Fabyan was waiting now in front of a large packing-case which stood, like an upright coffin, in the corner of the room. He began to swing at the lid of the packing-case with the claw of the hammer. Straw streamed from the ever widening opening as he levered against the lid to get it free.

'Stand back!' he yelled, as the final nails loosened. There was a shuddering, and Brodie was sure the ground moved. The lid of the case rocked slightly and then fell, as a cloud of dust and straw funnelled into the air.

Tusia covered her face and tried not to inhale. Beside

Colonel Fabyan

→ billionaire

Kept pet monkeys + bears

Lived at Riverbank USA

Got a letter from George L. Hart

dated December 1924

asked to look at some coded writing

That's what we do!

her, Sicknote reached for his asthma medication and gulped at it determinedly.

Brodie peered through the swirling dust as it cleared.

The case was crammed with weird objects. Giant ostrich eggs encased in glass; something which looked suspiciously like an Egyptian mummy; a small clay disc with strange hieroglyphs printed in a spiral; Native American headdresses and a necklace made out of shark teeth.

'What the low-fat yogurt is all this?' quizzed Hunter.

'Just trinkets. But this is what you have to see before we go!' Fabyan pulled out an enormous stack of envelopes and flicked through them like a poker player looking for the winning card. 'Aha. Here it is. Knew I'd packed it.'

'Packed what?' urged Sheldon.

'This. A letter to my great-grandfather.'

Brodie knew the story about Fabyan's great-granddad. Colonel Fabyan had also been a billionaire. He kept pet bears and monkeys in his home in Riverbank in the USA. And he collected unusual things from around the world. But what he was most famous for was his work on codes.

Fabyan flapped the paper flat with a flick of his wrist. 'This is a letter from a man called George L. Hart. It's dated December 1924 and it's asking my great-grandfather to take a look at some particular coded writing.'

'The Voynich Manuscript?' asked Tusia. 'MS 408?'

'No. This letter asks Fabyan to look at some coded documents by a certain Thomas Jefferson Beale. And once we're in the air to America I'll tell you all about them.'

'Ma'am, you can't go in there!' The secretary jumped up from her seat and a telephone earpiece fell from her head.

Kerrith wasn't listening. She had to see the Director. To explain what had happened before he heard from someone else.

The office, just like all the rooms she'd searched in the hotel at Birling Gap, was empty.

'Ma'am, please. This is a private office. Appointments have to be made. You can't just—'

'Where is he?'

'The Director's away on business. A very important meeting. I have to insist you leave and make arrangements to come back later.'

Kerrith steadied herself against the Director's desk. It was totally clear of paperwork except for a small scroll kept unrolled by a paperweight. A sword in a stone.

The families sent the passports to PO Box 111 for collection. Tusia's came with a long letter. She was red-eyed when she'd finished reading. Even Sheldon seemed a little choked by the note wrapped around his. Seemed his mum was missing him, although he wasn't sure if this was really because she missed his and Kitty's help in the kitchen.

There was no note with Hunter's passport. He checked three times.

'It doesn't matter, B,' he said. 'My parents have important things to do.'

Brodie didn't know what to say to him.

They walked together around the lake and she made sure that she took the worst of the splash from the water feature before they joined the others.

Chartering a private plane meant that any customs regulations about bird flu quarantine could be avoided. Fabyan's money had many advantages. It also meant the team could fly in total privacy and were free to talk about Thomas Jefferson Beale. But before they could get to him there was a new member of the team they had to talk about.

After months of leaving her at home while he worked, Mr Smithies had finally told his wife all about what Team Veritas were up to.

'I think it's about time she was involved,' said Brodie, looking down the plane at the rather scared-looking woman who was seated next to Smithies. It was easier for Brodie. She'd met Mrs Smithies before and knew all about how damaged she was.

'Did they really have a daughter who died?' whispered Hunter. 'That's terrible.'

'So terrible Mrs Smithies never recovered,' said Brodie. 'Smithies never told her about his work at Station X or any of the codes. But I guess he can't leave her behind any more. Not now we're going so far.'

'I think she'll be OK,' said Tusia wisely. 'I mean, we've got our fair share of damaged people here, don't you think?'

Brodie wasn't sure if Tusia was looking at Friedman or Sicknote but her friend had a point.

Hunter tapped Brodie gently on the arm.

'Hey, I'm not damaged,' she said defensively.

'OK. If you say so, B. I just thought, you know, losing your mum. And then the shock of finding your dad.'

Brodie didn't know where to look. 'I'm OK. Honest.'

Hunter didn't say any more, but instead he swivelled his chair round to face the centre of the cabin. 'So, Fabyan. How about keeping our minds off the fact that we're thousands of feet above the Atlantic Ocean and telling us about this Thomas Jefferson Beale character.'

'Sure, if you're all ready.'

Brodie was keen for Fabyan to start talking. Details about codes were probably just what she needed to distract her from how tangled up she felt inside. Two weeks wasn't long to know about having a dad. It was even less time to take on board that her granddad had known the truth and chosen not to tell her. She was nowhere near knowing how to work out how she felt about that. But stories and codes had taken her mind off things before. She just hoped they would again.

'The Beale Papers were a series of three coded documents written by Thomas Jefferson Beale,' began Fabyan. 'In 1820, Beale put the Papers in a box and gave them to a friendly innkeeper called Robert Morriss. Beale said that if he didn't return to the inn before ten years had passed, then Morriss was to open the box and try and decode the Papers. Beale promised he'd send Morriss extra things he needed to help with the code, but no documents ever came. And Morriss forgot all about the box. He didn't open it again until twenty-three years later.'

'What a Bourbon biscuit,' groaned Hunter. 'Don't tell me. When he opened the box he had no idea what the codes said.'

'Exactly,' said Fabyan. 'He couldn't solve a thing. After a while, addled by years of trying to break the secret, Morriss handed the Papers to a friend. This friend used the words of the American Declaration of Independence as a key, and deciphered one of the codes.'

Brodie felt her skin prickle with excitement. 'The Declaration of Independence?' she confirmed.

Fabyan looked surprised by her enthusiasm. 'Yes, why?'

'Because we found a copy at Shugborough Hall.'

'Seriously?' he said. 'That's great.'

'So this encoded Paper,' said Tusia, pushing forward. 'Once it was translated, what did it say?'

'That Beale had hidden a huge amount of treasure in the hills in Bedford County, Virginia, USA. It explained the other encoded Papers would reveal *who* should inherit the treasure when it was found and *where* exactly it was hidden.'

'And no one's broken the other two codes?' asked Hunter.

Fabyan shook his head. 'Which is why this letter was written to my great-grandfather asking for his help.'

Brodie had to admit the prospect of finding treasure hidden in the mountains of Virginia was exciting and the story was certainly helping her relax.

But she wasn't quite sure how any of this would help them find Avalon. 'What's the connection with MS 408?' she asked.

Fabyan looked around for help, deflated a little like a balloon which had sprung a slow leak.

It was Kitty who answered. 'We think this woman called Lucia that Thomas Jefferson Beale was paid to look after had been to Avalon, right?' she said tentatively.

There was a murmur of agreement.

'And perhaps she had treasure from Avalon?'

'That's what we thought,' said Sicknote. 'Nothing definite but that's what we worked out at Shugborough.'

'Then perhaps she gave some treasure to Beale,' Kitty said, 'and he buried it and hid details about where it was, in the three coded Beale Papers.'

'So,' said Brodie cautiously. 'If we find the Beale treasure, what we *might* be finding is treasure from Avalon! Perfect!'

The Home of the Boron Diamond

The limousine had blacked-out windows. The Director of Level Five of the Black Chamber could see what was happening outside but no one could see in. This was how it should be. There were only certain things the general public needed to know. Beyond the window, a reporter held a camera and aimed wildly at the car like a child trying to master the art of paintballing. The Director smirked. Even if the junior hack did get a photo it would be disposed of and he'd be dealt with. The Tyrannos Group had rules about that. They had rules about everything. Absolutely no press reporting of their activities was part of the deal.

The Director had waited nearly ten years to get an invitation. The yearly meetings of the group were open to a select few: the greatest brains in the world; the most influential members of society; the richest. The meetings covered a range of subjects, the discussions were far-reaching. Control of knowledge, though, was always number one on the agenda.

The group had toyed with him for months now. The scrolls they'd sent to him had been a tease. Notifications edged with black and stamped with an emblem in each of the four corners made it clear he was being watched. He'd left the latest scroll on his desk but he could see it in his mind – the letter 'T' embossed in gold and raised at the centre. This scroll was an invitation to join.

The air in the limousine was humid despite the attempts of the air-conditioning to keep the temperature controlled. He reached forward and pressed the button on the side of the window. There was a small electric hum and the window slid down a crack. The opening was tiny, just a slice, but allowed in enough daylight for him to notice the face of the reporter as a suited man took his camera from him. The Director tried to read the reporter's face. His expression struck him as sad and this was an uncomfortable sight. Distasteful even. The Director grimaced and pressed the switch once more. However stifling the air inside the limo was, it was better than the air outside. The window slid closed but not before a mosquito had found its way into the car. It landed on the back of the Director's neck. The Director shook his head in annoyance but the frantic insect, rattled by its unexpected confinement, bit into his flesh. The Director swore, shook the insect away and thumped his hand hard against the window. The squashed body of the mosquito smeared across the blackened glass leaving behind a bloody trail. The Director turned away.

It was a while before he moved once more to face the glass and by then the limo had pulled up the gravelled drive and stopped outside the hotel. Doormen scuttled forward to greet guests as they emerged from their vehicles. The Director joined the throng and made his way up the steps into the hotel foyer where waiters carrying silver trays offered drinks and cocktails. He took a glass and swilled the amber liquid over the ice cubes before taking a sip. The drink burned his throat as he swallowed, but it was a pleasant sensation, one he enjoyed.

'So, you made the invitation list at last,' came a voice from behind him.

The Director turned and a tear of alcohol splashed from his glass and trickled down his wrist.

'Periander. Good to see you.' The Director tried to hide the note of irritation in his voice.

The other man beamed a smile; his whitened, American-straight teeth flashed as skin devoid of wrinkles pulled tight beside his eyes. 'I wondered, if you pestered them enough, whether they'd eventually let you in. How goes it over the pond on that little island of yours?'

The Director sipped once more from his drink. It was hardly fair to refer to a country which once had control of the British Empire as a little island.

'I heard rumblings about amateurs messing with MS 408.'

The Director kept the glass at his lips.

'You see, my thinking all along was *they* should have shredded the thing the moment it turned up in 1912. All this trying to play things cool was a bad move if you ask me.'

The Director didn't remember ever having asked him.

'I mean, a really tight rein's got to be kept on the whole thing. Any investigation, or attempts to make sense of the manuscript, stamped out from the start, I reckon.'

The Director moved his glass in an ever decreasing circle. 'We've got the situation under control,' he said in a way he hoped sounded convincing.

'Under control or just under observation?'

The Director considered for a moment. 'We went with trying to close them down quietly. We've gone with disruption to the personal dynamics and we've got eyes on everything "the amateurs" do. Besides, whatever you've heard, these guys messing with the manuscript are small fry. "Has-beens" and "nothing-yets". Three descendants of code-crackers from the past who reckon they've got skills with story, shape and number. And some new fairly new kid who reckons he's good at music but managed to get himself thrown out of more than one school. The adults are oddballs. They've worked at the Black Chamber before but they're nothing special. And then there's Kitty. She's new. None of them have got a hope of piecing it all together and if they do, like I've just said, we've got them covered.'

The American nodded, although it was obvious he wasn't convinced. 'You're here because *they* are worried,' he said, gesturing towards unseen forces in the sky. 'Worried the whole thing could unravel if we're not all really careful. If you've been asked here *they* must want reassurance everything's really in hand. Things can't get messy. You must exercise control. Control is key, you know.' His eyes sparkled like the notion excited him. 'It's like the problems we faced in our own backyard when we were trying to educate the natives.

27

And in Australia too. "Assimilation" – that's what's required. Bringing everyone round to the "right" way of thinking. One clear world-view. People don't need their own stories and their own histories. We've got to make them see there's a right way to view the world and things can't afford to be cluttered. Got to keep things simple. Our way is best.' He thumped the Director hard on the shoulder and the ice cubes jangled in the glass. 'No one said it was going to be easy. Good job you're here. It'll give you a chance to be reminded how important our task is.'

The Director nodded. Things were under control. He was sure. Site Three was working overtime with the new detainees moved on from London and abroad. He was going to explain the whole system to Kerrith once he got back, and the scale of the underground operation was bound to impress her. It was true though. Those busybodies based at Bletchley were an irritation. But nothing more. They weren't, in any way, a threat. How could something so small threaten something so big?

The Director downed the rest of his drink and put the glass on the silver tray. Then he lifted his hand to the back of his neck. A small, raised lump throbbed under his skin. It hurt.

* * *

28

Brodie was pretty sure she was going to like America. Fabyan gave instructions to the drivers to take them 'to the Hyphen' and Brodie pressed her nose against the window trying to take in all the sights of New York City as the yellow cab crawled through the traffic.

'The Hyphen,' mused Hunter, chomping on something he'd retrieved from the bottom of his flight bag. 'Funny name for a hotel.'

'It's the Waldorf-Astoria,' explained Tandi. 'People here just use a nickname.'

Brodie's eyes widened as the car pulled to a halt in the middle of Park Avenue. She didn't mind what the locals called it. She just called it beautiful.

'Welcome to the Big Apple, ma'am,' said a smiling doorman dressed in black and wearing a peaked hat trimmed with white braiding.

Brodie beamed back eagerly. She'd absolutely no idea what she was supposed to say as he ushered her forward, his white gloved hands signalling the way.

Fabyan led them into the main lobby and the sounds of the traffic from the busy streets outside faded away. The ceiling above them was patterned white with gold. At the back of the lobby was dark oak panelling and the ceiling was held up by thick marble columns polished so brightly they shone like mirrors. In the centre of the lobby was a large golden clock on top of a carved

29

wooden tower. Brodie checked against the time on her New York watch. She felt a little strange. She guessed it was the jet-lag.

'Wow. So why are we staying here?' Hunter whistled through his teeth, turning round on the spot very slowly as if he was in charge of a minicam and wanted to capture every detail of the scene. 'Makes a change from the Plough or the Carthorse.'

'We're looking for a ring owned by someone called Astor,' said Fabyan. 'Makes sense to come to their hotel.'

'Oh. I see,' said Hunter, stopping his spinning. '*Astor. Astoria.* I get it. This place is connected to John Jacob Astor IV who owned the Knight of Neustria ring then, is it?'

Smithies seemed glad he'd worked out the connection.

'It's still totally over the top,' said Tusia, grimacing at the tall potted plants and ferns lining the edges of the lobby as if it were their fault they'd been chosen to fit into such a beautiful scene. 'When you think of all the poverty in the world and the conditions some people have to live in.'

'Can't complain about staying here, though,' said Tandi quietly. 'If it helps us get closer to answers.'

Fabyan turned from the front desk where he'd been

checking in. 'Exactly. So follow me,' he said, winking and leading the way towards a long corridor with black and white marble flooring and high domed ceiling hung with chandeliers. 'Time to see what I've arranged.'

'Why the Waldorf salad d'you want to go shopping?' groaned Hunter as he stood surveying the incredible stateroom Fabyan had guided them to.

Brodie had to agree, it did seem a bit strange to want to go to a shop so soon after they'd arrived, and she couldn't imagine there was anything at all they'd need to get themselves if they were staying in a place like this. Fabyan's rooms were called the Royal Suite and the parlour would certainly have fitted in completely with the decoration of the rooms at the Royal Pavilion in Brighton they'd visited so many months before. She stared at the golden curtain drapes, the thick rose-covered carpet and the crystal chandelier before turning back to face Fabyan.

'We don't all have to go,' he said. 'I mean, it's probably even better some of us stay here. But we're here to break secrets, not to vacation, remember. And there's one particular New York shop I think we should be taking a trip to, just as soon as we can. Tiffany's.'

'Who the peach Melba is Tiffany?'

'The most famous jeweller's in the world. And some of us have an appointment.'

Tandi stood in the office part of the suite. 'You need help with that, sir?'

Smithies laughed. 'We've known each other five years, Tandi. I think we've gone beyond formal titles.'

'You were my boss, Jon. Some habits are hard to forget.'

'But, yes. You can help me with these.' He was struggling with a large case that was stuffed with books. 'I know this looks more like the luggage Brodie would bring, but it's a little light reading I've been wading through.' He lifted the top pile of books and put them on the table.

Tandi took another pile and put them beside the first.

'I've been doing some research about Avalon,' Smithies explained. 'I think I'm nearly ready to talk to the kids about the sort of place it is.'

Tandi emptied the final pile from the case. A book by Archibald MacLeish was on the top. 'Poetry books?'

'Some of them. And some of them reference books. That author you have there has written quite a lot about the matter.'

'Not just poems, then?'

'And not just stories,' added Smithies. 'I think Avalon's a much bigger idea than the kids understand.'

'You think they're just hoping it's a place full of magic, then?'

'Oh, it's full of magic all right. But a much stronger type than the one they'll be thinking of.'

'So you should explain all this to them. Let them know what you've worked out.'

'I will. But I have to be sure they're ready first. And I have to be sure I'm ready too.'

Hunter flicked through the room service menu and jotted down a list of snacks for later when the rest of the team got back to the hotel. Friedman stood at the window looking out at the busy street. 'Is she OK, Hunter?' he said quietly, keeping his eyes firmly locked on the traffic.

Hunter put down his pen. 'B, you mean?'

'It can't be easy for her. I mean, finding out about me. She must've been so angry when I didn't come back.'

Hunter remembered Brodie's confusion when they hadn't known that Friedman had been kept captive by Level Five. How she couldn't understand why Friedman never returned to explain his side of the story. How she'd told him about her dreams. He decided it wouldn't

33

do any good to share any of this. 'She'll be fine. Honest. You just have to give her time.'

American flags flew from poles outside the store. The building was polished granite and each of the window displays was tiny, containing just a selection of intricate silver or white gold pieces. 'Real wealth doesn't have to make a peacock of itself,' joked Fabyan.

Brodie lifted her hands from the glass. 'So how much do those necklaces cost?'

The golden tooth in Fabyan's smile flashed. 'If you've got to ask the price, you can't afford it.'

There was a bell at the entrance and after Fabyan had waited patiently, the door was swung open.

'Mr Fabyan, sir,' beamed the doorman, once they were safely inside. 'It is, as always, our honour to see you here.'

Fabyan's tooth sparkled even more brightly under the powerful lights.

'Mr Young's waiting for you if you'd be so kind as to follow.'

The doorman led the way through the main store and into a darkened back office where an old man was seated behind a tall desk. He was hunched over, his shoulders bowed and his face contorted so a small tubular viewing device was balanced steadily in the folds of flesh against his left eye. Brodie couldn't think of a name for a person being less appropriate. The man seated before her was anything but young.

The door clicked closed behind them and the old man looked up, the viewing device still attached firmly in position. 'Fabyan,' he boomed in a voice surprisingly strong and loud. 'How good to see you again.' He stood up and the viewing device tumbled from his face and rolled across the green baize on the tabletop. 'You've found me with a boron, I'm afraid. Can't get enough of blue diamonds. Here, take a look.'

He picked up the viewing device and thrust it into Fabyan's eager hand, then motioned to a small black cloth positioned neatly under a bright light just to his left. Brodie could just make out a tiny stone lying on the velvet. Fabyan peered through the optical viewer and gave a sigh like a climber who'd finally reached a viewing point at the top of a mountain. 'Oh look, girls, look.' He passed the device along the line. 'See how the diamond slits the light.'

When it was Brodie's turn, she gasped out loud at what she saw. The tiny object lying on the black velvet shattered the light into splashes of rainbow.

'This beauty will have formed two billion years ago and been forced to the surface of the earth by volcanic eruption,' explained Mr Young. 'Magical, don't you think?'

Brodie thought it was totally magical.

'And so,' Mr Young went on, taking the viewing device from Tusia's rather reluctant hand. 'What brings you here to this part of Manhattan? Surely Tiffany's delivery service to our most loyal of customers could have met your needs.'

'It's your knowledge I'm after, sir,' Fabyan said deferentially. 'Not the sort of gift which can be packaged and tied with a Tiffany bow.'

Mr Young leant forward, intrigue lining the many wrinkles on his face. 'Go on then. You have my undivided attention.'

'It's about a ring,' Fabyan said. 'A very particular ring.'

'Rings *are* my thing.'

'Absolutely. So if anyone can help us, it's you, sir. As jeweller to the Astor family, I wonder if you'd ever come across a ring worn by Mr Astor on his very final voyage on the *Titanic*.'

Mr Young's eyes flickered a little and he moved his hands across his chest in the sign of the cross. 'A regrettable loss. To us all,' he said. 'The Astor family have been our patrons for many years, not least Mr John Astor, who was so tragically taken before his time.'

Fabyan allowed a few moments, acknowledging the jeweller's personal sadness. He took out of his pocket a copy of the painting from Shugborough Hall showing Lady Anson wearing the Coleridge ring on her finger. 'I'm afraid we're trying, if possible, to track down a particular ring Astor had. It's important.'

Mr Young looked offended. 'All jewellery's important, sir. It's an emblem of our love and loss. It's a representation of our most important commitments and achievements. It's a metaphor for all we hope to be, a sparkling gem amid the dust of time.'

The old man certainly loved his job, but Tusia was getting impatient. 'D'you know about Mr Astor's particular ring?' she cut in.

Mr Young flicked his head in her direction and his eyes were steely. Then, clearly made a little afraid by the question, he stood up from the chair and walked across the room to lower the latch on the door. 'It's a while since I've thought of Astor's ring,' he said. 'But a ring of such beauty's hardly something one would forget.'

'You know it, then,' pressed Kitty.

'I know it. It was beautiful and inspired. Many people claim it was that ring which prompted the idea of printing the name "Tiffany" simply and clearly on the jewellery we make here.'

Brodie wasn't quite sure what this meant but waited for Mr Young to explain.

'Oh, many jewellers decide to mark their goods with intricate emblems and designs, but here at Tiffany's the name pressed simply into the metal is enough. Many believe the idea was inspired by Astor's ring.'

'So this ring you're thinking of,' urged Brodie. 'It had a name pressed inside the band?'

The old man nodded.

'And do you remember the name?' she said.

'I remember the feel of the piece. The warmth of the metal and the sparkle and the lustre of the gems. But the name marked on the band, no. I don't remember.'

Fabyan stepped closer. 'Do you know, though, what happened to Astor's ring after the sinking of the *Titanic*? His body was found and he was wearing a ring. Was it the special ring you're thinking of? The one shown here in the painting?'

For a moment Mr Young was unsure how to answer. 'As a jeweller I'm allowed to know about the biggest decisions a man can make in his life. Sometimes, it's just me who understands that one sunny summer's evening a man will sink to his knees and ask a girl to join her life with his. I can be part of the biggest secrets and the biggest dreams, and sometimes, I'm afraid, the biggest disappointments.' He took in another breath. 'And it's therefore my duty, as jeweller to the rich and privileged, to guard safely that privilege they give me.'

Fabyan tapped the old man reassuringly on the shoulder. 'You're not breaking a code of honour. You're just helping a friend.'

'No,' the old man said calmly.

He obviously wasn't going to tell them.

'No. That's not the ring Astor was wearing when his body was recovered.'

Brodie's disappointment turned to despair. This was a disaster. If Astor hadn't been wearing the ring of the Knights of Neustria, and passed this ring on to his unborn son, then where had it gone?

The room was quiet. The electric bulb buzzed and the blue diamond on the velvet cloth splintered the light around it. Then the old man stepped forward and began to whisper. 'Astor didn't die wearing the ring, because by the time he died, he'd swapped it for another.'

The Director was woken by the sound of his BlackBerry beeping. He didn't sleep well on aeroplanes and he was more than annoyed to have been woken up.

He rubbed at his neck and fumbled in his pocket to find his phone. In his half-woken state he could see it was an encrypted message. He pressed the necessary keys to make the translation.

Now he was fully awake. And he was angry.

He'd trusted Kerrith. She'd assured him everything was under control. Accepting the situation had been dealt with was obviously a mistake. He tossed the phone on to the tray table and scratched at his neck. She'd better have answers for him when he got back. And she'd better have something in place to make up for her error.

Mr Young, the jeweller, lifted his head awkwardly, as if the weight of his skull was rather too much for him. 'What I'm about to tell you must never leave this room.'

'You can trust us,' urged Fabyan. 'We know about secrets.'

'And you'll tell no one else.'

'Only those in our party.'

'And you can trust them?'

'Totally.'

Mr Young patted the table, drawing strength from the diamond that still rested there. 'The ring was passed on to the Widener family,' he explained.

Tusia dug Brodie sharply in the ribs. 'Should we have heard of them?'

Brodie couldn't connect the name with anything

they'd discovered but there was something about it which made her think she should know.

'The Widener family are perhaps best known for their support of the Harry Elkins Widener Library at Yale University,' said Mr Young. 'The largest university library in the world.'

That must have been how she knew the name, thought Brodie. Any family who'd funded the biggest university library in the world must have been people she'd read about.

'Or perhaps you've heard of Harry Elkins Widener because he too lost his life aboard the *Titanic*.'

So that could be the reason why she knew the name.

'The library was funded in Harry's memory by his mother, who was also on the tragic ship but survived.'

'And this Harry,' said Tusia, edging forward. 'Did he know John Jacob Astor IV well?'

'Harry was a wealthy young man who liked to collect things. He was most interested, at the time, in collecting books, and so family records show he spent several hours with Astor one night during their time at sea, discussing a book Astor hoped to get hold of. It was a book which had come to Widener's attention quite recently.'

Brodie moved forward on her chair. A book which

Widener family

↓

Harry Elkins Widener memorial Library at Yale

↓

Largest uni. library in the world

died on the Titanic

R.I.P.

Knew John Jacob Astor IV

Heard about an unusual book in 1912

MS408 ??

he wanted the book!

~~~~~~~~~~~~~~~~~~~~~~~~~~~~~~~

Widener traded a ring for a book

↓

Astor gave his ring over first until the book was found!

The Knights of Neustria ring

had come to Widener's notice in 1912. A book wanted by a famous American billionaire. MS 408 had been discovered in 1912. Maybe it was MS 408 Astor was hoping to buy.

'And d'you have any ideas what this book was?' asked Fabyan, winking at Brodie.

'We're not sure of the title, but we do know a trade was struck between the two gentlemen on the night of the 13th April, 1912.'

'The day before the *Titanic* sank,' said Fabyan.

'And what did the trade involve?' pressed Tusia.

'A ring in exchange for this special book. But the trade was *never* completed.'

'So what happened?' urged Brodie.

'It was agreed that when Astor returned to New York he'd take possession of the book Harry valued so greatly and was sure he could get hold of for him. So aboard the ship, as they sailed unknowingly towards their death, Astor made his part of the bargain.'

'He gave Harry the ring?' said Kitty.

Mr Young nodded.

'And was the ring he gave away the Coleridge ring?' said Brodie, pointing once more at the painting.

'From the look of the picture I'd have to say yes.'

'So which ring did Astor leave to his unborn child, then?' asked Tusia.

'As I've explained,' said Mr Young, 'the trade was begun the night before the iceberg. And as a sign of the bargain struck that night, Astor took one of Harry's own rings and it was *this* ring which passed on to his unborn child.'

'But why would Astor do that?' said Brodie sharply. 'Give away this precious ring before he'd got hold of the book he wanted so much.'

'It was a gentlemen's agreement, young lady. A mark of trust.'

'But did the Astor family ever get the book they traded for?'

'No,' said Mr Young sadly.

'So where is it?'

'I don't know.'

'But do you know where the Coleridge ring is?'

'Of course,' said the old man, sitting up straight in the chair, his eyes burning brilliant blue. 'As far as I know the Widener family still have it.'

'I'm telling you. It's the same man,' hissed Friedman, turning from the window. 'The same black car cruising up and down. He's casing the place as he drives.'

'It's New York, Robbie. The city's crawling with sightseers. Of course he's checking out the building. It's one of the best hotels in the world.'

'There's something about it. The way he's looking. It's not—'

Smithies reached out his hand. 'Robbie. You've been through a lot. No one's doubting that. And it's going to play with your mind. It's bound to. But you need to concentrate on getting well. And getting to know your daughter.'

'And how can I do either of those things if they've followed us here?'

'Level Five are thousands of miles away, my friend. We're safe. You have to believe that.'

Friedman turned back to the window. He wasn't sure he knew what to believe any more.

Hunter was in the hotel lobby collecting post from the box system the hotel used for private mail. Fabyan had managed to have shipped over from Riverbank copies of the encoded Beale documents.

'Any luck at the jeweller's?' he asked as he joined those who'd been to Tiffany's waiting for the elevator.

'We've got a lead,' beamed Tusia. 'Fabyan's going to follow it up.'

'Great!' said Hunter, clutching the Papers close to his chest. 'And now we've got a code to crack!' He hesitated for a moment. 'You lot go ahead. I've ordered food.' The elevator doors opened and everyone bundled inside. 'But, B, can you help me just a sec?'

The doors to the elevator hissed close, leaving Brodie and Hunter in the lobby.

'What d'you do that for?' Brodie groaned. 'I'm starving too, you know.'

Hunter grabbed her arm and steered her towards a huge potted plant in the corner of the lobby. 'I know. I know. D'you think I want to miss out on our little buffet?'

This *did* seem unlikely.

'It's just I heard things,' Hunter explained. 'While you lot were gone.'

'And?'

'Friedman. He's worried. Thinks we're being watched, even here.'

'We can't be, can we? Not in America when Level Five are in England.'

'I don't know,' said Hunter. 'But I thought he was paranoid before, and look how that turned out. I just think we've got to be careful, you know. And also,' he added nervously. 'You'll give him a chance, right?'

'A chance to do what?'

'Be a dad, I guess.'

Brodie didn't know what to say.

'I just think he's trying, that's all.'

Brodie was sure she'd never seen Hunter look so sad.

46

* * *

Back at the suite, room service had arrived. After they'd eaten, Tusia spread the Papers across the rose-patterned carpet for everyone to see. She and Brodie skimmed through them so they could explain to the others what they'd been sent.

'Right,' said Tusia, taking a pencil from her topknot and twisting it like a baton. 'Let's go over what we know about this code. Morriss was the innkeeper who Beale left the Papers for. He was the one who didn't open the box when he should've done. And the one who could make no sense of what he saw when he did.'

'Makes it sound like a crime the poor guy couldn't read this stuff,' said Sheldon, rolling his eyes at the mass of pages spread across the floor.

'So,' went on Tusia, 'Morriss eventually asked a friend to help him. Except Morriss's friend couldn't read the Papers either. So this guy, Morriss' friend, asks his own friend. And his name was Ward, and Ward decided the best way to make sense of the code was to get as many people involved as possible.'

'The exact opposite of what the Black Chamber's done with MS 408, then,' said Hunter. 'They see a tricky code and their answer is to ban people looking at it. Ward's idea is to get as many people involved with the code as he can.'

47

'Exactly,' said Brodie. 'So Ward got the three Beale Papers printed in a pamphlet. He hoped if lots of people read the pamphlet, there was more chance of solving the code and finding the treasure.'

'So have we got the pamphlet amongst all this stuff?' said Hunter, licking his fingers and then sinking down to his knees so he could take a closer look.

'Sort of,' said Brodie. 'Fabyan's original copy's now part of the Friedman papers in a museum so apparently they couldn't send us that. But Riverbank Labs had some replicas. This note said there weren't many printed as a fire in the printer's destroyed most of the work.'

'A fire?' said Kitty, raising her eyebrows.

Brodie nodded. 'Sounds suspicious, doesn't it? The pamphlets on the Beale Papers were the only things destroyed. Makes you think someone didn't want these messages translated and so tried to get rid of them.'

'Well, that could link with the government wanting to stop people dealing with the code,' said Friedman. 'I'm just saying. It's not like those in power haven't been known to start fires to get rid of things they didn't want people to see.'

'The fire didn't destroy every copy, though.' Brodie held up the front cover of the pamphlet. 'Riverbank Labs sent over this copy made from the original.'

Thomas Jefferson Beale

wrote 3 coded documents

↓

1820 → Beale put papers in a box

↓

gave box to innkeeper Robert Morriss

↓

told him to open them after 10 years

promised to send extra details

↓

Morriss forgot + opened box 23 years later

↓

Handed papers to a friend

↓

1 paper deciphered using Dec. of Independence

↓

said ~~treasure~~ treasure hidden in Bedford County Virginia ?

? Other 2 codes... where? who will inherit?

'Looks kind of plain if it's trying to tempt people to search for treasure,' said Hunter.

THE

BEALE PAPERS,

CONTAINING

AUTHENTIC STATEMENTS

REGARDING THE

TREASURE BURIED

IN

1819 AND 1821,

NEAR

BUFORDS, IN BEDFORD COUNTY, VIRGINIA,

AND

WHICH HAS NEVER BEEN RECOVERED.

~ ~ ~ ~ ~ ~ ~ ~ ~ ~

PRICE FIFTY CENTS.

~ ~ ~ ~ ~ ~ ~ ~ ~ ~

LYNCHBURG:
VIRGINIAN BOOK AND JOB PRINT,
1885.

'I guess so, but you'll like the next bit.'

Brodie took the pages of the document and passed them over. Hunter looked like he was about to burst.

71, 194, 38, 1701, 89, 76, 11, 83, 1629, 48, 94, 63, 132, 16,
111, 95, 84, 341, 975, 14, 40, 64, 27, 81, 139, 213, 63, 90,
1120, 8, 15, 3, 126, 2018, 40, 74, 758, 485, 604, 230, 436,
664, 582, 150, 251, 284, 308, 231, 124, 211, 486, 225, 401,
370, 11, 101, 305, 139, 189, 17, 33, 88, 208, 193, 145, 1,
94, 73, 416, 918, 263, 28, 500, 538, 356, 117, 136, 219, 27,
176, 130, 10, 460, 25, 485, 18, 436, 65, 84, 200, 283, 118,
320, 138, 36, 416, 280, 15, 71, 224, 961, 44, 16, 401, 39,
88, 61, 304, 12, 21, 24, 283, 134, 92, 63, 246, 486, 682, 7,
219, 184, 360, 780, 18, 64, 463, 474, 131, 160, 79, 73, 440,
95, 18, 64, 581, 34, 69, 128, 367, 460, 17, 81, 12, 103, 820,
62, 116, 97, 103, 862, 70, 60, 1317, 471, 540, 208, 121,
890, 346, 36, 150, 59, 568, 614, 13, 120, 63, 219, 812,
2160, 1780, 99, 35, 18, 21, 136, 872, 15, 28, 170, 88, 4, 30,
44, 112, 18, 147, 436, 195, 320, 37, 122, 113, 6, 140, 8,
120, 305, 42, 58, 461, 44, 106, 301, 13, 408, 680, 93, 86,
116, 530, 82, 568, 9, 102, 38, 416, 89, 71, 216, 728, 965,
818, 2, 38, 121, 195, 14, 326, 148, 234, 18, 55, 131, 234,
361, 824, 5, 81, 623, 48, 961, 19, 26, 33, 10, 1101, 365, 82,
88, 181, 275, 346, 201, 206, 86, 36, 219, 324, 829, 840, 64,
326, 19, 48, 122, 85, 216, 284, 919, 861, 326, 985, 233, 64,
68, 232, 431, 960, 50, 29, 81, 216, 321, 603, 14, 612, 81,
360, 36, 51, 62, 194, 78, 60, 200, 314, 676, 112, 4, 28, 18,
61, 136, 247, 819, 921, 1060, 464, 895, 10, 6, 66, 119, 38,

41, 49, 602, 423, 962, 302, 294, 875, 78, 14, 23, 111, 109,
62, 31, 501, 823, 216, 280, 34, 24, 150, 1000, 162, 286, 19,
21, 17, 340, 19, 242, 31, 86, 234, 140, 607, 115, 33, 191,
67, 104, 86, 52, 88, 16, 80, 121, 67, 95, 122, 216, 548, 96,
11, 201, 77, 364, 218, 65, 667, 890, 236, 154, 211, 10, 98,
34, 119, 56, 216, 119, 71, 218, 1164, 1496, 1817, 51, 39,
210, 36, 3, 19, 540, 232, 22, 141, 617, 84, 290, 80, 46, 207,
411, 150, 29, 38, 46, 172, 85, 194, 39, 261, 543, 897, 624,
18, 212, 416, 127, 931, 19, 4, 63, 96, 12, 101, 418, 16, 140,
230, 460, 538, 19, 27, 88, 612, 1431, 90, 716, 275, 74, 83,
11, 426, 89, 72, 84, 1300, 1706, 814, 221, 132, 40, 102, 34,
868, 975, 1101, 84, 16, 79, 23, 16, 81, 122, 324, 403, 912,
227, 936, 447, 55, 86, 34, 43, 212, 107, 96, 314, 264, 1065,
323, 428, 601, 203, 124, 95, 216, 814, 2906, 654, 820, 2,
301, 112, 176, 213, 71, 87, 96, 202, 35, 10, 2, 41, 17, 84,
221, 736, 820, 214, 11, 60, 760.

'This is it?' he giggled, his eyes as wide as saucers. 'Just numbers? No words to clutter it up?'

'Just numbers,' Brodie said. 'Remember, the Beale Papers were made up of *three* coded pieces of paper. This is Paper number one.'

'And is that the one that's been decoded?' asked Sheldon.

'Nope. No one's got any idea what that one says yet.' Brodie turned the page. '*This* is the one that's been read.'

115, 72, 24, 807, 37, 52, 49, 17, 31, 62, 647, 22, 7, 15, 140,
47, 29, 107, 79, 84, 56, 239, 10, 26, 811, 5, 196, 308, 85,
52, 160, 136, 59, 211, 36, 9, 46, 316, 554, 122, 106, 95, 53,
58, 2, 42, 7, 35, 122, 53, 31, 82, 77, 250, 196, 56, 96, 118,
71, 140, 287, 28, 353, 37, 1005, 65, 147, 807, 24, 3, 8, 12,
47, 43, 59, 807, 45, 316, 101, 41, 78, 154, 1005, 122, 138,
191, 16, 77, 49, 102, 57, 72, 34, 73, 85, 35, 371, 59, 196,
81, 92, 191, 106, 273, 60, 394, 620, 270, 220, 106, 388,
287, 63, 3, 191, 122, 43, 234, 400, 106, 290, 314, 47, 48,
81, 96, 26, 115, 92, 158, 191, 110, 77, 85, 197, 46, 10, 113,
140, 353, 48, 120, 106, 2, 607, 61, 420, 811, 29, 125, 14,
20, 37, 105, 28, 248, 16, 159, 7, 35, 19, 301, 125, 110, 486,
287, 98, 117, 511, 62, 51, 220, 37, 113, 140, 807, 138, 540,
8, 44, 287, 388, 117, 18, 79, 344, 34, 20, 59, 511, 548, 107,
603, 220, 7, 66, 154, 41, 20, 50, 6, 575, 122, 154, 248, 110,
61, 52, 33, 30, 5, 38, 8, 14, 84, 57, 540, 217, 115, 71, 29,
84, 63, 43, 131, 29, 138, 47, 73, 239, 540, 52, 53, 79, 118,
51, 44, 63, 196, 12, 239, 112, 3, 49, 79, 353, 105, 56, 371,
557, 211, 515, 125, 360, 133, 143, 101, 15, 284, 540, 252,
14, 205, 140, 344, 26, 811, 138, 115, 48, 73, 34, 205, 316,
607, 63, 220, 7, 52, 150, 44, 52, 16, 40, 37, 158, 807, 37,
121, 12, 95, 10, 15, 35, 12, 131, 62, 115, 102, 807, 49, 53,
135, 138, 30, 31, 62, 67, 41, 85, 63, 10, 106, 807, 138, 8,
113, 20, 32, 33, 37, 353, 287, 140, 47, 85, 50, 37, 49, 47,
64, 6, 7, 71, 33, 4, 43, 47, 63, 1, 27, 600, 208, 230, 15, 191,
246, 85, 94, 511, 2, 270, 20, 39, 7, 33, 44, 22, 40, 7, 10, 3,
811, 106, 44, 486, 230, 353, 211, 200, 31, 10, 38, 140, 297,

61, 603, 320, 302, 666, 287, 2, 44, 33, 32, 511, 548, 10, 6,
250, 557, 246, 53, 37, 52, 83, 47, 320, 38, 33, 807, 7, 44,
30, 31, 250, 10, 15, 35, 106, 160, 113, 31, 102, 406, 230,
540, 320, 29, 66, 33, 101, 807, 138, 301, 316, 353, 320,
220, 37, 52, 28, 540, 320, 33, 8, 48, 107, 50, 811, 7, 2, 113,
73, 16, 125, 11, 110, 67, 102, 807, 33, 59, 81, 158, 38, 43,
581, 138, 19, 85, 400, 38, 43, 77, 14, 27, 8, 47, 138, 63,
140, 44, 35, 22, 177, 106, 250, 314, 217, 2, 10, 7, 1005, 4,
20, 25, 44, 48, 7, 26, 46, 110, 230, 807, 191, 34, 112, 147,
44, 110, 121, 125, 96, 41, 51, 50, 140, 56, 47, 152, 540, 63,
807, 28, 42, 250, 138, 582, 98, 643, 32, 107, 140, 112, 26,
85, 138, 540, 53, 20, 125, 371, 38, 36, 10, 52, 118, 136,
102, 420, 150, 112, 71, 14, 20, 7, 24, 18, 12, 807, 37, 67,
110, 62, 33, 21, 95, 220, 511, 102, 811, 30, 83, 84, 305,
620, 15, 2, 108, 220, 106, 353, 105, 106, 60, 275, 72, 8, 50,
205, 185, 112, 125, 540, 65, 106, 807, 188, 96, 110, 16, 73,
33, 807, 150, 409, 400, 50, 154, 285, 96, 106, 316, 270,
205, 101, 811, 400, 8, 44, 37, 52, 40, 241, 34, 205, 38, 16,
46, 47, 85, 24, 44, 15, 64, 73, 138, 807, 85, 78, 110, 33,
420, 505, 53, 37, 38, 22, 31, 10, 110, 106, 101, 140, 15, 38,
3, 5, 44, 7, 98, 287, 135, 150, 96, 33, 84, 125, 807, 191, 96,
511, 118, 440, 370, 643, 466, 106, 41, 107, 603, 220, 275,
30, 150, 105, 49, 53, 287, 250, 208, 134, 7, 53, 12, 47, 85,
63, 138, 110, 21, 112, 140, 485, 486, 505, 14, 73, 84, 575,
1005, 150, 200, 16, 42, 5, 4, 25, 42, 8, 16, 811, 125, 160,
32, 205, 603, 807, 81, 96, 405, 41, 600, 136, 14, 20, 28, 26,
353, 302, 146, 8, 131, 160, 140, 84, 440, 42, 16, 811, 40,

67, 101, 102, 194, 138, 205, 51, 63, 241, 540, 122, 8, 10, 63, 140, 47, 48, 140, 288.

Hunter's eyes were now the size of tea plates.

'And how did they decode this?' said Tandi.

'It's the one they used the Declaration of Independence for. I don't know how they worked out it'd help them. It's one of the most famous American documents ever written and they guessed, I suppose, it might work if they swapped numbers in the code for letters in the Declaration.'

'Like we swapped letters for numbers when we worked on the Firebird Code,' said Tusia.

'Exactly. Just like that. We used Sir Thomas Malory's work to give us the letters. Here in America, some genius decided the Declaration of Independence was the document they needed to help them read one of the Beale Papers.'

'Lucky guess?' said Hunter, still scanning the numbers.

'Maybe. Or maybe an educated guess like we made with the Firebird Code, breaking down a clue to get that idea. Either way, their idea worked.'

'And how'd they do it, exactly?' said Kitty.

'More simply than we did with the Firebird Code,' Brodie said, remembering the hours of careful numbering. 'They just worked through the Declaration numbering each word as they went. The first word of the Declaration was number 1, the second word number 2 and so on. The first number on the Beale Paper was number 115. So they looked at the Declaration and found the 115th word began with an "I". This gave them the first letter of their message. Once each number had been matched with a letter from the Declaration, they could read the complete code and understand the message.'

'So what'd it say?'

Brodie took a third sheet from the pile. She began to read.

I have deposited in the county of Bedford, about four miles from Buford's, in an excavation or vault, six feet below the surface of the ground, the following articles, belonging jointly to the parties whose names are given in number three, herewith:

The first deposit consisted of ten hundred and fourteen pounds of gold, and thirty-eight hundred and twelve pounds of silver, deposited Nov. eighteen nineteen. The second was made Dec. eighteen twenty-one, and consisted of nineteen hundred and seven pounds of gold, and twelve *hundred and eighty-eight of silver; also jewels, obtained in St. Louis in exchange for silver to save transportation, and valued at thirteen thousand dollars.*

The above is securely packed in iron pots, with iron covers. The vault is roughly lined with stone, and the vessels rest on solid stone, and are covered with others. Paper number one describes the exact locality of the vault, so that no difficulty will be had in finding it.

A hush fell across the room.

'So there are *two* loads of treasure,' said Smithies, pushing his glasses firmly up the bridge of his nose.

'Perhaps the original treasure was from a first journey to Avalon. Maybe it was on the ship we found out about when we were at Shugborough Hall – the *Covadonga*. And then perhaps the rest of the treasure was what Beale found later.'

'A second lot of treasure from Avalon?' said Tusia.

'Could be from Avalon, but we can't be sure,' reminded Miss Tandari.

'But we're going with that idea for now,' said Smithies.

'So maybe Beale found out about Avalon from Lucia, the woman who visited Shugborough Hall,' said Brodie. 'If her daughter, Renata, was buried at Shugborough in the Shepherd's Monument, and the message on the tomb said she'd been to Avalon, then that's how Beale learnt the place really existed. And if he knew about it, maybe he travelled there and brought more treasure back. If you find out where Avalon is, you're going to want to go there, right?'

The air pulsed with excitement. Brodie's words hardly needed saying.

'So if Lucia told Beale where to look for the treasure he may have travelled to find it and taken a second load,' suggested Sheldon.

'Fabulous,' said Hunter. 'So if we want to know where Avalon is we've got to work out where Beale travelled to between 1819 and 1821 because that's when he collected the treasure.' He took the encrypted Paper, which according to Brodie would tell them where the treasure was hidden, and stared at the series of numbers. 'Any ideas?'

317, 8, 92, 73, 112, 89, 67, 318, 28, 96, 107, 41, 631, 78,
146, 397, 118, 98, 114, 246, 348, 116, 74, 88, 12, 65, 32,
14, 81, 19, 76, 121, 216, 85, 33, 66, 15, 108, 68, 77, 43, 24,
122, 96, 117, 36, 211, 301, 15, 44, 11, 46, 89, 18, 136, 68,
317, 28, 90, 82, 304, 71, 43, 221, 198, 176, 310, 319, 81,
99, 264, 380, 56, 37, 319, 2, 44, 53, 28, 44, 75, 98, 102, 37,
85, 107, 117, 64, 88, 136, 48, 154, 99, 175, 89, 315, 326,

78, 96, 214, 218, 311, 43, 89, 51, 90, 75, 128, 96, 33, 28,
103, 84, 65, 26, 41, 246, 84, 270, 98, 116, 32, 59, 74, 66,
69, 240, 15, 8, 121, 20, 77, 89, 31, 11, 106, 81, 191, 224,
328, 18, 75, 52, 82, 117, 201, 39, 23, 217, 27, 21, 84, 35,
53, 109, 128, 49, 77, 88, 1, 81, 217, 64, 55, 83, 116, 251,
269, 311, 96, 54, 32, 120, 18, 132, 102, 219, 211, 84, 150,
219, 275, 312, 64, 10, 106, 87, 75, 47, 21, 29, 37, 81, 44,
18, 126, 115, 132, 160, 181, 203, 76, 81, 299, 314, 337,
351, 96, 11, 28, 97, 318, 238, 106, 24, 93, 3, 19, 17, 26, 60,
73, 88, 14, 126, 138, 234, 286, 297, 321, 365, 264, 19, 22,
84, 56, 107, 98, 123, 111, 214, 136, 7, 33, 45, 40, 13, 28,
46, 42, 107, 196, 227, 344, 198, 203, 247, 116, 19, 8, 212,
230, 31, 6, 328, 65, 48, 52, 59, 41, 122, 33, 117, 11, 18, 25,
71, 36, 45, 83, 76, 89, 92, 31, 65, 70, 83, 96, 27, 33, 44,
50, 61, 24, 112, 136, 149, 176, 180, 194, 143, 171, 205,
296, 87, 12, 44, 51, 89, 98, 34, 41, 208, 173, 66, 9, 35, 16,
95, 8, 113, 175, 90, 56, 203, 19, 177, 183, 206, 157, 200,
218, 260, 291, 305, 618, 951, 320, 18, 124, 78, 65, 19, 32,
124, 48, 53, 57, 84, 96, 207, 244, 66, 82, 119, 71, 11, 86,
77, 213, 54, 82, 316, 245, 303, 86, 97, 106, 212, 18, 37, 15,
81, 89, 16, 7, 81, 39, 96, 14, 43, 216, 118, 29, 55, 109, 136,
172, 213, 64, 8, 227, 304, 611, 221, 364, 819, 375, 128,
296, 1, 18, 53, 76, 10, 15, 23, 19, 71, 84, 120, 134, 66, 73,
89, 96, 230, 48, 77, 26, 101, 127, 936, 218, 439, 178, 171,
61, 226, 313, 215, 102, 18, 167, 262, 114, 218, 66, 59, 48,
27, 19, 13, 82, 48, 162, 119, 34, 127, 139, 34, 128, 129, 74,
63, 120, 11, 54, 61, 73, 92, 180, 66, 75, 101, 124, 265, 89,

96, 126, 274, 896, 917, 434, 461, 235, 890, 312, 413, 328, 381, 96, 105, 217, 66, 118, 22, 77, 64, 42, 12, 7, 55, 24, 83, 67, 97, 109, 121, 135, 181, 203, 219, 228, 256, 21, 34, 77, 319, 374, 382, 675, 684, 717, 864, 203, 4, 18, 92, 16, 63, 82, 22, 46, 55, 69, 74, 112, 134, 186, 175, 119, 213, 416, 312, 343, 264, 19, 186, 218, 343, 417, 845, 951, 124, 209, 49, 617, 856, 924, 936, 72, 19, 28, 11, 35, 42, 40, 66, 85, 94, 112, 65, 82, 115, 119, 236, 244, 186, 172, 112, 85, 6, 56, 38, 44, 85, 72, 32, 47, 73, 96, 124, 217, 314, 319, 221, 644, 817, 821, 934, 922, 416, 975, 10, 22, 18, 46, 137, 181, 101, 39, 86, 103, 116, 138, 164, 212, 218, 296, 815, 380, 412, 460, 495, 675, 820, 952.

'None,' said Brodie. 'In fact, there's lots we don't know about Thomas Jefferson Beale. Like what other documents apart from the Declaration of Independence he used to write his ciphers for a start? And why didn't he send them to Morriss the innkeeper, so he could work out what the ciphers said?'

'And what I want to know,' said Sheldon, 'is why Morriss waited twenty-three years before opening the box in the first place when Beale had told him to open them if he didn't make it back to the inn after ten years.'

Sicknote sipped from his mug, which was firmly chained to the ornately painted radiator. 'Why would

Beale Paper Already Translated

Use Dec. of Independence

When (1) in (2) the (3) course (4) of (5)
human (6) events (7) it (8) becomes (9) necessary (10)...

★ Code works like this:

Number 1 = W   because 1st letter of 'when'

Number 2 = I   because 1st letter of 'in'

Number 3 = T   because 1st letter of 'the'

SO

1, 2, 3, 4, 6 = witch!

anyone wait if there was a code to be solved?' he said.

Friedman shook his head in understanding. 'Yes, why would anyone wait? Why wouldn't cracking the code be the most important thing they had to do?'

And somehow, as Brodie gazed round the room, she knew not a single one of them could ever understand how anyone could resist the call of an uncracked code.

Kerrith ran the end of her finger along the tip of her thumbnail. The line of the nail wasn't quite smooth. This worried her. She needed to be on top of her game.

The Director didn't look up from his desk as she entered the room. His suit was slightly crumpled, suggesting he'd come straight from the airport. 'You're telling me they weren't there.'

Kerrith toyed with the edge of her nail 'No, sir. It seems Friedman and the others got away.'

'How did you let him live in the first place?'

She wasn't sure how to answer. 'I thought . . . it looked . . . I just left too soon.'

'You should have seen things through. Been totally sure that the situation was dealt with. How did he escape?'

'Sir, from what I can work out from the hospital reports, it had something to do with the children. I had no—'

62

The Director stood up from the desk. He'd heard enough. 'The situation is unfortunate, Miss Vernan. It's not as I hoped. You underestimated your enemy and that's always a fatal flaw. But we deal with *now*. We deal with the hand we've been dealt, and a little bit of shuffling will have the state of play back in our favour. I presume you've got things in place.'

She handed over a piece of paper. It was an air traffic control report dated a few days ago. It listed the departure and arrival of private planes.

'And tracking?'

'We have KM monitored, sir.'

The Director's scowl softened a little. 'Timing is everything, Miss Vernan. Let's see this as an opportunity to widen your education. We'll have a second chance to deal with the irritation from Station X. You must not fail again.'

'Special Delivery' to Ellen's Stardust Diner

Morgan Summerfield scribbled in his notebook. Kerrith Vernan was dictating at a speed of more than sixty words a minute. He was struggling to keep up. She'd obviously been reprimanded for the disaster at Beachy Head and now she meant to put things right.

'I've explained all this to them, ma'am,' he said. 'Just like you asked me to. They know to only watch things until ordered to take action. Nothing will go wrong.'

She didn't seem calmed by this. She took a stick of celery from the Tupperware container on her desk and snapped it in half, nibbling at the end as she strode up and down the room.

'And yes, there is a system of communication in place. We won't miss anything.' He pointed to the computer. Three lights flickered on and off in the centre of the screen, across the middle of the map of New York. According to the tracking system, the brightest light was signalling from inside the Waldorf-Astoria Hotel.

'You're telling me the Astor family helped set up this library?' said Brodie, hurrying up the steps to the front of the large imposing building where Sicknote had said they should begin their research.

'Yes, maybe even Tusia will forgive them their wealth,' mused Smithies, 'when she realises they used at least some of it for public good.'

Tusia mumbled something in reply but it was hard to hear her above the roar of the traffic and the honking of taxi horns.

'Do they *have* to keep doing that?' moaned Sheldon, who obviously found the racket uncomfortable for his highly musically trained ears.

'I'd like a library,' said Brodie, trying to ignore Sheldon's grimacing. 'As a way of being remembered, I mean.'

'Nice dream, B. I'll just have a gravestone with "he was quite good at maths" written on it.'

Tusia mumbled again and this time Brodie could make out something which sounded a lot like 'and the words "and being a pain" printed underneath.'

'OK,' said Smithies, clapping his hands together trying to defuse the tension. 'We've three hours to do some research on Beale. You need to split up and find out all you can. Where he was between the two dates when the treasure was buried and as much as you can about Bedford County and any likely places he may have chosen to hide treasure in.'

'And Morriss?' asked Sheldon. 'The innkeeper he trusted the information with? We should look into him?'

Smithies nodded. 'Yes. And Ward, too, the writer who took all the information from Morriss and put it together in that pamphlet which was so nearly destroyed in the fire. We need to know as much as we can about what was written and why.' He pulled himself up straight. 'I suggest you make your way back to the hotel when you're tired. Mr Bray and Mrs Smithies are taking a while to catch up with the time difference. Friedman and Tandi are doing some research of their own and Kitty was feeling under the weather. I left her sleeping. There'll be someone there for you when you're done.'

Brodie pushed her hands deep into her pockets and strode forward into the library. The noise of the traffic fell away like snowfall melting from a branch. She drank in the smell. It felt like home.

'Oh no,' said Hunter. 'BB's got one of her faces on.

You know, like the look she had in Westminster Abbey surrounded by all those dead people.' He grimaced slightly. 'I'll keep an eye on her. You lot come find us if you make any breakthroughs.'

Tusia led the others deeper into the library and Hunter followed the signs to steer Brodie towards the research room.

Brodie took a moment to centre herself. If she was told, in that moment, that she could never again leave the room they'd just entered, she was pretty sure she wouldn't mind. The tiled floor shone deep red, reflecting the light flooding in the windows. Above them a golden-edged ceiling was painted with clouds which scudded across a pale-blue sky. And the walls and a balcony above them were lined with books standing like defences between those inside and the noisy outside world of New York City.

'Erm, B?' Hunter steadied his hand on Brodie's shoulder. 'You still with me?'

Brodie found it hard to answer him.

'We're here to work, you know,' he whispered sharply in her ear.

Brodie shook her head. This wouldn't be work.

'OK. That's enough. I'm sorry. I shouldn't have pressed.' Tandi bent down by the chair. She rested her hand on Friedman's shoulder. 'We should leave it for today.'

Friedman had his eyes shut. 'It's OK.'

'You don't have to tell me everything yet. There's no hurry.'

'There *is* a hurry!' Friedman snapped, pulling away from her. His eyes were open now and they looked raw and red. He stood up and walked across the room. 'We need to work this out. There's people there, still trapped. An old woman from some institution in London. We can't just leave them.'

Tandi stood beside him. She rested her arm again on his shoulder. 'I know. Fabyan and I looked into it.' She pulled a notebook from her jeans pocket and passed it to him, open on a page labelled 'Missing'. The list of names below the title was long. 'We were making progress and then—' Now she didn't want to remember but she pressed on. 'Fabyan and I hacked into the Black Chamber files. We found lists of personnel. It helped us work out they still had you in custody. But we're no closer to knowing where they kept you. Except your files said you'd been sent "Down". We've no idea what that means. And maybe there's no way you'll remember. But . . .' She hesitated. 'The Black Chamber worked out we were watching. They sent us a message. So that way of finding information is closed to us now. We'll work out other ways to find out, Robbie. It'll just take us time.'

'But we've wasted so much time on all this.'

'Wasted?' Tandi couldn't hide her shock. 'You think all this effort to read MS 408 is wasted?'

'That's not what I said. It's just, how many lives are going to be ruined by this quest of ours? Are we really going to get answers?'

'We're *getting* answers. It's about Avalon!'

'But what does that mean? Avalon? What is that? Where is that?'

'Well, I guess the team are working on the where. And as for what . . . I think Smithies has been working on that too.' She pointed to the huge pile of reference books on the table. 'He thinks there's magic there. A *real* sort of magic. He's going to explain it all soon.'

'Good. I'm in the mood for answers.'

Brodie looked up from her notes and rubbed her eyes. They were prickly with tiredness. The sky outside the windows was now a darker blue than the sky painted on the ceiling. Brodie stretched her arms out in front of her and then looked down at her watches. Three o'clock in the afternoon here but getting close to late evening back in England.

Hunter shuffled closer to her on his chair. 'B. I have

69

to ask you. I mean, I've ignored it for months because everyone's allowed their thing. But you and the two watches. Why *is* that?'

Brodie looked up at the painted sky, fixed for ever in a moment in time. 'It's MS 408,' she said. 'Sort of.'

Hunter scratched his head.

She looked down at the two watch faces. Whichever time zone she used, she supposed it was time to tell him. 'My mother wore this watch,' she said, lifting the arm which had the New York timepiece. 'It was always set on New York time. I never knew why, but now I think I do. It's the time of the Manuscript, set for the same time zone as the one where MS 408 is kept. My mum left the watch at home when she went to Belgium on research. Granddad gave it to me just hours after her funeral. And I remember the time. On my own watch it was evening and she was gone. But on this watch; my mum's watch, it was still lunchtime and the time of the service hadn't happened. Like for a few more hours she was still with me. The time for her being gone hadn't arrived.'

Hunter looked straight at her.

'You think I'm odd, right?' she whispered apologetically.

'Oh, yeah. I think you're totally odd, all right. Nutty as a fruitcake. But I don't mind.'

Brodie's throat tightened. It felt OK to have told him. She hadn't thought it would, but it was. Like it had been OK to tell him about Friedman falling from the lighthouse in her dreams each night. For someone who spent so long joking, Hunter was a surprisingly good listener.

She lifted the pages of notes they'd collected and fanned them out across the desk. 'So? What have we got?'

'OK,' said Hunter. 'Well, looks like Thomas Jefferson Beale, the writer of the coded Papers, was in Sante Fe between the years when he supposedly hid the two loads of treasure. It's a town in America but it was a Spanish-run city built in 1610.'

'Spanish? Like the ship *Covadonga*, we think may have sailed to Avalon, was Spanish? That could be a brilliant link but how does it help?'

Hunter tapped his pen against his teeth. 'Well, it makes sense Beale hid what they found in Sante Fe, because it was a Spanish part of America and the *Covadonga*'s crew was Spanish.'

'OK. But at some time Beale went back to Sante Fe, collected the treasure from both journeys to Avalon, and moved it to the hills of Virginia, right?'

'He must have thought Virginia was a safer place to hide his secret treasure.'

'And then Beale kept the whole thing even more secret by coming up with the coded letters idea.'

'Exactly. Three Papers in a box. Given to a friend. And the friend is told he'll be sent all he needs to crack the code.'

'Perfect plan. But there's nothing in all these notes about why Beale didn't send Morriss the information he promised, to help him read the codes.'

'Perhaps he couldn't. You know. If he . . .' Hunter ran the tip of his pen across his throat, grimaced and then shuddered in a rather elaborate attempt to act out being murdered.

'You think Beale *died* before he could send the information on to Morriss?'

'Well, why else wouldn't he send it? If he'd promised he would? The whole system falls apart, doesn't it? If Beale didn't send Morriss what he needed to break the code, it's a pretty rubbish code.'

Brodie reached for the pen which Hunter was still holding against his throat. 'Maybe he *did* send it.'

'What, and Morriss just forgot about it?'

'Well, he forgot to open the box with the Papers in for twenty-three years when he'd been asked to only wait ten. Morriss was obviously hopeless at remembering things.' Brodie doodled an unopened box on the page in front of her. Then she crossed it out in frustration.

'Delivery box!' yelped Hunter.

Brodie thought for a minute he'd sworn at her. 'Excuse me?'

'Delivery box,' he blurted again. 'Suppose the parcel was sent to a delivery box, or a post office somewhere. We got our passports delivered to a PO Box back home and Riverbank Labs sent us the stuff on the code to the private delivery box at the hotel! Suppose whatever Beale sent Morriss was taken to a PO Box. And it was just never collected.' He pushed his chair out from behind him and stood up quickly. 'I reckon post back then went to the post office and you had to collect it.'

'Erm, where are you going?'

'To ask a librarian. About how things got delivered. Come on.'

The librarian gazed intently at the computer screen and rubbed a ruby-coloured stud shining in the side of her nose. 'Here we are,' she said. 'I've found a match.'

'You have?'

Brodie and Hunter had been leaning against the enquiry desk, waiting for what seemed an eternity.

'Aha.' The librarian seemed pretty pleased with herself. 'A link with the key words. Morriss and post office and the year you gave.'

'And?' Hunter was obviously trying hard not to be too pushy.

The librarian twisted the computer screen round so he and Brodie could see more clearly. She tapped the screen with fingernails which had a series of stars and stripes painted on them. 'Morriss, you said, right? A Morriss of Lynchberg, Virginia. Well, here's an article from the *St. Louis Beacon* newspaper published in 1832.'

'Ten years after Beale gave the box of coded letters to Morriss,' hissed Hunter.

'It's an open letter,' explained the librarian, 'published in the newspaper, saying there was a package waiting for Morriss to be collected at the post office.'

Brodie could hardly wait for the librarian to stop speaking. 'And did Morriss collect it?'

The librarian peered at her. 'Well, all depends on if he saw this newspaper. I mean, newspapers advertise all the time for people to come and collect things. Or come forward if they're relatives of dead people. Or witnesses to accidents. Or victims of crimes. Or people who've been wrongly sold a mortgage. Or—'

'Yeah. We get it,' interrupted Hunter. 'Newspapers print things all the time and people don't see them.'

'So what would have happened if this Mr Morriss didn't claim his parcel?' asked Brodie nervously.

'Well, I guess it'd still be being held at the St. Louis post office.'

'Still waiting?'

'Well, until this Mr Morriss claims it. Which ain't very likely now, is it, since he's dead.'

'So who could claim the parcel, then?'

The librarian snapped the screen back into position. 'Someone with an official interest, I guess.'

Brodie felt a surge of disappointment.

'Like a solicitor, or a relative, or a government body, library, or a charitable organisation. A journalist maybe,' mused the librarian. 'Someone like the Cobra could probably manage it.'

'Excuse me?'

'The Cobra.'

Brodie was totally confused.

'It's a nickname for a particular journalist,' the librarian explained. 'The Cobra. Maureen Dowd. When President George W. Bush was in office he had nicknames for everyone. Cobra was his name for a particular journalist.'

'Right,' said Hunter awkwardly. The librarian was careering well off track. How had they got to talking about nicknames when they were supposed to be discussing uncollected post!

There was no stopping the librarian though. She was

75

on a roll. 'George W. Bush had nicknames for everyone. It was from his time in a secret society when he was at Yale University. Apparently lots of secret societies have a thing about nicknames. George W. Bush called the president of Canada "Dino". It was short for dinosaur. He called Tony Blair, your prime minister at the time, "Landslide", as he won the election by a landslide of votes. His own vice president he called "Big Time". Cool, eh?'

Brodie had no idea how to get the librarian back on course.

'See, nicknames are a bit of a president sort of thing. My favourite president, our third, and writer of the Declaration of Independence, was Thomas Jefferson and he was known by the name "Red Fox". He had a hot temper, you know.'

Hunter looked as if he was struggling very hard to control his own temper and not demand the librarian tell them more about the uncollected post – what they'd asked her about in the first place!

'You'll be wanting me to put in a request, then?'

'Excuse me?'

'A request to the post office for the parcel which was sent to Mr Morriss?' said the librarian.

'You can do that?' said Brodie, hardly daring to believe that after all that chatter the librarian had something incredible to offer.

'What I was trying to tell you. Official organisations, journalists, law firms, libraries.' The nose stud glinted again in the fading light. 'Would you like to fill in a form?'

Kerrith had had enough of paperwork.

The visit to Site Three had finally been arranged. And she'd been fully prepared for the excursion.

The maps the Director had sent her had been shocking. A whole town, built underground and hidden from the public. It was almost too difficult to believe. Sixty miles of roads, which criss-crossed a blast-proof complex including hospitals, canteens, kitchens, storerooms, living areas and offices. There was a power station to generate electricity and an underground lake to provide drinking water. A self-sufficient universe, hidden below the surface of the earth.

Kerrith had been impressed enough with what she'd seen in London. Abandoned train stations and facades of houses hiding secret locations. But Site Three was on a scale she could barely imagine. The Director explained what she'd seen in London was merely the tip of the iceberg. Site Three was what really mattered. Where things were taken which needed to be hidden forever. And the plan was to show her where the interfering troublemakers from Station X would be taken before the net to catch them tightened fully.

Kerrith opened one of the maps across her knees and looked again at the plan. A prickle of excitement ran up her spine as the train thundered onwards. The rattle of the wheels along the track was reassuring. She closed her eyes and relaxed into the rhythm of the ride.

When Kerrith opened her eyes, the train had stopped.

She folded the map on her lap as the door slid open.

'Welcome to Corsham Quarry, Wiltshire,' said the Director, from beyond the door. 'I think, Miss Vernan, you'll be impressed by what you see here at what's known officially, but highly confidentially, as "Site Three".'

Kerrith took the hand he offered and stepped out of the train.

As in London on their underground visits, the air was cool and regulated against her skin, the darkness punctuated by electric lights. But this felt bigger than London. And deeper.

The Director seemed to sense her excitement and led her, without talking, down a twist of tunnels. There were street names pinned to the walls, roadways marked on the ground, people dressed in white uniforms striding about with purposeful steps. The Director led the way to a long double escalator and stepped aboard.

Kerrith tightened her grip on the handrail as the metal stairway took them even lower under the earth.

Once at the bottom of the stairway, the Director led Kerrith towards a wide entrance. He opened the doors. 'This is where we "manage" things,' he said in a voice of barely disguised laughter.

'Manage?'

The Director pointed up to a bank of plasma screens lining the walls. 'We manage things here at the Site and we manage life from above. By the time people have made it to Site Three, they're deemed a high risk to security. We need to watch their every move and we also need to be sure the information regarding the life they've left and the world above is carefully . . . how shall I put this? *Filtered*. Site Three is about controlling what's known above and below ground.'

Kerrith's eyes narrowed to take in the sights flashing across the screen. There were projected images of what looked like life outside in the open air. And there were screens showing life inside. And these images were shocking. Small, dirty, crowded rooms with battered furniture, lines of beds and people sitting, standing, sometimes rocking back and forth.

Her eyes focused on a grainy image in the top left-hand corner. A woman, fairly old, her shoulders hunched, was seated on a chair, one arm folded passively in her lap. The other arm was outstretched, her fingernails digging into the wooden surface of the shabby desk in front of her. Kerrith crinkled her nose and ran her own fingertip across her slightly crooked thumbnail. How could the woman be so ridiculous? What was she doing? And then, as Kerrith peered in more closely, she could at last make out what the woman was attempting to do. She was trying to scratch letters into the wood of the desk.

Kerrith peered closely at the woman. There was something unsettling about her, vaguely troubling.

The woman lifted her head only momentarily but just long enough for her eyes to lock on the screen. She stared directly forward. Kerrith returned the stare for a moment and then looked away, but not before the strangest of feelings washed over her – almost as if she was being squeezed through an old-fashioned mangle. Images and memories pressed down on her; a summer morning, the smell of newly cut grass, pancakes in maple syrup, guitar music. Kerrith shook her head and the images bounced from her mind like raindrops against a granite floor slab, but she felt oddly cold, as if she'd been soaked by the storm.

Kerrith didn't hold with such ridiculousness. She rubbed her eyes and when she looked again at the screen, the woman at the desk had looked away.

'Repulsive, isn't it?' the Director mused. 'We take all we can away from them and still they try to pass on what they know.' He pointed at the screen as the woman scratched again at the surface of the desk. 'Still,' he shrugged, 'what they know and what they should know are two different things and what we try to do here at Site Three is realign their learning. We make them forget all they've discovered and we try and assimilate them into our way of thinking.'

'And then you let them go?' Kerrith asked. 'When they understand how you want them to think and to see the world?'

The Director looked incredulous. 'My dear, we don't let them go. Site Three's the end of the line. It's where we make our last-ditch attempts to change their thinking, to drive out the need for their own views on the world. But the reality is, by the time they reach us here, there's really little hope for them. No, Site Three is where we keep the very worst society has allowed to be created and we suppress all they have to say and all they have to share. If they make it to Site Three, that's where they stay.' He patted his tie against his stomach.

'It's a lot to take in, I know,' he added at last, 'but the work of the Suppressors is so vast, we need a compound like this in order to function. When society decides stories need not to be told, then that's where the Suppressors step in. But making certain stories illegal above ground has never been enough. Taking stories and burning them has never been enough. There comes a time, eventually, when those who would fight to tell their stories no longer listen to our helpful advice. That's why Site Three exists. This place is the ultimate force in the suppression of stories.' The pride in his voice made the air ring. 'Over the years the Suppressors have been involved in the most amazing hiding of the truth. They've adapted history and destroyed stories and people with a skill and a dedication worthy of our utmost respect. You see, our stories make us who we are. It's important the stories we share are connected to the view of the world we want to be strongest. It keeps people in check. And for those stories which wouldn't die, for those stories which kept rising again from the flames, we built this place, the ultimate prison.' Above them the televised images flickered and crackled on the screen.

'Now, your education as an employee of the Suppressors is nearly complete, Miss Vernan. I think you're beginning to see the depth of the operation you're involved in.' He chuckled at his private joke. 'But there's aspects of your learning I've left until now.' He reached behind him and drew a large bound book from the shelves and then led her into a small dimly lit office where there was simply a single upright chair and a small wooden desk with a reading-lamp standing on one corner. The Director put the book on the desk. 'A few months ago I asked you to learn about the sinking of RMS *Titanic*, an unfortunate affair deemed necessary because of the mounting interest in MS 408 at the time and a ridiculous digging expedition in the River Wye which sought to uncover some Shakespearean secret which would change the world!' He snorted in disgust. 'We needed to distract the public.'

Kerrith looked down at the ground.

'And I believe I asked you to look with a little more care into the tragedy of the London smog disaster.' His tongue lingered on his final word, enjoying the taste of the letters and the image they created in his mind. 'In 1952, the burning of contaminated coal in London added to the destruction caused by the Great Smog and did much to quieten again the masses who were beginning to search for answers. But the work of suppression has stretched over centuries and over lands and oceans, Miss Vernan, and where better for you to spend time learning of our greatest exploits in the field, but here?' He tapped the top of the open book. 'Happy reading,' he said. 'The truth is a greatly guarded commodity. And it's now time for you to know the truth. The whole truth and nothing but the truth.' And with that he turned his back and walked away.

Brodie sat bolt upright in bed, her heart racing. The same dream. Once again she'd let Friedman fall from the lighthouse. She rubbed her face, clambered out of bed and moved quietly along to the suite sitting room to get herself a glass of water.

Friedman was standing by the window, the drape pulled back in his hand. 'They say this city never sleeps,' he said. 'I know the feeling.'

Brodie sipped from the glass and curled her toes in her slippers.

'I'm going to try and make it up to you,' Friedman said gently.

'I know.'

'And I am sorry. About all of it.'

'I know that too.' She ran her finger across the top of the glass. 'We are safe here, aren't we?'

Brodie saw Friedman's hand clench. He seemed to be struggling to find the words he needed and instead he let out a breath.

'I sort of hope that we'd always tell each other the truth now,' Brodie said awkwardly.

Friedman bit his lip. Brodie tried to read his face. She could tell he was choking back words. Then he turned away and looked down to the road. 'I'll do all I can to keep you safe, Brodie.'

He let the drape go and swing back across the glass. As he did so, the same black car made its fifth circuit of the hotel.

Hunter was on his second Frank Sinatra Burger at Ellen's Stardust Diner at the corner of 51st Street and Broadway.

'Do we *have* to keep coming to this place?' moaned Sicknote, as a waitress jumped up on to the benching between the seats and began belting out the song 'New York, New York'. 'We're staying somewhere with culture and class and you all insist on coming here.' He snuffled a couple of painkillers and washed them down disdainfully with a mouthful of Dr Brown's chocolate soda.

Sheldon waved his arms in annoyance. Obviously, as far as he was concerned, there was nowhere more cultured in the world than an American diner where the waiting staff burst into song at any opportunity while delivering fries and burgers to customers who tapped their feet in time with the big 'show-stopping' music. Besides, they'd left the diner's phone number with the librarian so she could reach them. Hunter had suggested Friedman might not like them giving Brodie's mobile number.

'Yo, Sheldon,' said one of the waiters, balancing a tray of blueberry muffins and black cherry pancakes precariously against his hip. 'You wanna join us?'

Sheldon shrugged his shoulders in a way he obviously hoped looked a little modest but in seconds he was up on the benching harmonising with the singing.

'This kid could go a long way, Grandpop,' said the waiter to Mr Bray, who was seated at the end of the aisle. 'If you need a good agent, I've plenty of contacts.'

Smithies leant over. 'Thank you, Dirk. We appreciate your help, but really, we all have plans.'

The waiter did little to hide his disbelief and Brodie couldn't blame him. They'd been waiting now for three days to hear from the New York Public Library about the package Hunter and Brodie hoped to collect, and after the others in the team had found loads of maps of the Blue Ridge Mountains there seemed little else they could do for a while. 'You sure, Mr S?' said Dirk playfully. 'You lot look like tourists at a loose end to me.'

Brodie fiddled awkwardly with her napkin.

Sheldon reached the swell of the song and was now getting into quite a high-stepped kicking routine which seemed to be causing a fair degree of alarm to the group of Japanese visitors seated to his left. Brodie was suddenly aware of a waiter gesturing to her from behind the bar. She slid along the bench seat and hurried over, nodding an apology to Sheldon who had just reached the climax of the song.

'Phone for you,' said the waiter, thrusting the receiver into her hand.

Brodie held the phone tight against her ear. 'Aha. Aha. Aha. Thank you loads,' she added as she hung up the handset and hurried back to her seat. Sheldon clambered down from the benching looking expectant.

'Well?' said Hunter, folding a French fry into his mouth.

'The package from St. Louis has just arrived!'

Back in Fabyan's Royal Parlour suite, Brodie opened the thin discoloured envelope addressed to Mr Morriss of Lynchberg, Virginia.

'Well?' pressed Kitty. 'Is it a map? Does it show where the treasure is?'

'Is it more numbers, B? Another sheet of figures?'

'Does it list the key texts Morriss needed to make sense of the codes?'

'Is there any mention of Avalon?'

Brodie held up her hands. 'If you would all just give me a moment!'

There was an awkward silence as she scanned the

paper. It was old, thin and brittle and the writing smudged in places, almost illegible. But it was clear it wasn't a map or a list of figures. It was a letter. From Thomas Jefferson Beale.

My dearest Morriss,

So many months have passed since I was fortunate to spend time in your company, that I fear you may well have given up the chance of ever seeing me again. But like the red fox of the mountains, my presence will never truly be gone. What is most important to the fox is clear. His home speaks of this. In the lining of his den, safe from the west and south-east winds, what is key to him remains. Men will list maybe two, or four or seven things of importance; or even two or six. But to the red fox there are only three. There are things he cannot live without and things for which he will be remembered.

I hope to join with you shortly, dear friend, but am resting a while in the care of Admiral Cockburn, a man of letters.

God's speed under one nation to you,
Thomas Jefferson Beale.

Brodie put the letter down on the table. She looked up. 'Anyone any ideas?' she said at last. 'Any at all?'

Hunter blew out his breath. 'Well, all I know is I'm not sure it was worth leaving half my Sinatra burger for. How's this help us?'

Smithies loosened the knot of his tie. 'It's obviously cryptic, Hunter. I'd have thought you'd realise that after all this time.'

'There's cryptic and there's bonkers, sir, and that letter's one marshmallow on a stick, cooking in the fire bonkers if you ask me.'

'Perhaps we should ask someone else, then,' said Smithies, turning to survey the room.

'Only joking, boss. I reckon it's time for the logbook, B. Your thing with the weird words, don't you reckon?'

'Oh I remember,' said Brodie, reaching for a pen. 'Like we did with the Firebird Letter. We need to make a sort of checklist of all the weird things, right?'

'Put his name on the top, then,' mumbled Tusia, winking at Hunter.

'Oh that's so old now!' He flipped the logbook open to a clean page and passed it to Brodie. 'OK. Weirdness. To list. From the letter. Ready.'

'Ready,' said Brodie.

It only took about two minutes. They were getting

- the red fox of the mountains
- most important to the fox
- His home speaks of this - lining of his den
- west and south-east winds,
- what is key to him remains
- two, four, seven
- two or six.
- But to the red fox there are only three.
- things he cannot live without
- and things for which he will be remembered.
- Admiral Cockburn. Man of letters.
- God's speed under one nation
- Thomas Jefferson Beale.

good at this. Brodie looked down at the checklist and then read aloud all the points they had listed against bullet points.

Brodie passed the note around and each person scanned the text thoughtfully.

'There's a whole lot of numbers in there,' said Hunter.

'Only one name though, apart from Thomas Jefferson Beale who wrote the thing.' Tusia looked down at the list. '*Admiral Cockburn. Man of letters.* That means he's clever, I think. Like, he has letters after his name because he's got a degree.'

'And the red fox?' said Granddad. 'Who's he?

Everyone turned to look at him.

Hunter slipped down to his knees beside his chair. 'You think it's a nickname? You think we need to be thinking about *someone* called Red Fox, not an actual thing.'

Mr Bray tapped his hand.

'So come on then. Anyone know who they called the Red Fox?'

'You're the nickname king, Hunter,' said Tusia. 'You're the one who seems to think it's OK all right to change someone's birth name and call them something totally different.'

'OK, Toots. Fair point. I was just asking, that's all,

if anyone knew who Red Fox was? No need to lose your temper.'

Brodie turned to face him. Temper. Red. Fox. The name meant something to her, but she wasn't sure what. For some unfathomable reason she had an image of a cobra snake in her mind. But did red foxes eat cobras? She couldn't see them coming off very well if they tried.

And then she remembered. The rambling librarian and her never-ending story about nicknames and presidents.

'I know who it is!'

'President Thomas Jefferson,' said Fabyan, leaning his weight against the fireplace. 'Of course. He was America's third president. Called the "Red Fox" because of his auburn hair and his dogged personality. He believed in getting things done. See, those lessons I had as a kid, on American constitutional history, paid off.'

'So he didn't have a temper, then?'

Fabyan looked surprised. 'I don't know, but what they taught us in school was all about how he wanted the best for people and how into equality he was. Didn't hear much about his temper. Why?'

Brodie decided against sharing the story about the rambling librarian.

'It's weird,' said Hunter. 'Thomas Jefferson's a great name. No need for a nickname really.'

Brodie didn't have the energy to point out there was hardly a name in the group Hunter hadn't replaced with a nickname. Instead she said the President's name again and again in her head. Thomas Jefferson. There was something missing but she couldn't work out what it was.

'Didn't Thomas Jefferson write some important American document?' cut in Tusia.

'The Declaration of Independence!' groaned Hunter. 'Of course. You went over that when we were back at Shugborough.' He looked across at Ingham, who seemed happy his lesson had been remembered.

Brodie rubbed her temple. Shugborough. It was nearly there. The thing she was missing. At the tip of her tongue. And then she blurted the word out loud. 'Beale.' That was it. The part which was missing. '*Thomas Jefferson Beale* wrote the Beale Papers,' she explained. 'He must have been named after the third president. That would explain why Thomas Jefferson Beale used the Declaration written by the president to help write his code. Perfect.'

Everyone looked like they agreed. Even Mrs Smithies was beaming.

'So maybe President Thomas Jefferson wrote other

stuff we need to help us work out what the other two Beale Papers mean,' Sheldon suggested.

'Sounds sensible,' said Smithies. 'You could be on to something.'

'So d'you think we should go to his home, then?' said Tusia, looking up at Smithies. She pointed at the part of the new letter about the red fox. '*What's most important to the fox is clear. His home speaks of this.*'

Brodie was getting excited. It did seem a logical jump to expect to be able to find clues they might need at Thomas Jefferson's house.

'Perhaps his home is the place to try for key texts,' said Smithies. 'But I'm not sure.'

Brodie felt a little deflated.

'Home might not mean the place where the person lives. Homes are temporary. We move on. And we're talking about a home in the past. I think we need to find a final home. We should try where we always look for people's most important messages. The *things for which he will be remembered*.' He pointed back at the checklist they'd made.

Ingham chuckled.

'Care to let us in on the joke?' asked Hunter, who was obviously confused.

Smithies folded the yellowed letter carefully and moved towards the door. 'I think it's time we paid the

- the red fox of the mountains ✓
- most important to the fox
- His home speaks of this - lining of his den
- west and south-east winds,
- what is key to him remains
- two, four, seven
- two or six.
- But to the red fox there are only three.
- things he cannot live without
- and things for which he will be remembered. ✓
- Admiral Cockburn. Man of letters.
- God's speed under one nation
- Thomas Jefferson Beale. ✓

president's final resting place a visit. That might be what the letter means by the "home of the red fox". His final home. The place where he's buried.'

Brodie took the logbook and put a tick by all the things on the list they'd already got their heads round. This was going to be fun. And, she dared herself to think it for just a moment, maybe even fairly easy.

In Nature's Workhouse

Kerrith Vernan woke up with a start.

The room was spinning, her pulse pounding in her ears. Her forehead was beaded with sweat. She leant against the mattress to steady herself and tried to breathe air deep into her lungs. It fluttered uselessly in her throat.

Site Three had scared her and she hadn't been scared for a very long time.

She wiped her hand across her face and swung her legs around the end of the bed. This was ridiculous. *She* was ridiculous. An understanding of exactly what the Suppressors did, and why, was something she'd wanted for years. Now she knew.

The Black Chamber was simply part of a worldwide

machine. Knowing the work of the Suppressors touched all parts of the world and times should have intensified her excitement. But something was wrong. There was a flickering of disquiet. A pain almost, inside her chest. And she didn't like it.

This was insane. She couldn't weaken now. Not after the Director had trusted her with so much.

She pressed her weight down on her feet and stood up and for a moment the room spun again. Then it steadied. Her world-view was restored. Everything looked once again just as it should.

The Director had said she could ask him any questions she wanted. It would do no harm to talk to him. Just to be sure of the details of all she'd read. He'd said he wanted her to know the truth.

'I'm just saying Monticello sounds like something you should eat,' joked Hunter, as the Gray Line coach they'd boarded in Washington turned left at the stoplight and pulled on to Route 53. 'I can't help it if I'm hungry!'

Brodie glanced down at the mounting pile of sweet wrappers and crisp packets littering the floor at their feet and rolled her eyes. The coach rattled as it passed under a stone archway then turned right on to the road leading to Jefferson's country estate. 'Monticello's where Jefferson lived and died, Hunter. It's not some sugar-coated chocolate bar.'

'Alrighty,' called the driver into a microphone buzzing with feedback. 'We've reached our destination. Please remember the number of the bus and be ready to depart from this parking lot at five and twenty after noon. We wait for no one.' Brodie was sure by the wideness of his eyes that he was absolutely serious. She scooped up the litter and the book on myths and legends she'd been reading on the journey and followed Hunter down the aisle.

Not everyone had come to Monticello. Fabyan wanted to follow up the leads they'd made about the Knights of Neustria ring so Mrs Smithies and Granddad stayed with him. Kitty stayed behind too, because she'd a few things she needed to do in the city. Tandi and Friedman planned to try and find out more about where the Black Chamber could be hiding missing people. Friedman seemed more willing now to talk about the details of the place where he'd been kept after Kerrith took him captive, and although Brodie was sad her father wasn't with them, it was good to see him helping. She could tell he wanted to be useful.

That left Smithies, Tusia, Sheldon, Hunter and Brodie. And of course there was no way Sicknote was missing an excursion to a grave. He'd been first off the coach and was scanning the map to find the quickest route across the estate. 'Looks like it's a bit of a walk,' he said. 'But that will give me time to run over a few facts about Jefferson on the way down there. Tell you all I can about the Red Fox.'

Brodie was keen to know more. They needed to start piecing things together if they were going to make sense of Beale's letter to Morriss.

'A check of the history books tells us the Fox bit of his name was given to him by someone called Alexander Hamilton who was the Secretary of State to the Treasury,' began Sicknote. 'Hamilton was one of the founding fathers who signed the Declaration of Independence. But he disagreed with Jefferson about things like freedom of speech.'

'Why?' asked Brodie.

'Jefferson thought everyone's freedom of speech should be protected by law but Hamilton didn't think so. He felt sometimes people should keep quiet about things.'

'So he didn't believe in everyone having equal rights to say stuff?' bristled Tusia.

'Not sure it was as simple as that. But apparently Hamilton believed rich people, and not common people, should make decisions about things.'

'And Jefferson was called a Fox because he disagreed

Thomas Jefferson ~~Beale~~ → nickname = Red Fox

Declaration of Independence

July 4, 1776

name given to him by Alexander Hamilton ↑ Killed by Burr

Loved his family ♡ ♡

Couldn't live without books

own way of numbering them   30 6
                             1429

gave books to the Library of Congress

1814 → British army burnt Library of Congress

tried to burn newspaper office

Admiral Cockburn → destroyed every 'C' ✗ ✗
                                          ✗ ✗

with that idea, then?' pressed Sheldon.

'I suppose. But then this is weird. Hamilton supported Jefferson when he decided he wanted to be president.'

'So Jefferson must have got him to agree with his view on things, then?'

'No. Hamilton just disagreed more with the other man who was running for president.'

'Who was that guy? Grey Wolf?'

'Someone called Burr. And in the end Hamilton and Burr had a duel and Burr shot and killed him.'

'Wow. Honestly. A duel. About politics. That's pretty serious.' Hunter looked quite shocked.

'If you're making decisions about what people can do and say and how they live,' said Smithies, 'then it *is* a serious business.'

'In all our investigations,' added Sicknote, 'the right to think and find out for ourselves has been everything. It's the most serious stuff of all.'

Brodie thought this sounded particularly brave coming from a man who was wearing pyjamas. The right to ask questions and think for yourself did seem like something everyone should have. She couldn't imagine why anyone would want to take that right away.

'So, sir? Any more nuggets of info about old Foxy?'

'He loved his family. And he said he couldn't live without books.'

'Sounds familiar,' mumbled Hunter.

Brodie smirked at him and then did a double-take. 'You're *not* teasing me?'

'No. I'm saying it sounds familiar. Like something on our list.'

'Oh. I see.' Brodie rummaged in her bag for the logbook and scanned their checklist of clues from the red fox letter. 'Here. *Things he can't live without.*' Books. She gave this item on their checklist a rather flourishing tick. 'Brilliant. *Things he can't live without.*'

Smithies smiled at her encouragingly.

'He actually had so many books,' went on Sicknote, 'that he had to come up with his own way of numbering them. It's called the Jefferson system. He gave his huge book collection to the Library of Congress in Washington. The most important library in the country. Said he wanted the things he loved to go to a new home.'

'What, the library didn't have enough of its own books, then?' asked Sheldon incredulously.

'Not when the British had finished with them.'

'What d'you mean?'

Sicknote was rummaging through his mind for historical details. 'In 1814 the British Army burnt down the Library of Congress in Washington.'

'Why?' yelped Tusia.

'Revenge. To get back at the Americans for attacking Toronto.'

'People from Britain burnt books in America as a form of revenge?' Hunter said in disbelief.

'I seriously wonder about you, Hunter. Freedom of speech and the control of knowledge in books – that's what we've been trying to find out about all this time. It shouldn't surprise you.'

'But burning books. That's what Savonarola did in Italy. Why did British people burn books in America?'

Sicknote stopped walking for a moment. 'If you destroy books, you destroy identity and history. You destroy a way of life. You take control of knowledge.'

'But that's awful.'

'It's reality.'

'And on the same day they burnt down the Library of Congress, the British tried to burn the newspaper building in Washington too, so the news could be controlled.'

'Tried to?' asked Tusia.

'Apparently, local women stopped the soldiers from setting the place alight. They begged with them not to start more fires as they were terrified their homes would burn. So instead, the soldiers dismantled the building brick by brick. The newspaper at the time used a printing-press where letters were attached to tiny little blocks. Each block had to be fitted into the printing-press in the right order to spell out words which needed to be printed.'

'Nice little technology lesson,' Sheldon whispered to Tusia. 'I think we understand how a printing-press works.'

'Well, here's the best bit of this lesson,' said Sicknote. 'The leader of the army at the time, Admiral Cockburn, insisted every block of type for the letter C was taken away so even if people tried to print a story of the events in the middle of all the chaos, they'd have no letter Cs to write his name with.'

'Cockburn. Admiral Cockburn. Didn't the red fox letter mention him?' urged Smithies.

Brodie looked back at the checklist. '*Admiral Cockburn. Man of letters*. So that bit didn't mean he was clever and had letters after his name. It meant he did special things with letters. We need to remember that.' She gave this item on the checklist a tick, but it was slightly smaller one than before as she wasn't entirely sure how this information about him helped. '*Admiral Cockburn. Man of letters.*'

'Thank you, Oscar,' said Smithies. 'You've given us loads to think about. But now we've got to focus on why we've come *here*.' They'd reached the end of the gravel pathway and in front of them was a tall obelisk. It was the grave of Thomas Jefferson, third president of the United States of America.

'This can't be right,' said Tusia, gazing up at the tall stone monument.

'What d'you mean?' said Smithies.

'The grave. The writing. What it says.'

Brodie peered at the inscription. She knew at once what Tusia meant.

HERE WAS BURIED

THOMAS JEFFERSON

AUTHOR OF THE

DECLARATION

OF

AMERICAN INDEPENDENCE

OF THE

STATUTE OF VIRGINIA

FOR

RELIGIOUS FREEDOM

AND FATHER OF THE

UNIVERSITY OF VIRGINIA

'He *was* the president, right?' she said quietly, for fear of being overheard.

'The third US president,' said Hunter. 'Why?'

'Because it doesn't say so on this stone.' Tusia had her hands on her hips, her forehead tightened in confusion. 'If you're going to write anything on a grave, then surely you write the most important things you've done. You said that once. Said they'd write "good at maths" on yours. And surely being president is up there, with the most important things?'

'He was vice president too,' added Brodie. 'And secretary of state. Those three jobs are the most important jobs you can have in America. Surely?'

'But you think the people who wrote the inscription didn't know that, then?' mumbled Sheldon, walking backwards and forwards in front of the imposing stone structure. 'They can't not have known. Look at the place. Look at who he was. How could they miss out that detail?'

'They didn't,' said Smithies, turning from a display board which gave information about the memorial.

'What d'you mean, they didn't.'

'*They* didn't write what should go on the stone,' he explained.

'Who the custard cream did, then?' asked Hunter.

'Jefferson! I mean, he obviously wrote it before he

died. He left instructions about what he wanted and everything he wanted is here. He wrote his epitaph himself.' Smithies waved towards the obelisk. 'Every word written on the stone was approved by Jefferson. That's what he wanted to be remembered for. Those three things and nothing more.'

'So this is awkward.' Friedman stood in the lobby of the hotel suite waiting for the lift.

Mr Bray had walked to stand next to him. Friedman was annoyed that, after all his successful attempts to keep clear of the older man, they were now alone together. The line of lights on the control panel glowed but the lift didn't seem to be getting any nearer.

'Robbie, there's lots we should probably say to each other.'

'What, about things we should have said a long time ago?'

The older man pressed the lift call button again. 'I thought I was doing the right thing?'

'For Brodie? For me?' Friedman turned his head to face him. 'For you?'

'For all of us, maybe.' The older man didn't sound too convinced of his own argument.

'I understand why you didn't tell Brodie that I was her dad. I get that. But not to tell me. Not to pass on the letter Alex wrote. Why would you do that?'

The old man seemed to think for a while.

Friedman was expecting all sorts of answers. Because he loved Brodie. Because he wanted to protect her. Because he didn't think Friedman would make a good father. When the answer came it was none of these things.

'Because I'd lost my precious daughter and I was scared.'

Friedman turned to look at the old man. His eyes were milky from years of seeing but they fixed Friedman with a determined stare and the old man didn't look away.

Friedman nodded.

The doors of the elevator opened. And they stepped inside together.

'I still say the man must have been an ice cube short of a Coke-on-the-rocks not to insist they wrote "President" on that thing,' said Hunter, leaning his back against the railing and lifting his head to look at the clouds.

'We've been through it,' said Brodie. 'The information board says after Thomas Jefferson popped his clogs a sketch was found of exactly what he wanted written on his memorial. So that's what they wrote. Just those things.'

'Three things,' said Hunter.

'What?'

'They wrote three things, B. *Just three things.*'

Brodie sat up straight. She had the checklist on her knee. They'd been looking at the memorial for ages, trying to work out what the rows of letters could mean and what secret message the writing might have for them. But it wasn't until now that Brodie felt a stirring in her stomach. The sort of feeling she felt when she was getting to the final pages of a book she was reading; the closing chapters of a story. 'How many encrypted Papers did Beale write?' she said quietly, scared that speaking the thought too loudly, too soon, would jinx the idea and pop it like a balloon.

'Three,' said Hunter. He turned his head. He looked directly at her. His eyes widened. Then, pulled somehow by an invisible cord, they both rose from the places where they'd been sitting.

'You two all right?' said Tusia.

Brodie nodded vigorously. 'D'you want to tell her, or should I?'

Sicknote and Smithies looked along the line from the railings on which they'd been leaning.

'Your call, B,' Hunter said brightly. 'I mean. The numbers thing was the clue, but I know you love a good story.'

Brodie rubbed her hands together.

'Well, come on, then,' urged Sheldon. 'Tell us what you've worked out.'

Brodie beamed. 'He wanted *only three* things recorded because they had to be clues.' She took a deep breath. 'Beale wrote *three* Papers and we know one of them used the Declaration of Independence to crack the code. And the Declaration of Independence is listed there,' she said, waving her arm at the tall stone monument.

'And?' Tusia was clearly not following the train of thought.

'So we're looking for *two more* texts to translate the *other two* Beale Papers, right? And the uncollected letter which was sent to Morriss to try and help him decode the Papers mentions the home of the red fox.'

'Which is why we're here.'

'And it says the fox lines his den with what's important. *Most important*, in fact.' The checklist was waving in her grasp like a tiny flag.

'So?' Tusia looked for a moment, a vein throbbing on her temple.

'So the other two documents we need to translate the Beale must be what are referred to here.' Brodie was very much aware that she now looked like a traffic police officer, and her shoulder was aching with the amount of waving she was doing at the monument. She lowered her arm. 'The second document needed to read the Beale Papers must be the Statute of Virginia for Religious Freedom.'

Tusia's eyes widened with understanding.

'And the third must have something to do with Virginia University.'

Brodie flattened the ruffled checklist.

- most important
- Red Fox only three
- what is key to him remains

Hunter clapped his hands together. 'Perfect, don't you think?' He grabbed a pen and gave each a tick. 'Christmas pudding perfect!'

Tusia grinned broadly. Then they looked along the line at Brodie.

'So where is it, then?' said Hunter.

Brodie felt the colour drain from her cheeks. 'Where's what?'

'The Statute of Virginia for Religious Freedom.'

'I don't know,' she mumbled.

When she looked up, Smithies was standing beside

her. 'I think you do,' he whispered.

'I do?'

'Sure. Where do they keep copies of every important book and document written in this country? In England every book that's written has a copy stored at the British Library. Well, what about here? Where do Americans send a copy of every book published for safe-keeping?'

Brodie still didn't know.

'The National Library, Brodie. The most important library in the whole of America. Where Jefferson sent every book that was important to him, to be stored?'

'Washington?' she ventured. 'The Library of Congress?'

Smithies nodded. 'Seems like as good a place as any to start our search,' he said.

The man in the suit tightened the knot of his tie then flipped open his mobile phone. 'The information was reliable,' he said quietly.

The answer made him smile. He slipped the phone back into his pocket and repositioned his sunglasses in front of his eyes.

And the toes of his pointed shoes clipped on the stone path as he walked away from Jefferson's grave.

In a Mirror to the Past

Kitty was waiting for them at the bus stop outside the House of Congress, as arranged.

'Did you get everything you needed sorted out?' Brodie asked.

Kitty nodded and shielded her eyes from the sun. 'And you?' she said. 'Found anything on Jefferson's grave?'

'Only three things. And not one of those was that he was the president,' said Hunter.

'So he was modest, then?' suggested Kitty.

'Or leaving a clue. The Declaration of Independence was mentioned on his grave. We've got that covered. That's been used to solve one of the Beale Papers. So we're working on the idea the other two things listed might be needed to crack the other two codes.'

'Brilliant. And are those things in Washington?'

'Probably,' said Sheldon. 'At least one of them is. The Statute of Religious Freedom. Smithies thinks that will be in the Library of Congress because that's where all official document and important papers are kept. So that's one reason we're here. And there's something else.'

'Go on.'

'Jefferson donated his own collection of books to this library. It was "home" for his books.'

'And the home of the red fox was important in the letter we got sent from the post office, remember?' cut in Tusia.

'So we're thinking there might be clues in this building like in Westminster Abbey back in London,' explained Brodie. 'The names, the pictures, the position of things. They were all laid out as messages there and so maybe there'll be clues here too.'

'So we've got to look really carefully, at everything we can,' said Smithies. 'The whole place might be heaving with signs for us and we've got to use the red fox letter to find what's important. But we've got to make sure we don't draw attention to ourselves. This place may be crawling with clues but it'll be crawling with security too. Understand? We can't afford for things to go wrong here.'

Tandi leant back in her chair. 'I think I get it.' The books Smithies had brought from England were splayed around her feet.

Fabyan put down a tray of drinks on the table. He passed round glasses to Mrs Smithies, Friedman and Mr Bray.

'We've got no further on *where* Level Five are keeping their prisoners,' added Tandi. 'But I think I understand, now, exactly *why* they've taken them.'

'It's not just because they don't want people spending time on MS 408?' said Mr Bray.

'No. It's because they don't want people knowing what it says.'

'And there's a difference?'

'Totally.'

'And when you say you've got it, you're not suggesting you've cracked the code, are you?' Friedman asked, leaning forward on his chair.

'Of course not. But I'm saying that if MS 408 is a book about Avalon then I think I know what it will be saying.'

'And you're going to share that with us?' asked Fabyan.

'Of course. When the others are back,' said Tandi. She took a sip from her drink. 'I think it's something we should share as a community.'

It seemed an odd word to use, but Tandi was obviously excited, so no one pressed her to explain.

'Have you seen what this part of the building's called?' said Brodie as they reached the top of the steps of the Library of Congress. 'Only the Thomas Jefferson building!'

'Now, that's a way to keep your name remembered,' Sicknote said as he led the way inside through the security system and into the great hall.

'Bit special, isn't it?' whispered Sheldon in an appropriate library tone. 'Kinda different to the mobile library which comes up near the Plough once a fortnight.'

'This is the sort of place where books *should* be kept,' Brodie whispered along the line, sure it was the most beautiful place she'd ever been.

Tusia stepped forward and craned her head to look up at the ceiling. 'Er, guys.'

Brodie readied herself for Tusia's usual rant about the waste of money on buildings and how at least half the world was starving and the money would have been better used to buy water systems or toilets.

'Guys?' Tusia's hiss was getting more demanding. She was peering up and pointing. 'We're supposed to be looking for clues, right? So check out the top of the walls and the ceiling.'

Brodie stepped forward to join her and lifted her own hand above her eyes so she could see more clearly. Sure enough, written in gold above each lattice window, were names. Brodie scanned the list and realised they were all famous writers. DANTE, HOMER, MILTON, BACON, ARISTOTLE, GOETHE, SHAKESPEARE, MOLIERE, MOSES, HERODOTUS.

Smithies pulled a copy of the red fox letter from his inside pocket and passed it to Hunter while Brodie got out the logbook checklist. Hunter scanned the words and then looked up again at the ceiling.

'What is Key to him is dear. His home speaks of this.'

Hunter flicked the page still and skipped on.

'Men will list maybe two or four or seven things of importance; or even two or six. But to the red fox there are only three.'

'These numbers have to mean something. We've covered the number three because of the three things on Jefferson's gravestone. But just suppose that list of writers on the ceiling isn't random? There's a billion writers in the world. They could have listed any names up there. So maybe we've got to match the other numbers from the letter with the names? What d'you think?'

'It's worth a go,' said Smithies.

Sheldon walked to the front of the group. 'So which numbers do we need, then?'

'Two and four and seven,' said Hunter, running through the checklist.

Brodie got ready to jot the names down in the logbook. 'Read them out, then,' she urged, as she hurried up the steps so the names, inscribed on scrolls in the centre of bright-yellow triangles below each window, came more clearly into focus.

Hunter led them round the balcony area, calling out the names as they walked. Brodie wrote them down. When they reached the beginning again she held out the list so everyone could see it.

DANTE
HOMER

MILTON
BACON
ARISTOTLE
GOETHE
SHAKESPEARE
MOLIERE
MOSES
HERODOTUS

Then she took a pen and circled three names from the list. Name two, name four and name seven.

Tusia clapped in excitement but Kitty looked confused. 'Tell me again why those three names are important,' she said. 'Because I guess by the smiles and the whooping and the clapping, you all think they are.'

Tusia began to explain. 'HOMER originally wrote about the island where people ate the lotus flowers, remember? Tennyson turned that story into a poem and Elgar set the poem to music. Homer was the inspiration. He had the idea of a magical island. So we already know he's important in any of the Knights of Neustria searching.'

'OK. And the other two?'

'BACON hid the ring for us to find, telling us about Avalon. He's vital to our search. Always has been. And then SHAKESPEARE's helped us loads with the anagram about the River Wye and the quote on the statue in London all about ignorance being darkness. Those three names are *all* connected with the Knights of Neustria and our search for Avalon.'

'This is fantastic,' said Hunter. 'Those writers are all linked to MS 408. That's got to be positive hasn't it, sir?'

Smithies was obviously trying not to look too enthusiastic but it was clear he was excited too.

'So what next?' said Hunter. 'I guess we should try and deal with the rest of the numbers. *Two* and *six* are in the next line of the red fox letter. We should try and find out what they mean. Look. There's more names there,' he said, pointing at the large cartouches along the east and west side of the walls.

Brodie stared at the names written in gold on the stone tablets and began to write once more in her logbook. This time the rest stood still until she'd written down every name.

CERVANTES
HUGO
SCOTT
COOPER
LONGFELLOW
TENNYSON
GIBBON
BANCROFT

She took her pen once more and circled the *second* and then the *sixth* name.

'HUGO. As in the French writer Victor Hugo, right? He wrote *Les Miserables*?'

'Well, that's a book about a revolution,' said Sicknote. 'That book was banned, you know. People used to burn it.'

'So we're back to book burning,' said Brodie quietly.

'Yes, probably not something we should mention here,' whispered Sicknote. 'But it does fit with the searching for firebirds and things saved from flames.'

'And then there's the other name?' encouraged Smithies.

Brodie didn't need to look down at the list. 'TENNYSON! Knight of Neustria. Cambridge Apostle *and* the writer of one of the most famous poems about Avalon and Arthur.'

They were doing so well. It looked like their visit to the library had already been worthwhile and they hadn't even come across any books yet.

'It does seem incredible that those names fit so closely with everything we've learnt,' said Smithies. 'Even I have to cautiously admit it's looking even more likely that Beale's treasure is linked to the Knights of Neustria and the secrets of Avalon.'

'So it's even more important we find the key texts to read the Beale Papers, then,' said Hunter, striding ahead. 'Come on,' he called over his shoulder. 'Let's get on with it!'

Brodie tried to tick the checklist as she hurried on. She could hardly believe they were doing so well.

Hunter led the way past a circular window. There was writing in bright-red letters sharp against gold.

TOO LOW THEY BUILD WHO BUILD
BENEATH THE STARS

Brodie liked that phrase. Her granddad had always

- the red fox of the mountains ✓
- most important to the fox ✓
- His home speaks of this - lining of his den
- west and south-east winds,
- what is key to him remains ✓
- two, four, seven ✓
- two or six. ✓
- But to the red fox there are only three. ✓
- things he cannot live without ✓
- and things for which he will be remembered.
- Admiral Cockburn. Man of letters. ✓
- God's speed under one nation
- Thomas Jefferson Beale. ✓

told her to aim for the stars. It felt odd to remember some of the things he'd told her. She still hadn't got over that he hadn't told her about Friedman. But she was trying. And it seemed like a good motto. This phrase was important. Brodie knew it. She just didn't know how yet.

'What you thinking, B?'

Brodie turned. 'I was just thinking about something I'd read.'

'You're *always* thinking about something you've read.'

'I mean something here. A quote on the walls which made me sure what we're doing's important.'

Hunter stopped for a moment. He seemed to drink in the smell of the air around him, allowing the stillness of the library to flood across him. 'It *is* important,' he said. 'Really important. And if you needed any more convincing,' he added with a smile, 'then take a look at those quotes there.' He gestured up to the writing across the domed lobbies at the head of each stairway at each end of the corridor. Brodie paced along the line as she read. Above the north lobby she read 'KNOWLEDGE IS POWER' by Sir Francis Bacon and above the south stairs was a quote in Latin by Horace, 'E PLURIBUS UNUM'.

'OK, Mr Ingham,' Brodie said, turning to face him.

'A bit of help, please. I totally get the quote from Bacon but I can't read the Latin.'

Sicknote peered forward.

'Hey, hold on,' interrupted Hunter. 'I can read that phrase, you know.'

'*You* can?' Brodie said, gulping down her surprise.

'Sure. It's a numbers thing. Something about "out of the many there is one".'

'He's got the right idea,' Sicknote said encouragingly.

'I guess it's like us,' said Hunter. 'A right pic-n-mix of people all chucked together in a goodie bag. Out of many people, one team.'

'That's really nice,' said Brodie.

'Yeah, well, don't let old Toots hear I said that. There's always one nut cluster with not enough chocolate and too many nuts.' But he was smiling as he led Brodie and Sicknote back to meet the others.

'So where now?' said Sheldon. 'We're looking for something Jefferson wrote about the Statute of Religious Freedom, aren't we? So where, in a collection of 111 million books, would you file a copy of something like that?'

'In the Thomas Jefferson collection, perhaps?' said Tusia, pointing out a sign which appeared to point the way. 'It says here, there's a display of the books the president passed on to the library. The books

126

he wanted to have a "home" here. That's got to be what we need.'

Brodie's anticipation grew. They were a team. They were in the biggest library in the world. And they were just about to find a book to help them translate the second Beale Paper which might help lead them to the treasure of Avalon. Could things get any better?

The security guard at the entrance to the Library of Congress looked down at his watch. Half an hour till the game started. Time to do one more walk-through. Then he was out of here.

He radioed Control.

He was just replacing his radio in its holster when someone called over to him.

'Can I help you, sir?' The guy didn't look like your regular tourist. That suit would have cost a fortune and the pointed shoes were obviously hand-crafted leather.

The guard stole a glance at his watch again. He really didn't have time for this.

The visitor moved closer, and tightened the knot of his tie.

'What a total and utter disaster,' hissed Tusia from behind her hand.

Brodie didn't need telling. They'd been so full of

hope. So sure the Jefferson collection would have the answer. That was, until they *saw* the Jefferson collection.

'How are you supposed to get to them?' groaned Brodie, looking forward despondently.

'You're obviously not,' replied Smithies.

The display of Jefferson's books was behind glass. Hermetically sealed and protected from damage and dust and humidity and light. But trapped all the same. If the text they needed was part of the collection then it was out of reach.

'Impressive, don't you think?' said a tour guide, moving over to join them. 'People are often overwhelmed, especially when they consider what the books have gone through.'

Brodie felt her curiosity growing despite her disappointment. The guide launched into a well-practised and rehearsed speech she never tired of telling. 'Jefferson sold 6,487 books to the Library of Congress after the fire of 1814. But then a second fire on Christmas Eve in 1851 burnt nearly two thirds of the Jefferson collection.'

That was awful. The books Jefferson gave to a new home were destroyed. This couldn't be good. Maybe the writing they needed about the Statute of Religious Freedom was in the two thirds of the books which were burnt. That would mean the end of the search.

The guide was still talking. 'We're trying to replace the books and you can see the replacement copies are marked with ribbons. And where we're still hunting for books, there's gaps along the shelves. You'll notice an interesting numbering system, too, on the spines.' Hunter stepped in closer. 'Jefferson had his own way of classifying things. A system used instead of the Dewey system, the most famous method of book numbering.'

Hunter's eyes lit up with interest. They'd talked about the Jefferson numbering system. But Brodie didn't know how this could make Hunter look happy. Didn't he realise the chances were the book they needed had been destroyed?

'It's just a good job,' went on the guide, 'that some of the most important and unique volumes were kept separately from the others and escaped the second fire. The most precious of the books, and the volumes Jefferson wrote himself, were actually kept in the Librarian's Room.'

'Children, you say?' The security guard was not really following the tourist's story. That was, if he *was* a tourist. He looked mighty smart to be on vacation. 'And some old guys. Alrighty. I'll look into it.'

He didn't have time for this. The game on TV

would have started by now and everything in him wanted to walk away and pretend he hadn't heard. But he knew the thought would nag at him. He'd never enjoy the game until he checked this fella's story out.

He took his radio again from his holster, radioed in the call and then turned to check some details. No going back now. Security alert would be in operation. He'd be here for hours.

But the man in the suit was making for the exit, his long-toed shoes clipping on the tiled floors as he walked.

'Come on,' Smithies mumbled, calling behind him as Sicknote, taking a quick blast on his asthma inhaler, struggled to keep up.

'Where we going now?' called Sheldon.

'The Librarian's Room, I think,' said Hunter. 'Smithies must reckon that what we need must've been kept in there.'

'Here,' said Tusia, stopping as she approached a large doorway and pointing out the sign. '*Reading Room Gallery: Access to Librarian's Room (by appointment only)*.'

Smithies nodded. 'Got to give it a go,' he said.

'And the appointment bit?' asked Sicknote.

Smithies shrugged.

Hunter pushed open a doorway and a draught of cold air hit them all. The gallery they'd entered was high, long and narrow, but the blast of air came from the space which fell away below the gallery. Brodie had loved the library in New York. She'd loved the entrance hall to this building. But she *adored* what she saw now.

'Steady on, B,' Hunter said supportively. 'Don't want you falling.'

Brodie looked up at the golden walls and the gleaming domed ceiling and the arches which led away to cases and cases of books behind the circles of desks and chairs each illuminated by a single golden light.

Tusia moved to stand open-mouthed beside her.

'Please don't spoil it by telling me it's a waste of money and the funds should've been spent on drainage and healthcare and for every book here someone could've bought a shelter or a—'

Tusia held up her hand. 'It's beautiful,' she said.

They stood for a moment in the golden glow and the silence and then Sicknote coughed quietly. 'Those statues,' he said. 'Around the edge. What are they?'

Brodie peered forward to see where bronze statues were looking down at the people who were reading in the space below. They each stood alone, looking kind of lonely. Vast spaces between them like they'd been arranged on numbers of a clock. Or . . . Brodie tried to think it through. The statues were arranged like points of the compass. She'd no idea why this made her feel excited.

'South-east and west,' mumbled Tusia.

Brodie turned to face her friend, whose mouth was still hanging open slightly. 'The red fox letter said something about south-east and west. It's talking about those statues. I'm sure of it.'

Tusia took the checklist then looked again across the reading room. She was grinning.

'Well, don't keep the egg boiling,' said Hunter, stepping nervously from foot to foot. 'What does it mean?'

'Those statues show different types of learning,' Tusia explained. 'The statue on the *south-east* wall's supposed to stand for Philosophy.'

Brodie peered at the golden statue clasping a book in his hand. It seemed obvious they had to look for a statue in the south-east corner, but why Tusia was so excited about what she saw Brodie wasn't really sure.

'Why are you happy about that statue?' asked Kitty.

'Because of the quote above it,' said Tusia.

132

Brodie peered to see more clearly as Tusia read aloud.

'THE INQUIRY, KNOWLEDGE AND BELIEF OF TRUTH IS THE SOVEREIGN GOOD OF HUMAN NATURE.'

'Very nice,' said Hunter, obviously not entirely sure why Tusia seemed so pleased with this statement.

'It's a quote from Sir Francis Bacon, one of our Knights of Neustria!' she explained.

'How the bacon butty d'you know that?'

'Because it says so. Look!'

Hunter's eyes widened. 'So what about the statue on the west?' he said, turning his head to see.

'That one's supposed to stand for History,' Tusia said calmly.

'What's that statue holding?' said Kitty.

'A book.'

'No. In the other hand?'

'A mirror!' gasped Brodie, as her mind flooded with all the work they'd done at Shugborough Hall involving mirrors and reflections.

'Like the Lady of Shalott?' said Sheldon.

'In more ways than one,' said Brodie, her smile widening. 'Look at the quote above her head.' She read the words aloud.

'ONE GOD, ONE LAW, ONE ELEMENT, AND

133

ONE FAR OFF DIVINE EVENT TO WHICH THE
WHOLE CREATION MOVES.'

'How's that like the Lady of Shallot?' said Sheldon.

'Because of who wrote that quote,' Brodie said. She
could hardly believe it. It was almost too neat.

'Who?' pleaded Kitty, peering forward to read the
name.

'Tennyson!' said Brodie. 'Our favourite Knight of
Neustria.'

Brodie looked again at the checklist. They were racing
through the clues and everything they found was
connecting to Thomas Jefferson or the Knights of
Neustria. 'It's like playing Scrabble and landing on a
triple word score,' she mused as she added extra ticks
to the list.

'Or getting to take the opponent's queen in chess,'
said Tusia.

'*But what does it all mean?*' groaned Kitty. 'I know
why you're excited. Bacon and Tennyson. They're sort
of vital to this whole quest thing. I get it. But the
quotes. What do they mean?'

'Maybe that finding out answers is what being
human's all about,' Smithies said. 'I think that's what
the Bacon quote means and I like that idea.'

'And perhaps the Tennyson quote means that

- the red fox of the mountains ✓
- most important to the fox ✓
- His home speaks of this - lining of his den
- west and south-east winds,
- what is key to him remains ✓
- two, four, seven ✓
- two or six. ✓
- But to the red fox there are only three. ✓
  things he cannot live without ✓
- and things for which he will be remembered. ✓
  Admiral Cockburn. Man of letters. ✓
- God's speed under one nation
- Thomas Jefferson Beale. ✓

something happened. Something important, and far away, which affected the whole of creation,' said Sicknote.

'OK,' said Kitty. 'But do they fit with MS 408 at all?'

Brodie thought about what the adults had said. 'Well, we're trying to find the truth, aren't we?' she offered. 'So that fits with the being human bit.'

'And maybe MS 408 is the story of what happened on that big event,' suggested Tusia. 'I mean, maybe things in Avalon changed then and so people wrote it all down in MS 408.'

'I get it,' said Kitty. 'Sounds good if you're right. Like we're getting closer to answers.'

There was a moment when everyone peered down at the statues.

It was Hunter who broke the silence. 'We might be getting closer to answers but we're no closer to the Librarian's Room. I think we should be making a move.'

'Excuse me?' The Director lifted his head, narrowing his eyes to peer forward. 'That seems a rather impertinent question.' He rubbed rather vigorously at the back of his neck and then reached into his desk drawer and took out a small container of tablets and pressed one under his tongue. 'You want to know *why*?'

Kerrith shuffled her feet slightly. 'Yes, sir. I did just wonder *why*.'

'I can tell you why I'm forced to take this ridiculous medication,' he snapped, through a mouthful of tablet.

Kerrith was entirely sure that wasn't the question she'd asked him.

'Infected insect bite. Blasted mosquitoes. Did you know I've recently discovered the mosquito's the most dangerous animal on the planet?'

Kerrith didn't.

'Half the humans who've ever died have been killed by female mosquitoes. One person dies every twelve seconds as a result of a mosquito bite, somewhere in the world. They carry diseases, you see. Fatal diseases.'

Kerrith looked down at her shoes. 'Sir, I'm sorry. I'm not really sure where this is going. I just . . .' Her voice tailed away.

'You've read the book at Site Three?'

'Yes, sir.'

'And it fascinated you. Let you see the scale and scope of the organisation you're involved in.'

Kerrith nodded feebly. 'And it made me just want to ask *why*, sir.'

The Director leant back on his chair. He took a deep breath and folded his arms across his chest. 'Let me explain it all to you, Miss Vernan. The Suppressors have been working for centuries to try and control the information and the stories around the world. It's important there's an accepted version of truth. A right way to see the world, and the Suppressors, throughout history, have been responsible for ensuring the correct version's always accepted and seen as the most powerful. Your reading will have shown you that the work of the Suppressors has taken many forms and been supported throughout many countries and populations.' His face was red with excitement. 'I explained to you, not long ago, about how we've manipulated history to ensure when people begin to ask too many questions their attention's diverted. National disasters, like fogs and sinking of great ships, are great ones for pulling attention away from our work. But of course, perhaps you hadn't fully grasped the role of the Suppressors in destroying stories.'

Kerrith looked once more at the ground.

'You see, if people understand their world because of the stories they have told to them or the stories they read, then that process has to be successfully managed. If you want to weaken a part of society, you take away their stories. The book you read at Site Three will have shown you that. Destroying stories destroys a culture and a way of life. It breaks the chain and kills secrets that should have been passed on. History's full of examples. The library of Alexandria devastated because of the stories it contained. The Library of Congress in America wrecked in 1851. The number of books destroyed topped 35,000. Stories which questioned the world-view we wanted to promote, eliminated like that.' He clicked his fingers. 'And if you cannot destroy the stories themselves, you weaken the people who tell them.'

'It was that section, sir. I hadn't really heard about it before.'

This news obviously pleased the Director. 'Across Australasia and the Americas there were native peoples whose stories of the world were different to our own. Their stories were rarely written down so they were more difficult at first to stamp out. But we did our work there by education.' He seemed to beam with pride at this point. 'We took children away from their aboriginal families and we educated them in the stories we wanted them to hear. We banned them telling their stories. Our aim was to "assimilate" the natives into our way of thinking. To make our stories theirs. Of course, we couldn't do this unless we made the telling of their stories illegal.' He seemed particularly pleased with this statement. 'Someone has to be in control, Miss Vernan. Someone had to monitor the stories told and the versions of truth shared. You ask me why and I tell you if we didn't, then there'd be chaos.' He snorted with laughter. 'We can't have people believing what they want to. There has to be control. And we as Suppressors manage that control. We always have. And we always will.'

Kerrith's head was thumping.

'I know this is a vast idea for you to comprehend. To see, for the first time, that throughout history and throughout time there've been those who've ensured the *right* stories survive and those which threaten the world order are destroyed. But that's the way of the world. The way of *our* world.'

'But I just wondered—'

'Now's not the time for wondering. Or questioning. What good's that ever done anybody?' He shook his head. 'No, my dear. What you've read in the history book at Site Three shows you how things are and how things will be. What we do is part of protecting society. Protecting it from itself.'

'And what we're doing with MS 408 is part of the plan?' she asked quietly.

'All part of the plan. Part of how we control what people read and share. The words of MS 408 could reveal a whole new world to its readers if they can make sense of the code. And we're not interested in a whole new world. We must keep control of the world we have.' He drew himself up tall in his chair. 'We suppress people's stories, Miss Vernan. We suppress their attempts to question and then, as you've seen at Site Three, if this doesn't succeed in keeping people quiet, we suppress the people themselves.'

6

Understanding the Fire Thief

The sign said they were in the south-west corridor. It also said again that the Librarian's Room allowed access only by appointment.

'We obviously shouldn't be in this part of the building,' said Kitty. 'Do we just carry on?'

'Course,' said Sheldon. 'We keep looking until someone stops us. So we need to be quick.'

The corridor extended onwards, looking out to the left on an interior court. Sheldon led the way. Sicknote was struggling to keep up. He leant one hand against the wall and signalled that he couldn't keep on.

Brodie began to wonder if perhaps they should have left the older members of the team outside.

Tusia stood beside Sicknote and nodded encouragement. 'We're nearly there, sir.' She leant her own hand against the wall then she stood up straight. 'Hey, look. That's not right.'

Brodie hurried back to join her.

'Below that picture.'

Brodie looked at the decorated panel. The title underneath explained that the picture showed Prometheus stealing fire from the gods. She liked that story. The idea that power was stolen by man and given out to others.

'Brodie!' Tusia snapped. 'Can you see it?'

Brodie jolted out of her thinking about the fire thief story. 'See what?'

'There's something weird about some of those letters in the quote,' she said. 'Below the picture with branches all round it. Look! Everything's decorated so perfectly here. But that quote looks all wrong!'

Brodie scanned the letters. It was true. Some of them looked a little thicker than the others. Bolder, like they'd been applied with extra force or care.

She opened her notebook and began to write out each emboldened letter.

*To the souls of fire, I, Pallas
Athena give more fire, and to
those who are manful, a
might more than a man's*

PGITAFETA

'Well?' Tusia said. 'Anything? A name we know? A writer? A possible Knight?'

'Nothing,' said Brodie. 'They don't make sense.'

Tusia looked disappointed. 'Doesn't matter. I was just thinking about the Admiral Cockburn thing and the clue about letters and I just wondered if this was connected. Especially with those branches curling round the picture. I thought it was a sign from a Knight of Neustria. Guess not everything was left here by them for us to find.'

'Never mind, Toots. You can't be right every time!'

Hunter jumped out of the way as Tusia swung her arm at him playfully.

'I'm OK now,' Sicknote interrupted. 'When you two have quite finished I feel good enough to go on now. The Librarian's Room? Haven't we got an "appointment"?'

'Shame we don't really have one of those,' Smithies said. 'It'd certainly make it easier to get in there seeing as the place is totally restricted.'

'Never stopped us before,' joked Hunter.

The security guard at the Library of Congress glanced at his watch. Fifteen minutes ago he should have been at home with a beer and watching the play-offs. That was if the guy in the suit and the sharp shoes hadn't given him 'information'.

He was annoyed. 'Control' said he had to wait. They were sending reinforcements.

He pulled his cuff down over his watch so at least he couldn't see the time, and the radio in his holster crackled into life. They were on their way.

This was ridiculous. Totally and utterly ridiculous. Kerrith was unused to this experience. Her mind couldn't focus. The discussion with the Director hadn't helped at all. The same image kept returning to her. A woman hunched over a wooden desk scratching her nails into the wood and making a mark. It was as if the woman was scratching the marks into her mind. Kerrith couldn't remember ever feeling like this before. She didn't like it.

There was something about the woman which

troubled her. Her eyes. The woman had lifted them only for a second. She couldn't possibly have known Kerrith had been watching her on the monitors in the control room at Site Three. She couldn't possibly know Kerrith was thinking of her now. But she had and she was and the thinking felt odd. It felt like 'worry'.

Kerrith shook herself. Worrying wasn't something *she* did. It wasn't her job to worry. It was her job to follow instructions and do what she was told for the good of the organisation she was part of. That's why she'd read every single page of the book the Director had given her. The work of the Suppressors thrilled her. It was exciting to know Suppressors had taken children away from their families and raised them to believe and follow agreed stories. It was wonderful to know Suppressors had the power to make the believing and telling of certain stories illegal. And she'd seen at once how all her work on the stifling of the work on MS 408 fitted into a global picture of keeping control. And for a while she'd felt nothing but joy and pride. She'd waited so long to understand everything. And yet that woman scratching at the table. Why had she done that? And why couldn't Kerrith forget?

Kerrith flicked her hair behind her ears and unfastened the blouse button at the base of her neck. A bead of sweat rolled down from her chin.

She was annoyed now. This was crazy. Why did she have to feel like this?

And all that rubbish about mosquitoes the Director had gone on about. Why couldn't she shake that from her mind either? She closed her eyes. The most dangerous animal on the earth. How could that be? She wiped the bead of sweat away. Mosquitoes were attracted to sweat apparently. They could smell weakness and were drawn to it. And she wouldn't be weak. This was all she'd wanted. To be part of the inner circle and to know everything. But now she knew. And now she'd seen that woman.

Kerrith looked down at her watch. Where was the Director? He'd told her he had to take an important call in the other room on the other line. That had been ages ago. Why wasn't he back?

She walked around to the window and stood behind the Director's desk. This was where the decisions were made and where everything was decided. Except it wasn't. Not really. She knew that now. The work of the Black Chamber in suppressing stories and ideas was controlled by people high above this. Not a national organisation, but an international one. She stepped closer to the desk. It was clear and uncluttered. A single fountain pen unclipped, resting on a small pile of papers, waiting for the Director's signature.

Kerrith folded her arms.

Then she saw the paperweight.

She'd seen it before, of course. The Director had talked in detail once about what it symbolised. A sword in the stone. Only one hand could remove the blade. That's how it worked. That's what the Chamber and the work of the Suppressors was all about. A sword in the stone only the rightful heir could release.

Kerrith curled her fingers around the hilt. She needed to feel it resist and to know the Director was right. That there was only one way to draw the sword.

But the sword slid effortlessly out of the stone.

The Librarian's Room was just in front of them. The door was closed.

'We do the hair grip thing?' whispered Sheldon. 'Like you did at Elgar's place?

'Or use a credit card?' suggested Kitty. 'Slide it between the door and the lock?'

'Or we could just try the handle,' Tusia said, allowing the door to swing open. 'Always best to try that way first.'

Hunter stumbled into the room behind her. Brodie remained in the corridor, her mouth gaping open.

One day, when all this was over, she'd have an office like this. Exactly like this.

Facing the doorway was a tall window topped with a stretch of glass shaped like a half-moon. In front of the window, framed by two flags, was a wooden desk. Behind the desk were rows and rows of books on shelves. The walls were panelled with dark oak wood running all the way up to a gold and blue domed ceiling.

'How d'you get to have an office like this?' asked Sheldon.

'You get chosen by a president,' said Smithies. 'Here, look, there's pictures of past librarians and . . .'

'You OK, sir?'

Tusia stood next to Smithies who was staring at a black and white photo.

'It's Archibald MacLeish.'

'Should we be pleased about that, sir? Was he a Knight of Neustria?'

'I'm not sure. He was a poet. I'd forgotten he was a librarian here. He said something interesting things we should discuss.'

Tusia looked slightly panicked. '*Now*, sir?'

'No. But soon. When we've found what we need.'

Brodie moved into the centre of the room. 'So how do we do that, then?' She looked up and on the very centre of the ceiling was painted a long streamer with words on it. 'LITERA SCRIPTA MANET'. She turned

149

to Ingham. 'What's it mean?' she whispered.

'That the written word endures,' he said. 'That it survives.'

That was good then. The written word enduring. It made her feel they were right to hope that in this room, where Jefferson's most important books and papers were kept, there'd be something connected to what he wrote about Religious Freedom.

They hurried to the shelves, scanning the spines of the books. 'Well?' called Sheldon as he reached the end of his own line. 'Anything?'

No one answered.

'There must be something here. A copy of what Jefferson wrote. The first copy. Surely.'

Still no answer.

'Anything at all?'

The silence was overwhelming. They'd checked every spine. Nothing here seemed remotely linked to Religious Freedom. But that's what they wanted. It was supposed to be one of the three most important things to him. The gravestone said so.

Brodie looked up again at the ceiling. If the written word endured, then where was it? The painted figure in the centre of the ceiling kept her face turned away as if she was afraid to meet Brodie's gaze. In response, Brodie turned away too and allowed her eyes to focus on the circled painting in the corner of the ceiling.

This painted figure was holding a musical instrument. Brodie looked to the next picture. This time the figure held an open book. Music and books had given them answers before. But this time they needed something more. She moved to the corner of the room and looked up at the third painting. It showed a woman holding a branch that was on fire. Underneath was a phrase in Latin.

'Mr Ingham. That writing. By the third painting. What's it say?'

Sicknote scanned the line of letters. Then he looked down and spoke the translation.

'IN TENEBRIS LUX . . . IN DARKNESS LIGHT.'

Brodie's head hurt. It was like the message at the very beginning of this adventure. Light is knowledge. But *where* was the light?

She reached for their checklist. She scanned it, underlining words with her mind.

The only phrase they hadn't ticked off in their search was 'lining of his den'. They'd thought it meant the library was important. It was the home for his books and all the clues were on the walls. But why go on about the lining of his den in a separate clue if they'd come to the library anyway?

- the <u>red fox</u> of the mountains, ✓
- most important to the fox ✓
- His home speaks of this - <u>lining of his den</u>
- west and south-east winds, ✓
- what is key to him remains ✓
- two, four, seven ✓
- two or six. ✓
- But to the red fox there are only three. ✓
- things he cannot live without ✓
- and things for which he will be remembered
- Admiral Cockburn. Man of letters. ✓
- God's speed under one nation

And whose den was it they were at? The red fox's in a way, if this was where all his precious books were kept. Rows and rows of books on shelves fixed to wooden panels.

'This red fox really isn't helping us,' said Hunter. 'Are we missing something to do with foxes and their dens. They're like dogs, right? Wild dogs?'

Something clicked in Brodie's mind. Coyotes. They were wild dogs. Like foxes in a way. So red fox could be another name for coyote.

Her mind began to churn the stories from the myths and legends stories her mum had told her as a child. A Native American version of a story they'd seen a picture of in the hall. In this version a coyote and not Prometheus was the fire thief. He stole the fire from the gods and he carried it away. Then man found the fire he'd stolen.

The understanding scalded her. Brodie jumped back. She knew what the last unticked item on the list meant.

'Fire thief!'

'What, B?'

'Coyote. It's another name for red fox. There's a link between Jefferson and coyote and Prometheus, the fire thief we saw on the painting just now.'

'Well, I'm not getting the link,' said Tusia.

'It's a different version of the myth,' explained Brodie. 'Coyote stole the fire – then he ran! He passed the fire from animal to animal. All sorts of things went wrong though. It's a way of explaining how animals look sort of different.'

Everyone was waiting for her to continue.

'Coyote passed the flame to squirrel and the fire burnt his back. It made his tail curl up behind him. Chipmunk took the fire next but the gods reached out to stop him. Their hands marked three stripes down the chipmunk's back. Fire was passed to frog and the gods grabbed hold of the frog and pulled his tail off. Then, the frog passed the fire to the tree and the tree swallowed the fire so when the gods came to search they couldn't find it. And then the tree fell into the water. The branches got covered by water so no one knew where the fire was. But it was hiding. The fire's always there, inside the wood, hidden and waiting and ready to be released. When there's darkness the light's ready to be freed.' Brodie pointed up at the ceiling and the woman who held the lighted wooden torch. 'In the darkness there's light and the answer's *in* the story like the fire's *in* the wood.' She spun around on the spot, stretching her hands out wide. 'Look at the panelling in this room. What we look for is *in* the wood.' And so she led them, pressing her hands against the panelling.

154

Then, from the other side of the room, where Tusia knelt on the floor, there was a click. 'Here. It's here,' said Tusia, and she drew her hand away.

The wooden panelling in front of where she knelt hung open.

Tusia reached inside.

'Well?'

'I've got it,' Tusia said.

But she didn't have time to tell them what she'd found.

Outside the door to the Librarian's Room, an alarm bell began to pierce the air.

'Security know we're here,' yelped Brodie.

Tusia scrambled to her feet and thrust the package she'd drawn from the panelling in the walls into the waistband of her skirt. 'We need to get out of here,' she blurted.

'You go,' urged Smithies. 'Make for the exit somehow and we'll find you.'

'But—' Brodie didn't have time to formulate her argument.

'Just leave me and Ingham here. We'll do the "aged English gentlemen stumbled into the room by mistake" thing. We'll make them think we're the reason for the alarm. There's no time, Brodie! Just go!'

Smithies' eyes were wide, his cheeks flecked with scarlet. Brodie tried to breathe and grasped at his hand for a moment before Hunter pulled her by the arm.

'Where will you find us?' Brodie yelled over her shoulder as she ran.

Smithies looked up at the ceiling and his eyes flickered for a moment. But he didn't breathe a word.

Brodie had no idea what he meant. She'd no idea where they were running to and no clue how to escape. But she moved with the others with Hunter leading the way. Behind them they heard a door slamming; feet running; shouting coming from the Librarian's Room. But they didn't wait. They didn't even look back.

Hunter surged towards a door marked 'Service Lift Only', and then pulled open a thick metal grille door. 'Inside!' he called, tugging Kitty in last and slamming the door back into place.

The lift shuddered and shook as it began to fall away into the darkness.

'Will they be all right?' begged Tusia, her eyes flitting from one person to another.

'They'll be OK. They'll be OK,' repeated Hunter, clearly attempting to reassure himself as well as the others. 'But we must make it worth the risk. We've got to get out with what we found.'

The lift shuddered to a halt and Sheldon clawed the

grille door open. In front of them, stretching as far as the eye could see, were rows and rows of yellow metal cages loaded down with books and texts, and moving up and down like mini elevators. It was obviously some sort of transport system for moving the books from storage into the library. Hunter rushed forward. The others followed.

Brodie stumbled at the rear. She couldn't seem to get any breath into her lungs. It was like her body had forgotten how to breathe.

'This way,' yelled Hunter, his arms raised scrabbling at the wall as he careered forward. The elevators clanged and juddered behind them as the floor space narrowed, funnelling down into a dimly lit corridor snaking away into the distance.

'Are we still in the library?' called Kitty, looking behind her as she ran. Tunnels crossed theirs. Corridors intersecting. A network of walkways and crossings hidden below ground.

They passed signs directing people to the Senate Offices, signs pointing towards the Capitol Building. Corridors stretching away into the dark.

'This must be how those in power get across the city,' panted Tusia. 'It's how they do it all without being seen.'

'Well, let's just hope we don't get seen, then,' Brodie

blurted as her feet pounded against the ground. 'We've got to get out of here. Up into the light.'

Hunter drove onwards. Brodie's side stabbed with a stitch. A sharp, hot needle jabbing into her side with every step as the air pressed down on them under a concrete sunless sky.

And then, like something seen by a diver, trying to swim up from a waterlogged reef, a pattern dappled across the ground in front of them like sunlight on the water.

'Here,' insisted Hunter, tugging Brodie's arm. 'Up here.'

Together they stumbled up the concrete steps and burst out into the light.

They were at the edge of the Washington Mall. Smithies and Sicknote were trapped behind them. But they were out from under the ground. And with the package they'd taken from behind the secret wooden panels, they were free.

7

The Temple Against Tyranny

'So were they dealt with?' Morgan Summerfield wasn't sure if he was supposed to be answering the phone. But as Kerrith's assistant, then surely he had to take the calls on her personal line if she wasn't in the office.

The voice at the other end was shouting now. Morgan was pretty sure there was swearing too, but the long-distance call was breaking up. Something about things going wrong at the Capitol. He wasn't sure he really wanted to be the one to pass on the message but the voice was insistent. And still swearing. So he guessed he had no choice.

He hung up the phone and opened the internal email system. He figured some messages were best sent in print rather than delivered in person. For some

159

reason this idea made him feel quite powerful.

Hunter turned from the front of the group. 'I don't know where we should go.'

They had escaped from the Library of Congress nearly three hours earlier and had been wandering the length of the Washington Mall ever since. Everything had gone wrong. They'd meant to leave the library as a team. They'd never intended to be apart, and now the Washington end of the operation was split in two they'd no idea how to re-form it. That was if Smithies and Sicknote had even managed to escape from the guards in the library.

'Why didn't they agree to take mobiles?' groaned Sheldon.

'To reduce the risk of Level Five tracing us, remember?' explained Hunter. 'Although all it's done is reduce the chance of us finding them!'

'I say we ring New York on Brodie's phone, then,' said Sheldon. 'We tell Tandi what's happened. We've got to take the risk.'

Brodie was desperate to ring. She was sure Tandi's calming voice would make her feel safe. But making contact with New York was bound to worry her granddad if he thought they'd been separated from Smithies. Then there was the worry they'd cause Mrs

Smithies. 'We can't ring New York yet. We've got to think about where Smithies and Sicknote would go if they did manage to get out of the library. And we go there,' she added, sliding the mobile phone back into her pocket. 'That's what we do.'

If only they'd come up with a sensible plan beforehand.

Brodie slumped down on to the grass and clutched her knees up to her chest. Above them the light was fading. Clouds thickening like a blanket. Kitty sat down beside her and tugged at the blades of grass. She didn't say anything and Brodie was glad.

Ahead of them pools of water stretched from the Capitol building down towards the Washington Monument. The first traces of moonlight were teasing at the edges of the water.

'Pools of reflection,' said Tusia eventually, as she too sank down on to the grass.

Brodie looked up.

'That's what they're called. The man-made ponds. Pools of reflection.'

Brodie let her mind play with the words. They'd certainly used the word 'reflection' to help them out in their earlier searches. Mirrors had been vital. She'd used Smithies' mirror to open the back of the book they'd found in the library at Shugborough Hall. He'd

161

a knack of always giving her what was needed. So why now, if he had even managed to escape, had they no idea where to find him? Why didn't she know what to do? In her mind she replayed the scene in the Librarian's Room. 'Where will we find you?' she'd said. And he'd just looked up. Why? Here they were, stranded in the capital city of a foreign country, surrounded by monuments to wars and presidents, and all he'd done to help her out was to look up at the ceiling!

'Oh, here we go,' said Hunter keenly. 'Have you worked it out, B? Something? Anything to help us?'

Brodie grabbed his hand and let him pull her up. How could it have taken her so long? 'Pass me the map,' she blurted.

Sheldon rummaged in his pocket and pulled out the free tour guide map they'd collected from a man who'd tried to tempt them to take a Segway tour.

'Come on!' urged Brodie.

Sheldon thrust her the map and she shook it open.

'Smithies looked up at the ceiling and I get it now.'

'Give her time,' said Hunter, holding out his hand to help Kitty stand. 'She likes to think things through *as* she says them, not before. No internal filtering of ideas. She doesn't go with putting the salad in the spinner first, she just dumps it all out there for us to sort, slugs on the lettuce and all.'

162

Kitty looked like she understood.

Brodie scanned the map. 'Smithies looked up at the words painted on the ceiling. That's our clue.'

'The words in Latin?' said Tusia. 'I don't remember all of them. There was a lot of Latin.'

'The written word endures,' said Kitty quietly. Everyone turned to face her.

'Exactly.' For Brodie things were slotting into place. Washington was a city full of monuments to make memories endure. Things people did; things people said; things people were. She glanced back down at the Washington Monument. A huge obelisk straining up towards the sky. A memorial for a president. But not the president *they* were interested in. 'If they've got away, then I think they'll go to the place the written word endures,' she said.

Hunter rubbed his head. 'What! Back at the library? Are you sure? I don't think that's right, B. If they managed to get free of the guards, they'd want to be well clear of the place.'

Brodie paced up and down, the map flapping in the breeze. 'Libraries aren't the only places the written word endures. We've spent hours on this search traipsing round looking at other words intended to last forever.'

'Graves?' said Tusia. 'You want us to look for another grave?'

Brodie shook her head. 'Not a grave. A memorial.'

'A memorial to who?' asked Sheldon.

Brodie pulled the map flat and jabbed it with her finger. 'Thomas Jefferson, of course,' and the rest looked down to the place where she pointed.

'I'm afraid this is most irregular, ma'am.'

Kerrith pouted. 'What d'you mean, irregular?'

'Well, we don't usually allow contact with the clients here, unless there've been instructions from the top.'

'Now, listen to me, young man. I *am* the top. The Director himself brought me down here only a few weeks ago. I'm a Level Five employee. I've read "the book" and I know what we do here and what we've done in the past. And I'm telling you now, I need to see a certain . . .' she searched for the word he'd used, '. . . client.'

'I'm really not sure about this. It really is—'

'I insist you allow me access,' Kerrith snapped. 'It's not your job to question.'

The young man based by the observation screen grimaced. 'Very well, ma'am. But I have to register my—'

'Register what you like! But you'll do what I say. That's how this place operates.'

The young man no longer argued. He took a large

164

ring of keys from the wall and slid them over his finger and then led the way out into the corridor. 'You realise there's hundreds of people here. I don't know how you expect me to remember who you saw on a screen last time you were here.'

'She was distinctive-looking. Her skin dark, her hair dark.'

'Yeah, well, that hardly narrows it down, ma'am,' he said petulantly as the keys clinked against his side.

'And she was scratching something into the desk she sat at, trying to write.'

The young man stopped walking. He lifted his head and angled it to the side. 'Oh I get you. I know who you mean now.'

'Well take me to her, then.'

'I wouldn't be wanting to spend time with that one, ma'am. She's really a striker short of a football team.' He fiddled with the keys. 'She's been here a while. Brought over from the United States. Taken from her husband, by all accounts. We're talking a while back now. She's one of the 408 detainees.'

'408? You mean the manuscript?'

The man nodded. 'We had a few. Brought in from London. A couple of old ladies. Can't see they'd really be any harm to anyone. And an old homeless guy. There was the past employee of the Chamber, of course.

Would have liked to have had my hands on his care. But seemed the Chamber had other ideas. He never made it down from London. Seems they let him go in the hopes that sending him back so messed up might weaken the resolve of the young 'uns.'

Kerrith felt a heat sweep across her face. It had nothing to do with the temperature of the air.

'Not sure if letting him back out there did the trick. But the woman you's talking about, she's been here for ages and there's no way she's being let out. She knows a little bit more than any of them ever did, if you get my drift.'

'She can read MS 408?'

'Oh no. There's no one around who can really read it, so I've been told. But this one knows things. Things others don't. That's why she's here.'

They'd reached the end of a narrow corridor. The light was buzzing above their heads.

'I'm still not sure I should be doing this,' the young man said, slotting the key into the lock.

Kerrith didn't bother to reassure him.

'*Finally*,' groaned Sicknote from his seat on the steps of the Thomas Jefferson Memorial building. He took a gulp from his asthma inhaler and rubbed his chest. 'Smithies was sure you'd work it out. But, I have to admit, I was beginning to doubt it.'

'I'm so sorry,' gasped Brodie. 'We took a while. I guess we were just so spooked after trying to get away, we forgot to work with the clues.'

'*You* were spooked! How do you think we felt?' joked Smithies, loosening the knot of his tie.

'So tell us what happened,' urged Hunter, flopping down on to the stone steps beside him. 'We were sure they'd catch you.'

'Oh, *they did*. But the "batty old tourist blundering into the wrong room by mistake" routine seemed to fool them.' Smithies pointed along the line at Sicknote. 'Guess after all these years, him wearing pyjamas turned out to be a good idea after all.'

'What was that?'

'Nothing. I was just explaining they were fine with us. Searched us both of course and found we'd nothing on us. Not even a working mobile phone, which of course if either of us had had, would've meant we wouldn't have had to sit here for hours waiting for you to work things out.'

'Oh, well,' said Hunter. 'Better late than never. Must have given you time to check out the place. Don't suppose you managed to get any food while you were waiting?'

Smithies leant to his side and produced four rather

large, but not so hot, hot dogs from paper wrappings and what looked like a vegetarian burger. 'Eat them first before we go inside. They have rules about eating here.'

Hunter didn't argue about eating quickly and Brodie made rapid work of her own hot dog before following Sicknote into the memorial building.

The structure was a huge open temple-shaped building with immense white pillars and a domed roof.

'Looks like the temple Mad Jack Fuller built on his grounds,' whispered Kitty, wiping away a trace of relish from her lips.

'Just a *little* bigger though,' Brodie said.

The place seemed even larger from the inside, with the ceiling stretching high above them, and in the centre of the open space an enormous statue of Jefferson peered into the distance.

'The red fox himself,' said Sheldon, circling the statue. 'Looks sort of kind.'

'And purposeful,' added Tusia. 'Like he knows where he's going and why.'

Brodie scanned the walls. 'This really is a place where the written word endures,' she said. 'Look at all the phrases written all over it. Where they all from?'

'Sections from his speeches and things,' said Smithies, skirting the statue. 'There's bits of the Declaration of Independence here.'

Brodie craned her neck to see. Her eyes hovered over the familiar phrasing and then latched on to the largest letters circling the domed ceiling. She spoke the words aloud. '*I have sworn upon the altar of God eternal hostility against every form of tyranny over the mind of man.*'

'He certainly believed in the right to think for yourself,' Smithies said, completing the circle and coming to a stop.

'And isn't it about time we began to look more closely at what else he believed, sir?'

'You weren't tempted to have a peek while you were lost?' Smithies said gently.

'No, sir.' Hunter sounded almost too convincing. 'Well, yes, sir, we were. But we agreed to find you first. Teamwork and everything.'

Brodie was almost sure that Sicknote was blushing appreciatively, but he turned his face away and stared at the statue before she could be certain.

Smithies nodded at Hunter. And then together they made their way from the memorial, out past the tidal basin and towards the centre of the city. The sooner they found somewhere to stay for the night, the sooner they could begin to look carefully at whatever secret document had been hidden in the wooden panels of the Librarian's Room in the Library of Congress. And the closer they'd come to solving the Beale.

Morgan Summerfield wasn't happy. His new job wasn't turning out the way he'd expected.

Kerrith Vernan was a force of nature. Someone not to be messed with. He'd been nervous about taking the job as her assistant. Seems he needn't have worried. Apart from that time on the helicopter flying to Birling Gap, he'd hardly seen the woman. Something was up with her, and nearly everyone at Level Five had noticed. He wasn't sure how long he'd be able to keep hiding her weird behaviour from the Director. And this was the evidence he needed that something was really wrong.

He'd found the chocolate bar wrapper on her desk. It was totally empty. Crumbs across her paperwork. Her Tupperware box of neatly cut carrot sticks and celery batons was untouched, the lid still tightly closed. Morgan's boss was losing it and he wasn't quite sure what to do.

But he had ambition of his own. He hadn't been chosen as an assistant on a whim. There'd been a strict selection process. It's true the helicopter ride hadn't shown him in his best light. He couldn't help that he was afraid of heights. But he wasn't afraid of hard work. And he wasn't afraid of showing initiative.

He took the lift to the basement of the Black

Chamber. He'd come to look at the Situation Board. Kerrith had shown it to him on the day he'd taken the job. She'd barely been down to see it since. But that didn't mean *he* couldn't check it out and do some research of his own.

Morgan scanned the photographs and report details – notes on Station X surveillance, inputs from the agent in the field and a whole board of notes and pictures taken from Friedman's place months earlier. Morgan scanned the board for something new. Something he could get his teeth into if Kerrith was going to leave him high and dry.

The report was tiny. A fragment from the IT department. A note about internal hacking. The reports below it suggested the event had been dealt with. The track of reports showed the hacking had produced an ideal way of warning the team about events at the lighthouse. That was all though.

Morgan ripped the paper from the board.

This team from Station X was resourceful and creative. But they were traceable. In more ways than one.

Cybercrime had always been of interest to him. Now he'd got an incident to investigate.

Tusia put the leather book down on the table of the

suite they'd checked into and looked up.

'That is quite a notebook,' said Hunter, cramming a square of Hershey bar into his mouth. 'Jefferson must have used it to keep all his notes and letters in while he wrote the thing on religion.'

'Well, something in here,' said Brodie, 'has got to help us crack the unsolved Beale Papers. When we get back to New York we'll have the numbers to work with.'

Hunter took another square of chocolate. 'And why are we waiting until we get back to New York?'

'Because, thankfully, we left the Beale Papers with Tandi and Fabyan,' said Tusia. 'Can you imagine if Smithies had been discovered with them in the Library of Congress? The guards might not have fallen for his "lost old man" routine then.'

'Fair point,' said Hunter. 'But can't we start trying to match some things from the notebook with the Beale while we're here?'

Brodie raised her eyebrows. 'Erm, could be a bit tricky without the numbers.'

'Well, I *know* the numbers. All we've got to do is try and find a note or a letter in the book which might work.'

'You what?'

'All we've got to do is find a note or a—'

'Not that bit. The bit about you and the numbers.'

Hunter looked more than a little surprised. 'What? It's OK for you to remember every story you've ever been told. But it's odd for me to have learnt the numbers?'

'*You've learnt the Beale numbers?*' gasped Brodie. '*Off by heart?*'

'Hey, don't get your strawberry milk all shaken, B. Numbers. It's what I do.' He rolled up his sleeves and grabbed a piece of paper and a pen. 'You get looking through that notebook of yours and find something which might be the key text. And me. I'll jot down the Beale.'

Brodie found it difficult not to watch him as he began to write.

'Oy,' he yelled, stabbing his pen into the page. 'Get on with finding the key text. We haven't got all night.'

They may not have had all night. But that's how long it took them.

Brodie's eyes were itching with tiredness. She was finding it hard to focus and the words in copperplate writing seemed to lift off the page every now and then and dance in front of her eyes.

It was so difficult to know which of the notes and letters crammed inside Jefferson's stolen notebook was the one they needed. Everything was somehow linked to the Statute of Religious Freedom, but which note or letter was the one used to encode the Beale seemed beyond their grasp to work out.

'Let me see,' said Sheldon, taking the book again.

'You've seen it a hundred times,' groaned Sicknote. 'You've all seen. Perhaps it's best we just call it a night. There's always tomorrow. It will all still be there in the morning. Nothing will have changed. The only people awake now are all-night cleaners and priests delivering the last rites to those who are dying.' These words seemed to amuse him as he rubbed his eyes and yawned.

'Yeah. Well, priests are something to think about if we're looking at notes and letters about religion,' said Tusia half-heartedly. 'Although . . .' Brodie wasn't sure if she was thinking hard, or on the verge of falling asleep. 'The word priest was in there, wasn't it?'

'It's a collection of notes about religion, Toots. It's going to mention priests.'

Tusia took the empty Hershey bar wrapper from the table and twisted it into a knot. 'Priestley. Was there a mention in there of someone called Priestley, though?'

Sheldon flicked through the yellowed pages. 'There's something here. Refers to a man called Priestley. It's a letter from Jefferson to him. Why?'

'No reason,' said Tusia. She took the book. 'It's just I remembered reading the name. But I didn't read the letter.'

Kitty came and stood behind him and began to read over Sheldon's shoulder.

'That's weird. Why's this letter in here? It's not about the Statute of Religious Freedom. It's about the University of Virginia.'

Hunter bounced up from the edge of the bed. 'But that's the other thing listed on Jefferson's grave, wasn't it? The Statute of Religious Freedom and the University of Virginia. Maybe this letter's important if it links the two. Might make it clear that it's the thing from the book we need to use, if it combines two things listed on Jefferson's grave.'

'So go on, then,' urged Smithies. 'Read the letter. What's it say?'

Kitty scanned the copperplate writing and traced the formation of each word with her fingertip. Then she looked up. 'The gist of it's that Jefferson was friends with this guy called Priestley. Looks like they chatted lots about religion. Jefferson wanted Priestley's opinion on how to deal with religion at the university in Virginia he was going to build. Priestley had friends in England and these friends wanted to emigrate and live in the US and set up a sort of community. It had a name and

PANTISOCRACY

Utopian idea → 1794 → Samuel Taylor Coleridge

+

Robert Southey

Egalitarian Community

↓

Fair Rule for all

← New society built by River

Sir Francis Bacon → his book → New Atlantis

⇓

New Atlantis = Lost Avalon

ASPHETERISM → ownership of property by everyone

everything. It was called the Pantisocracy.'

'Oh this is good!' said Smithies. 'Very, very good. This fits with everything I've been reading about Avalon. A pantisocracy means where there was equal rule for all. There's lots I've got to explain to you about that. But go on about the friends. Did they make it over from England?'

'Not according to this letter,' said Kitty. 'Something stopped them coming.'

'And do we know the names of any of these friends?' said Smithies. 'The people who wanted to come but didn't.'

Kitty looked down at the letter and scanned the writing. 'Here. It's going to list them here. It's . . .' She turned the page.

'Come on, Chaos,' urged Hunter. 'You've got it, right? Who the chips and vinegar were the friends?'

'It lists twelve couples,' she said. 'But at the head of the list's one particular name. A name you've told me about before.'

'Is it a Cambridge Apostle?' asked Tusia.

'A Knight of Neustria?' quizzed Sheldon.

Kitty put down the page of the letter so they could see. The name was both of those things and more. The name was Samuel Taylor Coleridge.

* * *

Tandi hurried across the tarmac and climbed up the steps of the private plane. Friedman, Mrs Smithies and Mr Bray were already inside.

'Fabyan's really OK with us going without him?' asked Friedman.

Tandi sat down and did up her seat belt as the plane began to taxi. 'He's fine. He's got something to collect and then he'll join us.' She looked across at Mrs Smithies. 'You have the name of the hotel Jon rang from?'

Mrs Smithies nodded. 'It's quite appropriate,' she said quietly. 'They're staying at The Jefferson.'

'Great. Flying time to Washington is just over the hour. We should be with them by morning.'

'A man has to eat,' groaned Hunter, munching through his third Hershey bar of the night.

Tusia paced across the room. 'And a "man" who's learnt the number of the Beale Papers off by heart has to be able to make sense of the code when the key text's been found. Surely,' she urged. 'Come on! The first translated Beale Paper told us all about the treasure. The other two are supposed to tell us who's meant to inherit it, and where it is. You need to focus. This Paper will probably tell us who Beale thought should inherit all the stuff. You have to use the Priestley letter to break the code to tell us.'

'I'm doing my best,' Hunter spluttered through a mouthful of hazelnut chocolate. 'If you think you can do any better, then by all means pull up a chair and have a go.'

Tusia rolled her eyes. 'Numbers are your thing, Hunter. You have the numbers from the Beale Papers. You have the letter we need from Jefferson's secret book. *All* you have to do is fit the two together.'

'Well, maybe I would be able to do a better job of it if you didn't keep twittering in my ear, Toots!'

'Look,' said Kitty, glancing down at her watch. 'This isn't helping anyone. You're right. Numbers are Hunter's thing. So why don't we leave Hunter to his work and have a look at the story?'

'What story?' asked Brodie, suddenly energised.

'The story behind the letter. If Samuel Taylor Coleridge, one of our most important Knights of Neustria, turns up in one of Jefferson's letters, then we need to check out why. Maybe we should find out about his pantisocracy idea while Hunter works on the code.'

'And where will we do that?'

'Well, we're in Washington DC. Capital city of the centre of the free world. And we happen to be staying in a pretty nice hotel.'

'So?'

'So, because I've already used it, I happen to know, if we just take a walk down to the lobby, we'll find connection to most of the stories contained in the world.'

'We will?'

'A computer, silly,' groaned Sheldon, picking up his jacket to join them. 'I think what Kitty's trying to say is, if we journey on down to the lobby we can make use of the World Wide Web.'

'Finally,' groaned Hunter, swallowing the last of the chocolate. 'Let me know what you find.'

The computers in the lobby took tokens which Kitty collected from a very helpful receptionist called Frank. Sheldon stocked them up with cola from the vending machine near the entrance and then the three of them took up seats by the computer.

'Right,' said Kitty, typing the password she'd been given into the login screen. 'Let's get to the story.'

She typed the word 'PANTISOCRACY' carefully into the search engine and waited.

The page which appeared began with a simple definition. '*Pantisocracy was a Utopian scheme devised in 1794 by the poets Samuel Taylor Coleridge and Robert Southey for an egalitarian community.*'

'What's that mean?' said Sheldon, leaning forward in his chair.

Brodie read over Kitty's shoulder. It was complicated and she wasn't sure she totally understood. 'Try looking up *egalitarian*,' she suggested.

More clicking and the definition popped up on the screen. 'I think it's the idea of fair rule for all.'

'OK. So let's go back to the original page. OK. Look.' Brodie pointed to the screen. 'It says the scheme involved the American Joseph Priestley and Coleridge planning to build this new society alongside the Susquehanna River in America.' Kitty scrolled through the pages on the screen while Brodie read. 'The idea was to live more simply here in America than they were in Britain. And the plans were going well. But something stopped Coleridge and the others coming to America.'

'Does it say what?' asked Sheldon.

Brodie shook her head. But she'd seen a name she recognised. 'Oh, this is brilliant,' she said. 'Look, look.' Her finger made a scratch in the dust on the screen. 'Look at who else wrote about the idea of a pantisocracy.'

Sheldon leant forward and read the name aloud. 'Bacon. Sir Francis Bacon. My life! It's all connected. The idea of Coleridge's society linked to Bacon's book.'

'Which book?' said Kitty, wobbling on the chair.

'Bacon's book! *New Atlantis!*'

'I don't get it,' said Kitty. 'Why's that important?'

Sheldon began to explain. 'Months back now, when we'd just started and were first trying to make sense of MS 408, we found a ring buried in the River Wye. It was Bacon's ring and we found it because we followed clues linking Elgar's music to stuff Tennyson had written. We found this ring Bacon had worn and underneath the gems of the ring there was a code.'

'And the code said?'

'NEW ATLANTIS was LOST AVALON.'

'I'm confused,' said Kitty. 'I can't keep up.'

'The code explained Avalon wasn't a made-up place,' said Sheldon. 'It was really the place described in a book Bacon had written about New Atlantis.'

'And how does that connect to Coleridge and what he was trying to do?' asked Kitty.

'It connects because Coleridge was a Knight of Neustria. He knew about Avalon. And all this,' he said, jabbing at the computer screen, 'could mean Coleridge was making plans to go to there. It looks to me like he was coming to America to set off and find Avalon. All this stuff about building a new society called a pantisocracy might have been a cover. Seems more likely that, instead of building a new society, he was going to set off on a journey to find an old one. D'you think that's what it means, Brodie?'

'I think so,' she said. 'And look.' The cursor was hovering over one of the words. 'It says here the society Coleridge wanted to join was built on two principles. Pantisocracy, which means government by all. And something called aspheterism.'

'What on earth does that mean?'

'No idea,' said Kitty. 'Let's find out.' She selected the dictionary option again.

Brodie read the definition. 'Perfect! I reckon the word aspheterism makes sense of the code Hunter's trying to break upstairs with all his numbers.'

'It does?' said Sheldon.

'Aspheterism means ownership of property . . . *by everyone*,' Brodie said calmly. 'I bet when Hunter works out the code in the Beale Papers, we won't be surprised at all about who's supposed to inherit the treasures of Avalon.'

'I'm not here to discipline you.' Morgan Summerfield was enjoying the fact that the IT worker was squirming, but the guy being so defensive was making it tricky to get to the truth. 'I'm not interested in stock rotation either. I just want you to tell me about the hacking. How it happened.'

'Ms Vernan dealt with it,' the man behind the desk said warily. 'We used the hack to get a message to them.

In the end, it worked in our favour.'

'I understand that. And I appreciate how effectively you used the situation to help us.' The man seemed to relax a little. 'But I'm interested in knowing who got in. And what they saw.'

'We guessed it must have been Tandari,' said the man. 'The hacker knew her way around the system so must have worked here. And it was a woman who—' The man had said too much. 'Look, it's my job just to watch the system and monitor movement and I noticed security had been breached and I reported it. I did my job.'

'Again, I say I'm not here to investigate you, my friend. Only them. Tell me again why you think it was Tandari.'

The man fidgeted with notes on his table. His face was flushed.

'You saw her, didn't you? You didn't just *notice* the system had been broken into. You knew *in advance*.'

'Look, mate. I know you're new but this job's important to me. I made a mistake. I should have said something earlier. But like I say, it all turned out OK, so what I knew and when I knew it, don't matter.'

Morgan considered the situation for a moment. He could drive home his advantage but then the man would tell him nothing else. It was time for the soft approach. 'It was Tandari, then. OK. Let's leave it at that. But I want all her previous login details, email addresses, the whole works.'

The man was relieved to have something to do. He clicked on several screens, running the cursor backwards and forwards, and then pressed 'print'.

'Good,' said Morgan, taking the pieces of paper he'd been offered. 'Now you need to tell me what she saw before you blew her cover.'

'Personnel files mainly. I could track which ones she'd opened. There was one on a guard. He's gone missing but she checked out his details.'

'Anyone else?'

'There was a "hover over". A file labelled "KM". She didn't open it though, which is good news for us.'

Morgan nodded his head in agreement.

'And she looked at Ms Vernan's, of course.'

'Obviously.'

'You won't say anything, will you? I'm a reformed character, honest.'

Morgan doubted this was true. But now the man had mentioned honesty, maybe there was an opening he could follow up. 'Ms Vernan's files. You're saying Tandari opened them all.'

'Oh, no, sir. Not all of them.' He leant forward so

that he could whisper. 'Miss Kerrith Vernan has protected files. Ones that aren't on this system at all.'

'Is that usual?'

'Not at all, sir. But then according to those secret files, Miss Kerrith Vernan isn't what you'd call altogether *usual* either.'

'I've done it,' said Hunter, looking up smugly from the pages of paper scrawled across the end of the bed.

Brodie winked at Kitty. 'And?' she said. 'You've used the letter Jefferson wrote to Priestley to crack the Beale code about who should inherit the treasure. So? Who is it?'

Hunter pushed forward the piece of paper with his decoding on. 'You'll never, ever guess,' he said, folding his arms across his chest. 'Not in a million sugar-coated years.'

The words on the paper were clear.

The treasures of Avalon
should be inherited by
everyone.

Brodie thought it seemed rather unkind to tell him they'd worked out that would be the answer.

* * *

The knock at the door jolted Tusia out of her celebratory dance.

Brodie looked instinctively at her watches. Nearly five a.m. Maybe other guests had complained about the noise. Then Brodie went cold. Hunter had said they had to be careful. Could Level Five have tracked them here?

'Erm, hello!' came a whisper through the door. 'Bit tired here. Any chance you're going to let us in?'

'Tandi!' yelped Sheldon, opening the door wide.

Several moments of hugs and welcomes followed and then Mrs Smithies, Granddad, Friedman and Tandi sat themselves down.

'Fabyan not with you?' asked Sicknote.

'He's finishing off some business back in NYC,' explained Friedman. 'But we thought we had business to attend to here.'

It sounded like he had things to tell them, but there was so much to explain about what they'd worked out about the Beale Papers, everyone fell over themselves to explain that first.

'So you've cracked the second Paper,' said Mr Bray. 'That's brilliant news.'

'And it explains the treasure of Avalon is for everyone,' said Hunter. 'So we're thinking there must be a banquet load of treasure.'

'Well, treasure comes in many forms,' Tandi said. 'And though I'm sure there'll be lots to find in the mountains of Virginia if we can manage to work out the location, while you've been away I've been looking at some of the stuff Smithies has been reading about Avalon. I think I've got a better idea about what the treasure could be.' She took out a stack of notes and papers from her bag.

Smithies looked impressed.

'After everything they've just found out, don't you think it's time we explained the real magic of Avalon to them?' said Tandi.

Brodie was exhausted. They'd spent most of the day lost and scared. They'd been up all night solving codes. But this was a story she was desperate to hear.

'OK,' said Smithies. 'Time to tell you the truth about Avalon.'

He stood in front of the window and behind him the sun began to rise.

'All the stories talk about it being magical, right? A place where swords and scabbards are created that can make you invincible. A place where King Arthur went to be restored when he was injured. But you have to understand that these ideas are fantasies. Made-up things about a wonderful place.'

Brodie felt disappointed. 'You mean Avalon isn't magical?'

'Ah, but it is. But in a way that's much more powerful and real than in fantasies. The stories we read have been told to give us an idea of the magic. A way of helping us understand how the place works.' He picked up Jefferson's notebook. 'The Priestley letter, and the explanation of what Coleridge and his friends were looking for, gives us a glimpse of what the magic really is. And the writings of Archibald MacLeish make things clearer too.'

'Archibald who?'

'The librarian, right?' said Hunter. 'The photo you pointed out to us in the Library of Congress. Never forget a name, me!'

'Absolutely, Hunter. Well done. Archibald MacLeish, Librarian of the Library of Congress, poet and writer.'

'And he explained what Avalon's magic really is?' asked Tusia.

'Yes. He and others did.'

'And?'

'Avalon's magic is that it's a perfect society.'

Brodie didn't understand why this was magic and it was obvious from the silence that no one else did either.

'Way back in the 1500s, about the time MS 408 was written in fact, the writer Thomas More came up with a word for it. You've heard of it. Utopia.'

'That means perfect place?'

'Well, it really means perfect imagined place. People have been writing about them for centuries. Bacon's Atlantis. Even Arcadia. We've made the connection before when we were at Shugborough. A link with perfect places. But people haven't just written about them. All sorts of people have tried to set up perfect societies. New Lanark in Scotland; Ohu in New Zealand; Los Horcones in Mexico.'

These names meant nothing to Brodie but she guessed Smithies had done his research.

'But the difference is that in all the stories that you read, and all the attempts to set up real places as utopias, something always goes wrong. People aren't perfect, are they? So surely a perfect society where everyone is treated equally and where every need is cared for isn't really possible. Don't you see? That would be *truly magic*.'

'So Avalon is like all the other utopias, then? It started off as being perfect but things went wrong?' asked Brodie.

'No. That's the point,' cut in Tandi, looking down at her notes. 'In Avalon, things haven't gone wrong. It's the place where people really are treated equally. There's no poverty, no unfairness, no war. And that's its magic.'

'OK. Sounds nice and everything, but if Avalon has managed to be perfect then why doesn't everyone know about it? Why haven't people gone there and found out how it's done?'

'Well, Plato had a theory.'

'Oh, I remember,' said Brodie. 'We've talked about it loads of times. The cave story and how even if someone saw how the world should really be then no one in the cave would believe them.'

'That's part of it,' said Smithies. 'But Plato also believed that a real perfect place couldn't be too large. It could only be big enough for everyone to chat together and talk through ideas. Become too big and the magic would be lost.'

'So that's why the real location of Avalon has to be kept secret, then?' said Hunter. 'In case too many people went there and ruined the magic?'

'Exactly.'

'So why did the Knights of Neustria leave a trail of clues? Sounds like it would be a bad idea if it was found.'

'As a form of protection, I guess, in case the people of Avalon ever needed to send out a cry for help; there had to be a way of hiding the secret in plain sight. And also, more than that, it's important for those who aren't in Avalon to believe that a perfect place is possible to achieve. You don't have to go there in order to soak up the magic from knowing that there's a place where all people are treated fairly. That idea is like magic in itself and can drive you on. That's why most of the Knights of Neustria were poets and writers. They had to believe in the true possibility of Avalon. MacLeish said that the reality of Utopia is all about hope, and the moment humans give up hoping then the life goes out of them. That makes sense of the magic, doesn't it? Hope gives life. You can't get more powerful than that!'

'I think I get it,' said Brodie. 'But why does Level Five want to stop people knowing that Avalon as a perfect place exists? What's wrong with knowing a perfect society is possible and hoping for that?'

Smithies pushed his glasses up on to his forehead. 'Because it's the way they maintain power! If you make people believe that a perfect society isn't possible, then you keep control. If people believe that there'll always be unfairness and that there's nothing anyone can do about it, that there'll always be wars, poverty and starvation and that we just have to sit back and let that happen, then people don't try to change things. But, if they believe that equality and happiness for everyone is possible, then they would start changing the world they lived in. They'd stop looking away every time someone was hurt. They'd do something! Not just a few people who dreamt that things could be better. But everyone who *knew* things could be better. Can you see what would happen?'

'Not really,' said Tusia. 'I'm trying to get it, honestly.'

'There wouldn't be a divide any more between them and us . . . those in power and those who don't have any. If people knew that Avalon was real, it could affect the power structure of the whole world. And that's a type of magic to really take notice of.'

8

Remembrance at the Rotunda

The room was dark and tatty; just as it appeared on the screens in the control room. And the woman. She was the same too. Her shoulders bent, one hand in her lap, and the other scratching at the wood, digging at the desk.

Kerrith stepped inside and the young man, with the keys raised, pursed his lips in a way which said 'I told you this wasn't a good idea', before he turned and shut the door behind him. Kerrith coughed quietly into her hand.

The woman looked up.

It was then Kerrith understood.

The worrying and the puzzling and the questioning. In that moment. In that look. It all made sense.

'Hantaywee?' Kerrith's voice was shaking. 'Is it really you?'

The woman lifted her nail from the desk and her face smoothed in surprise. And there was a flash of recognition in her eyes. A spark of a distant memory flickered like a flame. 'Kerry.' Her voice was husky, dry and unused. 'Kerry. Really here?'

Kerrith nodded awkwardly. No one called her Kerry. Not since . . . She couldn't remember the last time.

The woman from the desk reached out and clutched at Kerrith's arms. 'Oh, Kerry. When did they bring you in? When did they take you? How did they . . . ? It's such a terrible place. I've no idea how . . . My husband. They took me from my husband . . .'

Kerrith held her arms up in an attempt to stop the flow of words. But the woman wouldn't be silenced. She babbled on; a deluge of questions in a voice wavering and thinned from lack of use. Eventually, Kerrith steered the woman back towards the chair and sat her down. 'Tell me what they've done to you, Hantaywee.'

The woman nodded and a single tear ran down her cheek.

'Tell me from the very beginning.'

And so the woman explained. She told Kerrith how she'd completed her studying at the American university where they'd met so many years ago; the first of her Sioux family to gain a degree there. She explained how she'd left the university and travelled. And how she'd fallen in love with a man who was kind and clever and had lots of money. A family fortune. But she'd loved him for his courage and his knowledge of the world and his interest in the unusual. Everything had been wonderful.

Kerrith nodded to let her continue and so Hantaywee ploughed on. She explained how one day she'd found a letter at home. A letter written to her husband's great-grandfather. She'd heard stories of his cleverness. He'd used his vast wealth to work with the brightest minds in the world on solving puzzles. People wrote to him for help. And one such person was a man called Hart who asked for help with some coded documents. Finding that letter, and the reply her husband's great-grandfather had drafted, had changed everything.

Kerrith interrupted then. 'So did your great-grandfather-in-law manage to read the coded documents he'd been asked to look at?'

The woman looked away and tears flowed freely. 'He'd made sense of parts of them. And he'd discovered connections with an important ancient manuscript. And that connection . . .' she fought to find the right words, '. . . could change the world.'

'And what did your husband say when you told him what you knew?' Kerrith pressed.

'I never had the chance to tell him,' the woman sobbed. 'They came in the night. My husband. He never knew why. I'd told someone, you see. What I'd read. I trusted them. And they betrayed me. My family never even knew what I'd found.' She could hardly continue. 'I suppose my husband thinks I walked out on him. Left him in the night to go back to my Sioux roots. He must believe I chose to leave. And if that's true, he won't even have looked for me. For him, I may as well be dead.'

Kerrith didn't know what to say.

The woman at the desk looked up. Her dark eyes were wide. 'I never believed I'd ever see a friendly face again. I was all alone and now, like a miracle, they bring me you.' Her smile was fleeting. 'Tell me your story, Kerry. Why've these terrible people brought *you* here?'

The Clifton Inn in Charlottesville wasn't quite the New York Waldorf-Astoria or The Jefferson of Washington DC but the hotel was so small the team were able to take it over completely which meant conversations could be held in the dining room without danger of being overheard.

Brodie was so incredibly glad the team was back together. She was particularly pleased her dad was here. Friedman was looking stronger, his hand less bandaged, and the darkened rings below his eyes had paled a little with time. She wanted to reach out and hug him. But she didn't. She sat next to him though, and that felt nice.

Mrs Smithies was looking brighter too as she sat beside Tandi. Miss Tandari did have a knack of making people feel looked after. Mrs Smithies had proudly shown everyone the new shoes Tandi had bought for her. The leather shone a little.

But nothing shone as brightly as Fabyan's surprise.

'It's THE ring,' blurted Brodie, as Fabyan held his hand out across the table. 'THE ring from the *Titanic*. Coleridge's ring!'

Fabyan rocked back on his chair. 'It's THE ring all right. Seems it was worth staying in New York while you lot were breaking secrets in Washington.'

'But how? When? What?' The questions came thick and fast and Fabyan had to hold up his hand to silence them.

'The Widener family lost so much aboard the *Titanic*,' he said at last. 'But this ring traded with Astor had been in the family ever since.'

'And you actually bought it from them?'

Brodie could see Hunter was performing mental gymnastics in his mind trying to work out a likely price.

'How much did you pay?'

'When you're a billionaire, money matters little, Hunter. It's availability that's the key. And for a while I kinda feared the Wideners wouldn't go releasing the ring however much I was willing to pay.'

'But?'

'To them the ring's simply a reminder of what they've lost. Not what there might be to claim. Without the true history and the connection of the ring to the Knights of Neustria, the ring's just some tragic item of jewellery. It's strange then how quickly money seems an attractive alternative.'

Brodie leant forward across the table. The ring sparkled in the beam of the lantern above, shattering the light into a spectrum of colours. 'It's so beautiful,' she breathed. 'Do you think we've got to take it apart like the ring we found in the River Wye?'

'I don't think so,' said Fabyan. 'I think the message we need to find is already there. Mr Young at Tiffany's was right, look. Printed on the inside band of the ring is a name. Martin de Judicabus. It's got to be important somehow.'

Brodie rocked the ring backwards and forwards in

her palm. Then Tusia reached forward and took it. 'Can I?' she said, preparing to slip it on.

'To be honest, it's probably the safest way to keep it,' said Fabyan. 'By wearing it, I mean. Be sure you don't take it off.'

'Oh, I won't!'

Brodie reached up and took hold of the locket her mother had left her. She knew all about the importance of not taking things off. And she also knew, as Mr Young had told them, that jewellery, like codes, was all about making connections.

Smithies went through to the coffee machine in the lobby. He pressed the button and a cup fell from the dispenser and filled with steaming liquid.

'You should add sugar to that,' said Fabyan. Smithies jumped a little so that the coffee splashed on his hand. '*New York Post*,' Fabyan said, passing over the front of a folded newspaper.

Smithies scanned the article. A man found drowned in the River Thames, London. A distinctive dragon tattoo on his arm the only identifying feature. Smithies recognised the guard from Station X. 'He left,' said Smithies slowly. 'Moved on.'

Fabyan took the paper back and refolded it. 'He was conflicted. Tandi and I spoke to him a few months back. Warned him that if the Chamber is after you, they stop at nothing.'

'You think his drowning is down to Level Five?'

'I don't know how they work, Jon. But it's a possibility, isn't it?'

A new splash of coffee ran down Smithies' hand. 'You mustn't say anything,' he ordered. 'To the kids or to Robbie. They think they're safe here and he's twitchy enough as it is.'

'But d'you think it's possible?'

'Anything's possible as far as the Black Chamber's concerned.'

'You OK?'

Friedman was leaning in the porch, his arms folded tight across him. 'Not sure,' he joked to Tandi, who'd followed him outside. 'You?'

She shook her head.

'Really? What's up?'

'I know you think we're being followed. And I've got a bad feeling too.'

'You've seen someone watching?'

'No.'

'So why the nerves?'

'I checked my emails before I came here. Some of the ones I don't remember reading had been opened.'

'You sure you're not just tired? You might have forgotten.'

'I haven't.'

'Anything else?'

'A few silent hang-ups on the hotel phone to my room back in Washington.'

'Could have been Reception dialling the wrong number.'

'Could have been.'

Friedman sighed. 'Look, it's good we're worried. Means we're alert. On guard and all that. But Smithies is right, we mustn't let the kids know.' He tried to smile. 'We'll be OK, Tandi. Really. We will.'

'So,' said Fabyan, taking the coffee Tusia offered him. 'I think it's time you gave us an update on what exactly you've been up to in the capital.'

Brodie watched the stone on the ring sparkle. 'You want us to catch you up with all the other stuff we know?'

'That's what you do,' said Fabyan. 'I buy expensive things and you keep us all up to date with the story.'

Brodie took a deep breath. 'OK. We came to America for two reasons. One to find the ring Coleridge wore which we thought had been inherited by a passenger on the *Titanic*.'

We came to America: 2 reasons ✈️

1) Find Coleridge's ring from the Titanic 💍

   ↓

   Found! → has name Martin de
            Judicabus on it

2) Beale Papers 📄

   ↓

   Thomas Jefferson Beale → worked at
                            Shugborough Hall
                                ↓
                         servant to Lucia 🌸🌸
                      mum of Renata → shep's monument

   ↓

   Hid treasure from Avalon 🗺️

   ↓

   Used things written by Thomas Jefferson ✏️
                          to hide clues

   1) Declaration of Independence 🇺🇸
   2) Priestley letter
   3) Something from uni. of Virginia?

'Job done there then,' said Hunter.

'Except we don't know yet who this Martin de Judicabus is or why his name's written inside the ring and how he connects to the Knights of Neustria. But what we do know's a lot more about Thomas Jefferson Beale and his three encoded Papers.'

'So come on then,' urged Fabyan. 'Spill!'

'OK. Beale Papers. Put together by Thomas Jefferson Beale who worked for a while at Shugborough Hall in England. There was this woman there, who had a child who'd been to Avalon. She was the child the Shepherd's Monument at Shugborough was for. Of course, her mum was all upset about the death of her child, so she went back home to Italy. And Thomas Beale went with her. Sort of as a servant, we think. He brought with him from Shugborough some treasure taken from Avalon. We think it was part of his pay. He then made his way to Virginia, America and buried the treasure.' She paused for a moment to make sure everyone was following the story. 'Years later, Beale found some more treasure from Avalon which was being kept in the town of Sante Fe. He buried that with the first load and then wrote three Papers in code about the treasure. The first Paper can be read using the Declaration of Independence written by the third president, Thomas Jefferson. That Paper tells the story of the treasure. The second Paper can be translated using the notebook kept by the president when he was writing the Statute of Religious Freedom for Virginia. We worked all that out by making connections to myths and stories from all these codes hidden around the Library of Congress. The notebook's full of letters and writings from Jefferson. And the letter we used to make sense of the code was written to a man called Priestley.'

'And why d'you use his letter?' asked Tandi, seizing a break in the explanation to ask her question.

'Because his letter linked back to one of the original Knights of Neustria and the man who was the reason for the founding of the Secret Society at Cambridge University, the Cambridge Apostles,' said Brodie.

'Which man?'

Tusia laughed and moved her hand so the light danced on the stone on her ring. 'Samuel Taylor Coleridge. The original owner of this ring.'

Fabyan rubbed his face with the palms of his hands. 'It's really all connecting,' he said.

'But,' interrupted Hunter, 'we've one coded Paper from Thomas Jefferson Beale left to read. If we can make sense of the third Beale Paper we should be able to find the hidden treasure from Avalon.'

'So where do we look now?' Friedman said.

'University of Virginia,' said Hunter. 'It was the third most important thing to Jefferson. The third thing listed on his grave. So it must be where we find the third document which we can fit with the numbers on the third Beale Paper.'

'So what do we know about Virginia University?' asked Tandi.

Tusia looked down at some notes she'd made on the journey from Washington and began to read. 'Well, they started to build it in 1822 but it wasn't finished until 1826. Sadly, Jefferson died before the buildings were complete, but he planned the whole design. Apparently it's unique.'

'Why?' asked Sheldon.

'Well, most universities built before then,' began Tusia, 'had a church as the centre of the campus. But Virginia had something else.'

'A cafeteria?' joked Hunter. 'That'd be excellent. A café right slap bang in the middle.'

Tusia made her disapproving face. 'There wasn't a café at the middle of the campus,' she said curtly. 'But the place at the centre's where we should start our search tomorrow.'

'OK,' said Brodie tentatively. 'So what is this place?'

Tusia grinned. 'The university library.'

* * *

Smithies stood in the hotel hallway. He was keeping his voice down. 'They were just security guards, Robbie. It was wrong place, wrong time. That's all. You have to relax.'

'I'm telling you, Jon, I saw the same guy over and over again in New York. I think they're tailing us. I'm convinced they know we're here.'

'How can they know? You've got to be rational about it. Level Five is in England! We flew out on a private jet. No one knows we're here.'

Friedman fiddled with the fraying edge of the bandage on his hand.

'And Tandi. She's sure someone's watching her, and you've got to admit Level Five are going to be fed up with the both of us. She was never supposed to hack into their computers. I was never supposed to escape!'

'I know it's hard, mate. I can't imagine what you're going through. But we haven't been followed. We can't have been. You've got to believe me. Tomorrow we'll check out the university. You'll feel better there, I'm sure.'

Friedman tried to smile. He'd worn a hole in the end of the bandage.

'But it looks exactly like the Jefferson Memorial in Washington,' said Hunter. 'I mean, except for the being closed in bit, and having books inside and not being by water.'

'Actually,' said Tusia. 'You're right.' It was obvious this sentence stuck a little in her throat. 'The designs are similar. The architect of the memorial in Washington had the Library of the University of Virginia in mind when he made his plans.'

Brodie was sure Hunter was mumbling something which was far from polite under his breath.

Tusia ploughed on regardless. 'This building was actually designed by Jefferson himself,' she said. 'This was the first university where students could study astronomy, and Jefferson planned to have the ceiling painted with stars. Sadly, this never happened. But it's still amazing, isn't it?'

Brodie had to agree. She was impressed. This Jefferson guy could run a country, write important documents and design things. He'd have made a perfect addition to Team Veritas with all those skills. 'So this place could've been a mixture of Mad Jack Fuller's temple building and his observatory,' she mused, staring up at the circular building.

'So another reason to connect this part of the world with MS 408,' added Tusia.

'Are we going inside, then?' asked Sheldon, stowing his harmonica in his pocket. 'To get looking for clues?'

Tusia led the way.

It was as Brodie looked down at the ground that she noticed a large letter Z painted across the steps leading to the rotunda. 'What's that all about?' she said, pressing her feet firmly against the white of the paint. 'A team from Station X standing on a painted letter Z. Why would anyone paint that? What's it for?'

'No idea,' said Tusia. 'Seems a bit weird, if you ask me.'

A rumbling of voices seemed to be swelling from behind the building. Shouting and calling and the sound of running.

Brodie pressed her feet down hard against the steps and she felt for the moment the oddest sensation. A sort of tingling in her toes and a light-headedness. Her heart rate quickened and the tiniest bead of sweat lifted on her brow. Then her feet burnt.

'B?' said Hunter, slowing to stand beside her. 'You OK, B? You worked something out? Some clue about the letter Z? Something about the rotunda? Cos you've got that face on. You know, the face you wear when you've worked something out.'

Brodie shook her head but the movement caused her pain. Images seemed to collide inside her brain. Images of MS 408 and the unreadable script and then suddenly, surging and growing, images of flames and fire.

'B? B? You OK? Cos you're worrying me now. You're kind of scaring me!'

Brodie reached out her hand and grasped tight to Hunter's arm. She looked up into his face but he seemed to be so far away. And he seemed too, to be ringed with fire. Crimson flames reaching up into the sky. And behind him Tandi. And the flames seemed to wrap around Tandi's body, choking the life from her. Smoke curled in tendrils from her midnight-black hair.

'Brodie, please.'

Hunter's hands steadied her, and she stumbled along the steps to a small wall and he helped her down, afraid she'd fall if he let go of her. 'Brodie. You OK?'

And from her seat on the wall, Brodie looked up, and the fire she'd seen was real and yet Hunter and Tandi were safe. The flames didn't touch them. Instead, a rabble of students seemed to be pouring out from behind the rotunda carrying paper lanterns that flickered with fire. And they called as they moved, shouting things, but nothing they said made sense. And then from the end of the line of students, a group of four men dressed in suits appeared and they carried, spread between them, a man. They held the man high in the air. He was totally still. And Brodie felt herself falling and folding into a tunnel of noise.

Then all went totally dark.

Brodie felt water trickle from her face and into her ear.

'Sorry about that,' said Sicknote, peering down at her. 'You fainted. Best way to bring you round.'

Brodie rubbed her face with the palm of her hand and tried to sit up. Her vision swam in front of her and the rancid smell of ash clogged her nostrils. 'Fire! There was fire! And a man! There was a dead man being carried!'

She slumped back into arms which held her. Bandaged arms. 'There was definitely fire and . . .'

'Shh,' whispered Friedman. He smoothed her hair with his wrapped hand, wincing slightly as he did so. 'It's OK. We can explain.'

'You can?'

'Well, *we* can't exactly. But she can.' He pointed at a small woman of about twenty who was crouching beside them, holding an empty plastic beaker.

Brodie squinted. 'You threw water over me and I'm expected to listen to you explain things?'

'Gee, sweetheart. I was only acting under orders of your friends here. And yes, if you want to understand what you've seen then, for sure, I'm your best bet.'

Brodie shrugged and pulled herself up to a sitting position, leaning her weight against Friedman. He smoothed her hair again but this time he didn't pull his hand away. Brodie blew out a breath and peered behind the crouching woman to where the crowd at the top of the steps still called and shouted among a circle of fiery lanterns. This would certainly need some explaining.

'It's the Festival of the Rotunda Remembrance,' explained the American.

The definition did little to help.

'Every year we mark the occasion of the burning down of the library rotunda due to a terrible fire in 1895. It was a terrifying night. A small fire, caused by faulty electrical wiring, broke out in the annex. The tiny fire may just have burnt itself out if some well-meaning engineering professor hadn't tried to stop the spread of the fire by dynamiting the bridge between the annex and the rotunda.'

'This didn't work?' chipped in Tusia.

The student shook her head. 'Unfortunately, what it actually did was blow a hole in the rotunda and the fire was then able to spread more quickly.'

'Not the best move in the world, then,' said Sheldon.

'No. Not one of the better ideas originating from this university.' A droplet of water splashed from the edge of the plastic beaker and on to Brodie's knee. 'So each year, we mark the occasion of the burning by making paper replicas of the rotunda and setting them on fire. I'm sorry if we scared or freaked you out.

Students can be a little rowdy, you know.'

'But there was a man,' blurted Brodie, sitting up more sharply again. 'There was a man being carried from the fire. He was injured, dead maybe.'

'He was made of marble, sweetie.'

'What?'

'The man you saw was made of marble. A life-size replica of Thomas Jefferson. It's a source of great pride to us that the students of Virginia were able to rescue the thing they treasured most from the fire. The statue of our founding father. We carry him out every year to celebrate that success at least.'

'So no one was hurt, then?' sighed Brodie, sinking back again.

The student shook her head. 'Not then, at the time of the fire. Or now, on the occasion we've chosen to mark the anniversary. Unless of course we count you.'

'Me?' Brodie was embarrassed. She'd no idea what had come over her. Lack of sleep maybe. They'd been awake for hours over the last few days. Tension perhaps. But everyone had been tense and no one else had flopped to the floor like she had.

The student looked down distractedly at her hands. 'Tell me – when you came over all faint – where were you standing?'

'Standing?'

'Yes. Where exactly were your feet?'

Brodie wriggled a little and lifted her toes. 'I don't know. I was on the steps.'

There was a spark of understanding. 'Where exactly on the steps?'

'On the letter Z,' said Brodie.

'Let's get you inside,' the woman said softly. 'I think I have some more explaining to do.'

The Wonderful
Secret of the Z Society

'More tea? British people like tea, right?'

Brodie tried to stretch her face into a smile. 'Some of them,' she said.

Caitlin, the American student who'd explained all about the rotunda burning, had taken Brodie into one of the dorm rooms, where she was busily trying to make Brodie feel at home. It wasn't really working. 'Come on. Drink up,' she said, stirring the rather generous helping of tea bags in the very small spotted teapot. 'There's plenty more where that came from.'

This was what worried Brodie. The tea was the colour of tar. It clung to her tongue and the roof of her mouth, refusing to be swallowed.

The others in Team Veritas had been dispatched to explore the rest of the university and catch the last moments of the burning ceremony. Caitlin, meanwhile, insisted that in order to make Brodie feel better, she needed to speak to her alone. That was another thing worrying Brodie. Caitlin seemed odd. She stood a little too close when she spoke, so her breath was hot on Brodie's skin. And her eyes never focused forward. She was always looking behind her. Checking she wasn't being watched. Finally, when the last mug of tea had been poured, Caitlin put the pot on the table and cleared her throat to speak. 'You felt funny, yeah? When you stood on the steps? A sort of weird falling-away feeling when your feet were on the letter Z?'

'I was tired. Things have been quite stressful. It must be that.' Brodie tried to make it look like she was sipping at the tea, although her lips remained firmly clamped shut, the smell itching at her nose.

'I think it's more than that.' Caitlin's eyes darted to the door. 'I think you must be one of *them*.'

'Them?'

Caitlin clasped her hands together. 'What I'm about to tell you may make you a little nervous. But you must understand, I tell you this to warn you. To try and convince you to "hang on" before it's too late.'

Brodie winced slightly and put the mug back on the table, all pretence at trying to look as if she were drinking forgotten.

Caitlin leant forward in the chair. 'The letter Z's the sign of a secret society which meets here on the campus of Virginia University.'

Brodie knew all about secret societies which met at universities.

'The Zeta, or Z Society for short, was founded in 1892 and it's made up of outstanding student leaders who give time and talent and recognise excellence.'

'*Is* made up?' said Brodie. 'You mean it still exists?'

'Oh yes, the Z Society's still in operation. I'm a member.' Caitlin's eyes darted once more towards the door.

'What's this got to do with me feeling ill?'

Caitlin bit the edge of her lip before answering. 'Ancient societies exist to keep secrets and pass down information throughout history.'

Brodie knew all about that too.

'The Z Society has deep and important beliefs about what people can know and understand, and it's the belief of the Z Society that certain types of information are best understood by those who approach learning with an open mind. Who are willing to see things with

217

the sort of openness that a child sees things.'

'I still don't understand what this has to do with me feeling ill.'

Caitlin held up her hands. 'The Z Society gives lots of weight to the work of two famous English poets, Wordsworth and Coleridge.'

'Coleridge?' Brodie heard the excitement in her own voice.

'The two men were great friends and their poetry is full of important information. Wordsworth wrote about a child who was playing in a stream. Rivers were important to them.'

Brodie knew all about the importance of rivers too. Her mind darted back to Westminster Abbey and the poems on the graves.

'Wordsworth pointed out the child playing in the stream could know answers to big ideas. He said, *"one on whom truths do rest; which we are toiling all our lives to find"*.'

Brodie shook her head and the tiniest bead of perspiration ran down her forehead and soaked into her eyelashes. She was trying to keep up, she really was. 'Please. I really don't understand why you're telling me all this.'

Caitlin's eyes narrowed as if she was concentrating even harder on trying to make sense. 'The Z Society tries to encourage people to look at big questions like children do. To try and work things out using the brilliance of the mind of a child. And here, in this centre of learning, we mark the ground with the sign of the Z to remind people how powerful kids' thinking can be. And we've got a legend. A founding myth if you like, that there are those who will come to the university who'll stand on the marks we've made and they'll begin to forget how to see things like a child.'

'And that's what you meant when you said I could be one of *them*?'

Caitlin blushed. 'Few experience what you did because very few come to this place who still think with the openness of a child anyway. But the legend is that some who stand on the Z will lose the ability they had.'

'But that's a crazy idea.'

'Of course it is. It's a totally ridiculous legend that's filtered down through time. It's just a myth. But it's one some of us believe in.'

Brodie felt a coldness sweep across her. 'But I always see things like a child. I'm all about stories and adventures and . . .'

Caitlin looked mildly panicked. 'Don't overexcite yourself. Have more tea.' Then she added quietly, 'I'm sure it's nothing. Nothing at all. But here's a question to help you remember my warning.' She sat up straight. 'Do you like sprouts?'

'Pardon?'

'Sprouts. The vegetable. Do you like them?'

This was a question she felt best suited for Hunter. 'Well?'

Brodie shook her head. 'I can't stand them.'

Caitlin laughed. 'The taste buds of a child are several hundred times sharper than those of an adult. We begin life with thousands of taste buds and our ability to taste is at its strongest when we're children.' She looked awkward. 'Few children like sprouts, Brodie. Their taste is so strong it attacks every taste bud we have. But as we age, our taste buds begin to die. Our ability to really taste grows weaker. Many of us then, simply because we cannot really taste them fully, begin to be able to eat sprouts. Even enjoy them.' A nervous grin flitted across her face. 'The Z Society exists at the University of Virginia, formed by the founding father of this nation, to encourage everyone to hang on to the tastes of their youth. Our myths and legends may be only stories and you feeling faint on the steps of the rotunda may have had more to do with the smell of the fire and the heat of the day.' Her grin flickered and was gone. 'But it might be a warning.'

* * *

'You OK?'

Brodie wasn't really sure how to answer Tandi.

'She didn't upset you, did she, that student? I wasn't sure we should have left you with her, but she seemed so keen to try and explain what happened. Did it make sense?'

'About as much sense as MS 408 does.'

'Oh. Not much then.'

Brodie sat down on the seat outside the Library building next to Mrs Smithies, who'd waited for her too. The rest of the team were trying to find out as much as they could about the rotunda burning festival. 'You'll feel better soon,' the older woman said reassuringly. 'It'll just take time.'

Brodie took a deep breath. She'd been thinking on her walk to meet them, trying to work out what Caitlin could mean about looking at things with the eyes of a child. It sounded weird and Brodie wasn't sure there was another way of looking at things. She fiddled with the end of her plait. 'Can I ask you both something? When you look at the pages of MS 408, what do you really see?'

Tandi considered for a moment. 'I think the colours of the paintings. You?'

'It's the words. All those hundreds of words. They're so beautifully written. And I know the

221

pictures are amazing and everything, but it's always the words.'

'What about you, Sarah?' asked Tandi, turning to Mrs Smithies.

'Ah, well. It's newer to me, isn't it? I haven't spent hours on it like all of you. But I think it's the stars.'

Brodie was confused. 'There's stars in there?'

'Yes. Lots. Zodiac pages and stars scribbled in the margins. They're everywhere.'

'Really?' Brodie tried to wrack her brain. She supposed there were lots of stars now she thought about it.

'Why do you think you noticed the stars?' Tandi asked.

'I'm always looking for stars,' she said. 'You see, we didn't have a gravestone for our daughter, Corriss. Jon didn't want that. Not somewhere cold and dark. She might have been scared.'

Brodie wanted to interrupt but Tandi rested her hand on Brodie's arm, signalling for her to wait.

'And so we bought a star. You can do that, you know. They give you a certificate and everything and we chose the name. Corriss, of course. And now we can see her. Every night when it's dark. And I like to think she's not scared any more. Even if I am.'

'So that's why you see stars in MS 408,' said Tandi.

'I guess it is,' the older woman said, and Brodie

noticed that her face suddenly looked younger, almost childlike.

'It's really important we don't rush her.' They'd travelled back from the university to the Clifton Inn virtually in silence, and only when Mrs Smithies had gone up to bed did Tandi tell the others what happened.

'But we should celebrate. We should do something. Something special,' blurted Smithies. 'I've been waiting so long for her to get involved with the code and this is brilliant. Shows she's moving on.'

Brodie didn't like to explain that everything Mrs Smithies had said was connected to her lost daughter. She wasn't sure it proved she was moving on at all.

Sicknote stood up from the table. 'Don't rush it. The pain which kept her locked away from the code won't be gone because of what she said today. She's taken her first steps, that's all.'

Smithies looked crestfallen. 'So what did she say?'

Brodie looked round the table and felt the weight of responsibility resting on her shoulders. 'It was about what she could see in the pages.'

Fabyan looked confused. 'See? What d'you mean, see?'

Brodie searched for a way to explain. She wasn't sure she could. 'I just wondered if everyone sees the manuscript differently. Because it makes no sense,

I mean, do we all focus on different things? Well, Mrs Smithies focuses on stars.' Brodie shuffled uncomfortably where she sat. 'I think stars are important.'

Hunter shook his head. 'Look, with all due respect, B, I'm as excited as a chicken dipper in a bath of ketchup that Mrs S has got herself involved and all. But I don't get where this is all going. I thought we came to the university to search for writings by Jefferson and now you want us to think about stars and stuff. You weren't feeling well. Maybe you should rest, you know. Get over things a bit and—'

'I'm fine,' snapped Brodie, determined not to dwell on what had happened with Caitlin and her strange messages about childhood visions and sprouts. 'I just think the stars thing's important. Look.'

She held out the copy of MS 408 and pressed the pages flat so everyone could see.

'There are star pages all through this book. And I just wondered if we should think about why.'

'You think we should be travelling to other planets?' asked Sheldon. 'You think that's where Avalon is?'

'No. Maybe. I don't know. But look at this page.'

Tusia leant across the table and peered in more closely at the circular sketching centred by a blue and red drawing.

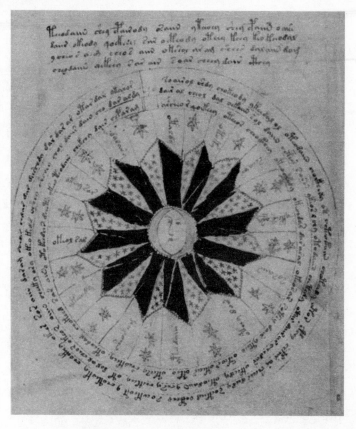

'You see the star?' said Brodie.

Tusia nodded.

'It could be important, couldn't it? You remember the weird water horse animal we saw in the Anson family crest when we were trying to solve clues back at Shugborough Hall? And then, d'you remember when we saw the picture of the little beast in MS 408?' The others nodded. 'Well, maybe these star pages are important too.' She was trying to sound convincing. She was pretty sure it wasn't working.

Tusia scratched her head. Then she leant forward and narrowed her eyes. 'Extraordinary,' she said.

'Of course it's extraordinary, Toots,' puffed Hunter. 'We've been looking at the manuscript for months and I think it's fair to say, if the thing wasn't extraordinary then we wouldn't have trekked across the Atlantic looking for answers.'

'No. This page. This exact page. It's extraordinary.'

Brodie turned to look at her.

'It reminds me of something. Something else. Something I've . . .' Her voice tailed away. 'Oh, my life.' She jumped up from the table and ran out of the room, returning with her arm laden with papers and booklets and documents. 'The university rotunda,' she said. 'While you were having your funny turn, Brodie, and getting over feeling weird and that, the rest of us went inside the rotunda. There were guides and I asked them about the rotunda and the fire and what happened.' She tried to catch her breath but her ideas were running away with her. 'And they showed me some blueprints for the original building and then how it changed.' She spread the notes across the table.

'Changed? I thought you said the rotunda was Jefferson's design,' said Sheldon.

'It was! But it altered after the fire. The building was adapted and then in 1973 the building was brought back to look like the original design Jefferson had. But for some years it was different.' She ploughed on with her explanation. 'They got rid of the middle floor and the skylight was widened. It was fine. It looked great. But people felt it was important, *really important* the building was returned to how it was. And here's why.'

Tusia took from the pile of notes and leaflets a rolled-up blueprint and unfurled it flat across the table.

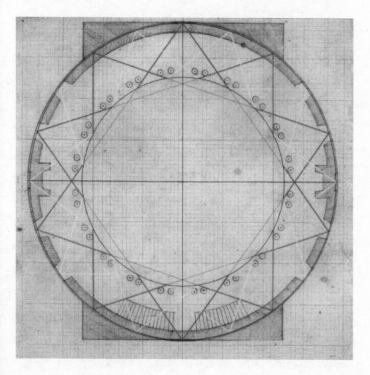

'People believed they had to change the rotunda back to the way Jefferson had planned it, because the original design provided balance and precision.'

'And why was that a good thing?'

'It was how it was supposed to be.'

'And does this plan show how that was?' said Kitty, waiting for Tusia to lift her hands from the blueprint.

Tusia stepped away.

There on the table, clear as anything, was Jefferson's plan for the internal arrangement of the rotunda.

Brodie could hardly breathe.

What the plan clearly showed, without any question or doubt, was stars.

Morgan looked up at the screen. The inbox was flashing.

Kerrith wasn't here to open the message. He'd hardly seen her for days.

That didn't matter. He was beyond waiting for her to get back.

He clicked on the message. The screen went white and beside it a map of America appeared. A flashing red light hovered over the location of Virginia.

'I can't believe we're doing this,' giggled Kitty, racing to catch up with them. 'Breaking and entering. *Again.*'

'Where have you been?' groaned Hunter.

'Nowhere.'

Brodie could tell Hunter was about to argue with the ridiculousness of this answer. How could anyone be nowhere?

Sheldon spoke before Hunter had a chance to argue. 'We're going to end up with a criminal record at this rate.'

Brodie was exasperated. 'We won't end up with records,' she puffed defensively. 'And we're not breaking and entering. The rotunda's always open.'

'Really? Even in the middle of the night?'

'Jefferson wanted it to be the centre of the campus, like a church. So it's always open, like a church.' She strode to the front of the group holding tightly to Mrs Smithies' hand. She'd tried to catch her up with all that had happened. She'd hoped Mrs Smithies would say something. Anything. To show she was excited. She said nothing. But her hand was tight in Brodie's own. It felt comforting and warm.

'OK,' said Smithies, drawing the group together. 'Let's see what we can make of the pattern in the stars.'

Hunter raised his hand. 'Eleven,' he said confidently.

'Excuse me?' said Smithies, lifting his glasses and resting them on his forehead.

'Eleven. That's what I make of them.' Hunter took the page of the rotunda blueprint and opened the facsimile of MS 408. Then he put them on the ground outside the rotunda and stepped back, and shone a torch directly on them. 'What d'you notice?'

'They're sort of the same,' offered Sheldon.

'Which is why we're here,' added Tusia. 'And not back at the hotel catching up on our sleep.'

'Yeah, yeah. I know. They're very similar. Which is why we've come. Two outer circles. Two inner circles. I get that. And then, inside both of them, a star marked in two colours. So far so good.'

'But?' asked Sicknote urgently.

'There's a difference between the stars.' He drew himself up straight and shone the torch across the group. 'Seems now's the chance for you to do your thing, Toots. D'you think you could copy the star from the picture in MS 408? Just the star?'

Friedman handed Tusia a piece of paper and she drew a pencil from the bun in her hair. With the others watching, she sketched the star and then handed the finished drawing to Hunter.

He began to tear the paper.

'Erm? What you doing?' said Fabyan defensively. 'Tusia's done what you asked and now . . .'

Hunter let the edges of the torn paper flutter to the floor. 'I'm just getting things ready,' he said, showing them the star now free of the paper edging. 'There's something you must see.'

Taking the paper star in his hand, he put it down on the blueprint of the rotunda. Then he stood up straight.

'What we supposed to be seeing?' asked Kitty quietly.

'No idea yet,' said Smithies, allowing his glasses to slide down from his forehead on to the bridge of his nose.

'It's the points of the stars,' Hunter explained. 'The MS 408 star has twelve points and the rotunda star's got ten. The number between those numbers is eleven. And it's the "in-between bit" that's important, like the filling in a sandwich!'

'Why?' urged Sicknote.

'Look at the points of the MS 408 star,' Hunter went on, 'and how they all rest inside the points of the rotunda star. Except in one place.'

Brodie peered forward to see.

'Here,' said Hunter, making it easy for them. 'Every point fits inside the red points of the rotunda star except these two points and they sit either side of this one point. The important point.'

'And how does this help us?' asked Kitty.

'Jefferson was interested in design,' said Hunter. 'He felt what he did here was so important it needed to be remembered. So if he wanted to leave something behind for us to find – something so important it was referred to on his gravestone – then I reckon he'd hide it here,' he tapped the page again with his finger, 'in the point of the star.'

They circled the building. Tusia used the blueprint to show them that the place Hunter felt was important was the part of the rotunda just above the entrance hall.

Torchlight filled the room, illuminating their steps as they walked. Shadows stretched along the walls like flames and Hunter led the way.

'He was going to paint stars on the ceiling of this place,' whispered Tusia.

'Who was?' asked Granddad.

'Jefferson. I don't mean paint them himself but have others paint them. He wanted to help students as they studied astronomy.'

Sheldon stopped walking. He lifted his head and looked at the unpainted ceiling and, because he was nervous maybe, he began to hum. Brodie recognised the tune. It was the Firebird song. 'Nimrod'. And it made her feel safe.

'Hey. Keep up,' hissed Sicknote, stumbling into Sheldon's back. 'We've got to check the point of the star and it's an awfully big star. We've had enough scares with American security guards for a while. We need to be quick about this and get out before we're seen.'

'So hurry up, then,' encouraged Hunter, obviously stressed that the crocodile of people following him was slowing and breaking up. 'We're in the space marked on the map,' he said, widening his arms. 'We just have to hunt around here till we find something. Anything that'll help.'

Brodie searched the shelving, behind the pillars, ran her hands along the panelled wood of the walls as they'd done in the Library of Congress. They reached up behind books, searching titles which seemed important, scanned through pages likely to hold a code.

'Why any particular book out of all the ones here?' asked Smithies, rejecting volume after volume. 'It has to be more precise. How in the world are we supposed to find what's important?'

Sheldon stopped humming. 'How about, *how in someone else's world* are we going to find what's important?' There was something about the tone of his voice which persuaded Brodie that what he was saying was important enough for her to stop searching. Sheldon slid his hands across his face and then crouched down to the ground, running his fingers along the floor like he was playing a tune on a keyboard, as if this action was forcing all his thoughts to line up and make sense. 'The keys on the piano,' he said quietly. 'The clue we needed to solve the very first code left by Elgar.'

Hunter tried to look supportive but his voice made him sound frantic. 'We've moved on from Elgar, mate! We're in the United States of America trying to find codes left for us by Jefferson.'

'You're wrong.'

'I'm not wrong.' Hunter didn't sound cross. Just confused.

'No. You are. You really are.' The silence that followed

was uncomfortable. 'Not wrong about the point of the star. Or being here. Or moving on to America. But you're wrong about moving on from Elgar.'

'So help us out, mate.'

'We never moved on from Elgar. Not really. We keep coming back to him, like we keep coming back to Coleridge and Bacon. Remember how we found a link between Tennyson and Elgar which brought us here. So what about a link between Elgar and Jefferson?'

'I don't know what link you're talking about.'

'One you'll like,' said Sheldon. 'The number 88.'

Brodie looked from one to the other. She'd no idea how this was helping and she could see Hunter struggling to understand. 'Hold on. I thought we were thinking about the number eleven and finding whatever Jefferson's hidden in this part of the rotunda.'

'But look at the space, Brodie. It's huge. We need to be more focused if we're going to find what we're looking for.'

'So how does the number 88 help us?'

'Like it helped us before! The number 88's the number of keys on a full-sized piano. But it's also the number given to a constellation in the sky.'

Brodie's mind was trying to reach backwards to dredge up the answers from her memory. The information she needed just wouldn't arrive. And then, like a firebrand burning in her skull, the words came. 'Phoenix constellation?' she blurted.

'Exactly.'

'Oh, please. I can't keep up with you lot. What on earth are you talking about now?' pleaded Kitty, her face red with the effort of trying to understand.

'Nothing on earth, but beyond it,' said Friedman, obviously remembering too.

'The phoenix constellation is constellation number 88,' added Sheldon. 'Knowing that helped us link the Firebird Code and Elgar's *Enigma Variations* and first find out about the Knights of Neustria.'

'But how does that help us here?' Kitty begged.

Tusia was obviously trying to pull the ideas together. 'We need to find the space where the blueprint and the MS 408 and the phoenix *all* meet. How can we do that?'

Sheldon's fingers were pressed hard against the ground. He looked as if he was in pain; the tune he played in his head had ended.

'Jefferson's numbers,' gasped Hunter.

'What?' Sheldon looked hopeful.

'Jefferson put numbers on the book spines. He came up with his own way of numbering books a bit like the Dewey system,' he blurted. 'Don't you remember? The guide in the Library of Congress told us, when she was showing us round the Jefferson collection. See if you can find any books, in this space here, which have the number 88 printed on their spine.'

Smithies darted along the lines of books, Friedman hurrying behind him. But it was Tusia who was the first to call out. 'Here,' she yelled. 'Here. I've found them. Books with numbers that include 88.'

'And are any of them helpful? Any of them written by Jefferson?'

Tusia shook her head.

'Of course not!' groaned Hunter. 'It's not enough. It's not *all* of the code.' His face was strained as if he was working out the final stages of an important calculation. 'But I think I've got it now!'

'You've found a book?' called Brodie.

'No. But I've worked out *exactly* where to look.'

'Well, tell us then!'

'The Library of Congress. If we've taken our clue about the numbering from the Library of Congress, then there might have been other important clues there.'

'Well, yes,' agreed Tusia. 'There were lots of clues. About Prometheus and the fire and the—'

'About the stars, Toots!' Hunter interrupted, the exasperation cracking in his voice. 'There may've been another clue about the stars.'

'I remember!' said Brodie. 'There *was* a quote about stars. I knew it meant we were involved in something big!'

'So what did it say?' pressed Smithies.

'*Too low they build who build beneath the stars.*'

'So we've got to look above the number 88!' Hunter explained. 'Beneath the stars is too low! It's got to be with the stars. Or where the stars would have been if Jefferson had ever had his way and they'd been painted on the ceiling!'

Brodie grinned. He was right, she knew it. They were moments away. 'Tusia. I reckon it's up to you.'

'Me? Why me?'

'Because moving on with the clue involves one of us taking a climb.'

Tusia didn't argue. Instead she reached her hand up the side of the pillar which supported the ceiling next to the shelving numbered 88. She linked her legs around the pole and, as if she were climbing the rigging of a giant boat about to sail away across the stars, she began to pull herself upwards.

Brodie craned her neck to watch her.

Then Tusia stopped. Her legs tightened and her hands clutched at the top of the pillar. There was a gentle click. It was the sound of a tiny door in the ceiling, swinging open.

In the Shadow of the Blue Ridge Mountains

The Director held the receiver against his ear for a moment. Then he lowered his hand and put the phone back on the cradle. Things were going as they should now. He was relieved.

Since the group meeting in Europe, he'd been a little unsure. It had seemed a dangerous game to allow those at Station X to continue at all. It would have been safer perhaps to haul them all in. Goodness knows there was enough room for them at Site Three. But it was the whole 'children issue'. Children were a special case. Of course, historically, the Suppressors had dealt with large numbers of native children by taking them from their families and re-educating them. Then the numbers involved were vast. That could be explained away then as a national policy. A 'Protection Board' set up even, so anyone with half a care to look and see what was going on could see the needs of the children were apparently being catered for. But a small group of modern children? Random children drawn together from a range of backgrounds? That was more difficult to explain. More tricky to stamp out the irritation of a troublesome few than a whole group. People seemed to go for that. The television news each night focused on stories of a lone child falling from a balcony and breaking his arm, or a single child suffering some terrible disease. That got people's attention and made them sit up and notice. But whole groups of children starving in a land far away? This didn't have the same news value somehow. No. The 'Station X few' had always been more problematic, more difficult to deal with. And he'd doubted several times that Level Five was approaching the problem in the best way possible. Now he was reassured. Those in the Chamber may have ignored the work of Station X initially; they may have treated the situation with more care to try and minimise public interest. But now things were going to happen that would put the irritating little team out of business for good.

The Director ran his finger across the top of the telephone receiver. Then he lifted the handset and dialled.

The phone continued to ring.

He wasn't a patient man. The lack of answer annoyed him.

He put down the phone and tried another number. 'I'm trying to reach Miss Vernan,' he said at last. The voice at the other end was apologetic. Kerrith's new assistant, Morgan, was obviously floundering around trying to work out what to say. The Director grimaced. 'What do you mean, she's gone home ill?'

There was a mumbled answer at the end of the line and the repeating of a phone number. Then some muttering about how even if Kerrith wasn't available then he, as her assistant, was. The Director considered for a moment. He supposed it wouldn't hurt to have Morgan more on board. The man seemed to be capable of showing initiative. And more important than that, he was actually here.

The Director scheduled a meeting with the new guy in his diary and then hung up the phone.

Then he looked down once more at the notepad in front of him and dialled the number he'd been given. If Kerrith Vernan was too ill to talk to him at work then he'd talk to her at home. The number connected. There was a soft hum. Then the phone began to ring.

* * *

'My head hurts!' groaned Brodie as she rubbed her temples.

Hunter was striding up and down the room in front of her. 'We're getting there, B,' he said. 'We're totally getting there. You just have to push through the pain.'

Brodie took a deep breath, folded her body forwards and banged her head on the table. 'There's too many numbers.'

Hunter didn't even answer this time. He simply strode up and down with more purpose and vigour.

The team had travelled to Riverbank Labs after their exploits at the University of Virginia, with Mrs Smithies taking special charge of the envelope Tusia had retrieved from above the shelving in the rotunda.

Riverbank Labs was all Brodie had known it would be. An eccentric mix of the weird and the wonderful. There were more zebras, as Fabyan had only shipped his favourite pair to Station X. There was a troupe of monkeys roaming around the estate with the freedom Brodie was more used to seeing cats wander around with back in England. And there was the windmill. Riverbank's own Tower of the Winds. And it was in the tower the team tried to decipher the message they'd found.

The code was totally different to what Brodie had expected.

The envelope contained three separate documents. One was a sketchily drawn map of the area around Burford's Tavern in Virginia. The second was a sheet of yellowed paper containing letters and dashes. The third was a handwritten note.

'So who's this guy, Professor Patterson, who wrote the note?' asked Sheldon.

'A professor of Mathematics,' explained Sicknote. 'He wrote to Jefferson often, apparently, about the need to form a perfect cipher. There's evidence Patterson did develop what he thought was a perfect way to write in code. But this note here was written way before he worked out his cipher system.'

'Might explain why it's such a useless note, then,' said Tusia.

It was hardly the most expressive of communications. Brodie glanced at the wording again.

Jefferson,
The need for perfection comes from order and being clear about what is important.
Patterson

If this handwritten note was little help to them then the third piece of paper was even worse. 'It's the ramblings of a madman,' said Sicknote as he surveyed the writing.

Brodie couldn't disagree.

She pressed the paper flat again on the table and traced her finger along the first few lines of writing.

egl/ o/ yan/ etc/ rueate/ g/ n/ rJ/ aht/ i/ ce/ vw/
eh/ ./ o/ f/ n/ / o/ iy/ r/ h/ lhh/ tco/ t   ueal
lp/ e gs/ l sd/ t/ u/ oa/ yssf/ d/ s/ h/ ,e/ it/ o/
uf/ o, t/ ecy/ eoeohawngsre tb/ g/ nw/ en/ y/ at/
hf/ n/ p/ r/ hd/ eanyrn   l/ e/ A/ fsinso   nr/
hnh/ r/ n/ t/ o t/ id/ c/ n/ dpe/ w/ l/ pln/ ./ i/
hs/ p/ th/ ese/ alto/ ff/ i/ sc   rmf/ kp/ sh/
adaaey   l/ oo/ s   d.osmneu/ Na/ e/ ue./ rtu
deteerhmei f/ rr/ oone ht hel/ a/ o/ f Time of
acrhusing ttrhe i/ welec.tors, adnAdTi/ n/ d/ bo
thes/ ie/ n/ dm/ tu   ko   oqDobev/ ias/ ./ a/ h/
wyht/ n/ we e tponr/ ffe/ ota whileh thgrey shall
gievnre ethueir kvotex/ hs;o/ ts rwhitch they
shralaoll   giveo   i/ rtehoeeih/ vrg/ i/ s   yvotes;
Gwhicah Dad/ ky shall bte trhe tsame t
hroughout theo/ r united states B/ lNeo pewrsoon
except ma natuwural eboron tcitsizen,or a cibBt
dizen o f fthe un itedm/ r states, at tphreu tkime
of the Adopt ion of this co/ aofnstitutfion, hshall
be eligible to the lioffice of Presindenot ;neither/

tsth uall any person be eligible to that kofffice wmho shall neot ahoave attined to the age of thuirty five years,eand befen fourteen years a Resdident within the unfitted states.before ne enter on the ex e/ rec ution otf hias o ffice, he shall taken the rfolmloowing Oath or An/ tffir mhation:'I do so lemnlosya swear that I will faithfully execute n/ geathse office t/ iof the un ited States,anaad will to ethe beset of my Ability, preserve, protect and defend the constitution of the United states.'the president shall be the commander in chief of the Army and Navy of the United States; of the militia of the several states, when called into the actuall service of the united states; he may require the opinion, in writing, ohf the principal officer in each of the executive departments,upon anysubject relating to the duties of their respective offices,and he shall have power to grant reprieve s and pardons for offenses oagainst the united states, except in cases of impeadchment. He shall have power by and with the advice and consent of the senate to make treaties,provided two thirds of the senators present concur;and he shall nominated, and by and with

245

the advice and consent of the senate, shall appoint
Ambassadors, other public ministers and consuls,
judges of the supreme court, and all other officers
ofl the united states,whose appointments are not
herein otherwise provided for, and which shall be
established by law: but the congress may by law
vest the appointment of such inferior officers.

The writing was totally and utterly bonkers, the first few lines a mess of slashes across the page. 'How on earth does this fit with the unsolved Beale Paper?' Brodie moaned again. 'I just don't see how it'd work.'

'It doesn't,' said Hunter matter-of-factly. 'There's not enough words to fit with the numbers.'

'How can you possibly know that?' Brodie exclaimed. 'Have you counted the words?'

'Err, yes, B. That's what I do. 2,260 is the highest number in the Beale Paper . . . and there's just not enough words in this message to make them fit together. So I reckon we've got to number the letters this time and not the words.'

'OK. So let's do that,' said Tusia.

'But we've got another problem,' groaned Hunter. 'There's 2,356 characters in this weirdo piece of writing, if you include all the spaces and the slashes. So that's *too many* letters!'

71, 194, 38, 1701, 89, 76, 11, 83, 1629, 48, 94, 63, 132, 16,
111, 95, 84, 341, 975, 14, 40, 64, 27, 81, 139, 213, 63, 90,
1120, 8, 15, 3, 126, 2018, 40, 74, 758, 485, 604, 230, 436,
664, 582, 150, 251, 284, 308, 231, 124, 211, 486, 225, 401,
370, 11, 101, 305, 139, 189, 17, 33, 88, 208, 193, 145, 1,
94, 73, 416, 918, 263, 28, 500, 538, 356, 117, 136, 219, 27,
176, 130, 10, 460, 25, 485, 18, 436, 65, 84, 200, 283, 118,
320, 138, 36, 416, 280, 15, 71, 224, 961, 44, 16, 401, 39,
88, 61, 304, 12, 21, 24, 283, 134, 92, 63, 246, 486, 682, 7,
219, 184, 360, 780, 18, 64, 463, 474, 131, 160, 79, 73, 440,
95, 18, 64, 581, 34, 69, 128, 367, 460, 17, 81, 12, 103, 820,
62, 116, 97, 103, 862, 70, 60, 1317, 471, 540, 208, 121,
890, 346, 36, 150, 59, 568, 614, 13, 120, 63, 219, 812,
2160, 1780, 99, 35, 18, 21, 136, 872, 15, 28, 170, 88, 4, 30,
44, 112, 18, 147, 436, 195, 320, 37, 122, 113, 6, 140, 8,
120, 305, 42, 58, 461, 44, 106, 301, 13, 408, 680, 93, 86,
116, 530, 82, 568, 9, 102, 38, 416, 89, 71, 216, 728, 965,
818, 2, 38, 121, 195, 14, 326, 148, 234, 18, 55, 131, 234,
361, 824, 5, 81, 623, 48, 961, 19, 26, 33, 10, 1101, 365, 82,
88, 181, 275, 346, 201, 206, 86, 36, 219, 324, 829, 840, 64,
326, 19, 48, 122, 85, 216, 284, 919, 861, 326, 985, 233, 64,
68, 232, 431, 960, 50, 29, 81, 216, 321, 603, 14, 612, 81,
360, 36, 51, 62, 194, 78, 60, 200, 314, 676, 112, 4, 28, 18,
61, 136, 247, 819, 921, 1060, 464, 895, 10, 6, 66, 119, 38,
41, 49, 602, 423, 962, 302, 294, 875, 78, 14, 23, 111, 109,
62, 31, 501, 823, 216, 280, 34, 24, 150, 1000, 162, 286, 19,
21, 17, 340, 19, 242, 31, 86, 234, 140, 607, 115, 33, 191,

67, 104, 86, 52, 88, 16, 80, 121, 67, 95, 122, 216, 548, 96,
11, 201, 77, 364, 218, 65, 667, 890, 236, 154, 211, 10, 98,
34, 119, 56, 216, 119, 71, 218, 1164, 1496, 1817, 51, 39,
210, 36, 3, 19, 540, 232, 22, 141, 617, 84, 290, 80, 46, 207,
411, 150, 29, 38, 46, 172, 85, 194, 39, 261, 543, 897, 624,
18, 212, 416, 127, 931, 19, 4, 63, 96, 12, 101, 418, 16, 140,
230, 460, 538, 19, 27, 88, 612, 1431, 90, 716, 275, 74, 83,
11, 426, 89, 72, 84, 1300, 1706, 814, 221, 132, 40, 102, 34,
868, 975, 1101, 84, 16, 79, 23, 16, 81, 122, 324, 403, 912,
227, 936, 447, 55, 86, 34, 43, 212, 107, 96, 314, 264, 1065,
323, 428, 601, 203, 124, 95, 216, 814, 2906, 654, 820, 2,
301, 112, 176, 213, 71, 87, 96, 202, 35, 10, 2, 41, 17, 84,
221, 736, 820, 214, 11, 60, 760.

'Can't we just ignore some letters?' Tusia offered.

Hunter turned to face her.

'If there's too many,' she said. 'I mean, as long as
we can match a number to a letter on the text we should
be OK.'

Hunter's face was marked now with deep worry
lines. 'But *which* letters do we ignore? The whole
piece of writing's just a jumble of nonsense.'

Brodie looked down again at the document. She let
her eyes scan along the lines searching for the story or
the sense hidden inside. And then, as if water was
beginning to move under the ice of a frozen lake, she
began to see movement. Letters seemed to group

together in front of her, forming words she could recognise. Not at the beginning of the writing where slashes marked the page like scars, but deeper into the text, so the further you journeyed into the maze, the closer you came to finding the answer.

'Look,' Brodie said sharply. 'Here. Can you see? Words. That actually make sense.' She pointed her finger and with the tip of her nail marked out the words 'United States' and 'President'.

'Unbelievable,' breathed Smithies. 'There's sense hidden there.'

Brodie peered in closer. Every now and then random letters seemed to sit inside the words trying to trick the reader and make them stumble. '*Presindenot*' hid the letters '*o*' and '*n*' inside it but it was clearly the word '*President*'. '*Natuwural eboron tcitsizen*' had to be the words '*Natural born citizen*' simply cluttered up with extra letters. And after peering hard enough, Brodie found the word '*constitution*' hidden in the chunk of letters and slashes '*co/aofnstitutfion*'.

'There *is* sense in here,' she gasped. 'It's just cluttered up with extra stuff.'

Sicknote ran his finger along the line of his collar. 'There's always sense hidden in the ramblings of madmen. If you look carefully enough.'

Looking carefully took some time. 'There,' said Tusia loudly, stepping back from the table. 'The sense in the nonsense. See.'

Brodie read what they'd found out loud.

'The Congress may determine the Time of chusing the electors, and the day on which they shall give their votes; which day shall be the same throughout the United States. No person except a natural born citizen, or a citizen of the United States, at the time of the Adoption of this constitution, shall be eligible to the office of the President; neither shall any person be eligible to that office, who shall not have attained the age of thirty five years and been fourteen years a Resident within the United States. Before he enter on the execution of his office, he shall take the following Oath or Affirmation: "I do solemnly swear that I will faithfully execute the office of President of the United States and will to the best of my ability preserve, protect and defend the Constitution of the United States." The president shall be the Commander in Chief of the Army and Navy of the United States of the militia of the several states , when called into the actual service of the United States; he may require the opinion in writing of the principal officer in each of the executive departments, upon any subject relating to the duties of their respective offices, and he shall have power to grant reprieves and pardons for offenses against the United States except in cases of impeachment. He shall have power, by and with the advice and consent of the Senate, to make treaties provided two thirds of the senators present concur, and he shall nominate, and by and with the advice and consent of the Senate, shall appoint Ambassadors, other public ministers and consuls, judges of the supreme court, and all other officers of the United States, whose appointments are not herein otherwise provided for, and which shall be established by law: but the congress may by law vest the appointment of inferior officers.'

There was a general hush. 'This is all about the powers of being president,' said Brodie proudly.

'Brilliant,' said Granddad.

'No. Not brilliant,' offered Tandi.

'Why not brilliant?'

'It wasn't important, was it?' she said. 'To Jefferson, I mean. All this,' she said, flapping the paper in her hand. 'Being president, choosing judges, granting pardons. All that stuff, wasn't what was most vital to the man. You worked that out from his gravestone. It wasn't what he wanted to be remembered for.'

Hunter picked up the small handwritten note from Patterson. 'And it's not what the professor said he should think about either,' he said. He reread the note from Patterson aloud.

'Jefferson,

The need for perfection comes from order and being clear about what is important.

Patterson'

Then he tightened his hand on the piece of paper. 'That's it,' he said quietly. 'That's what we ignore.'

'Ignore?' said Brodie.

'All this stuff about the constitution, and being president. That's not where we're going to find the translation of the Beale. That's just there to hide the real message.'

'So where's the real message hiding?' yelped Tusia.

'*In the order*,' groaned Hunter. 'We need to number every letter in the jumbled key text, and then match it to the Beale. But I'm betting you, all the stuff about presidents is just a bluff. There's a word for that, isn't there, sir?'

'Disinformation,' said Sicknote. 'You could say the extra letters are "nulls" in the code.'

'Nulls, like not being any good,' said Hunter. 'I like it. So maybe the message about the president is the nulls of the code. The unneeded letters which make up the text.'

Not everyone seemed to totally understand what he meant, but Tusia suddenly jumped in to help. 'Remember the tablecloth?' she said. 'Way back when we were being tested to join Team Veritas? Remember how there were all these letters on the top of the table and we had to cover the table with the cloth to let just some letters peep through the holes. It's how we found the message. We covered up the disinformation to find the information we needed. This is like that!'

Sicknote seemed to be glowing with pride at Tusia's explanation.

'What we need to find is the letters hidden inside those words and around those words,' agreed Hunter. 'That'll be our real message.'

Brodie grimaced. 'But didn't you say there's too many letters? It won't match exactly.'

'That's why there are slashes! The message is hidden side by side, and so when there's letters separated by slashes then either one of the letters could be the one we need to solve the code. When the letters are on their own then they count as one number but when the slashes appear, then the letters next to the slash must count as one group. A group is equal to one number and we've got to make a choice about which letters in that group work best with the code.'

Brodie was sure she'd nearly got it.

'It's to do with ORDER and IMPORTANCE,' Hunter said. 'Take number 71. That's the first letter in the code. If we count along the key text page, counting each collection of letters close to a slash as being one letter, then when we get to number 71 we find l/e/A/f. Well, that could mean "l" or "e" or "A" or "f" according to what word we need.' He highlighted the beginning of the page. 'See.'

Brodie looked down at the start of the message.

eg/ o/ yan/ etc/ rueate/ g/ n/ rJ/ aht/ i/ ce/
vw/ eh/ ./ o/ f/ n/ / o/ iy/ r/ h/ Uhh/ tco/ t uea/
lp/ e gs/ l sd/ t/ u/ oa/ yssf/ d/ s/ h/ ,e/ it/ o/
uf/ o, t/ ecy/ eoeohawngsre tb/ g/ nw/ en/ y/ at/
hf/ n/ p/ r/ hd/ eangrn l/ e/ A/ f sinso

'But I'm thinking we choose "A",' Hunter continued, 'because it's a capital letter and we're at the start of the message.'

Brodie tried to allow the logic to seep into her brain. There were too many letters but *not* if you grouped the letters around the slashes and counted them as one. If you did this, you had the right number of letters for the code!

'Come on,' encouraged Hunter. 'We've got to start numbering! Oh, this is pizza perfect.'

Brodie could think of lots of words for the activity. 'Perfect' wasn't one of them. The slashes and choices of letters were a pain. Brodie's head was pulsing and her eyes itched with fatigue. But as the early morning sun began to filter in through the windows and fill the air with natural light, Hunter put down his pen.

'We've done it,' he said.

And they had.

The translation of the Beale Paper was in front of them.

Clear and as bright as day.

And so to the location of the vault four miles from Burford's. The iron pots wait buried some six feet beneath the ground for fear of plunder. They can be found at the quadrant meeting of Goose Creek, Bear Wallow Gap, Peaks of Otter and Blackhorse Gap. Know the fire passes through the line and gives power and transformation to all who carry her spark. And when you find the treasure, guard well the country of her birth for the sake of all the Knights of Neustria who have passed before you. Seek ye well good friend.

The Director placed the newspaper back on the table and folded his arms behind his head. He was not sure he would have chosen the River Thames as a way of dealing with the guard. It was perhaps too public. But no matter. The man had been missing from action for months and it was important that a message was sent out loud and clear to everyone involved with the Black Chamber. You didn't get to change sides. That's not how it worked.

There was a knock at the door.

'Special delivery, sir.' The visitor was holding a scroll in his hand.

The Director remembered how excited he'd been when the scrolls from the Tyrannos Group had first started arriving. It meant he'd been noticed. Now he feared they may have noticed too much.

He scratched at his neck and then unrolled the scroll.

It was not an invitation this time. It was an instruction.

It seemed a bit extreme. But it was simply moving on with the plan he had in place. And he supposed everyone had been waiting long enough.

'We'll let you know as soon as we find anything.'

Brodie hugged Tandi tightly.

'And we'll keep digging for answers here,' Tandi said.

Brodie noticed Tandi's eyes were shadowed, her forehead lined. She was tired. Or there was something she wasn't telling her.

'Are you getting closer, trying to find the people we know've been taken?' Brodie asked gently.

Tandi rubbed her eyes and her bangles jangled round her wrists. 'I'm not sure, Brodie,' she said. 'I don't know if we'll ever find where the Suppressors take people they want to silence. The records are so difficult to read. It's as if the people who've been taken never really existed. Their stories count for nothing.' Tandi reached her arm across Brodie's shoulder and drew her into another hug. 'But we keep looking. We won't give up. You and the words of the code, and us and the people it's claimed. We all have a job to do and we won't stop trying to make a difference.'

Brodie looked up at Miss Tandari and she suddenly remembered how determined she could be. 'You worked with Smithies, right?' she said quietly. 'When he was at the Chamber.'

'Smithies first showed me the pages of MS 408,' she said, 'and I knew then, nothing would stop me trying to find answers to that code.'

'And you don't mind that you're having to spend all your time looking for those who've been taken?' Brodie asked.

Tandi's dark eyes glinted. 'Many of them are captive because they love the code, Brodie. Because they dared to try and make sense of something which couldn't be read. What could be more important than helping those people to freedom, while the rest of you make sense of the patterns on the page?' She patted Brodie's arm again. 'Two sides of a marvellous coin,' she said. 'Knowledge and freedom. One without the other's really worth nothing at all.'

Morgan pointed to the flashing computer screen. 'The flashing dots are agents of ours.'

The Director nodded. 'These three?'

'Virginia, Illinois and Washington DC, sir.'

'Excellent. And we have contact.'

'With two of them, regularly. For the other it's more complicated, sir.'

The Director understood the system.

'And this notification?'

'Travel plans, sir.'

'Good. I think it's about time I made plans of my own. See to it that the plane is made ready.'

* * *

'I want to come with you.' Friedman's eyes were wide. 'I *need* to come with you.'

Brodie shuffled awkwardly in the foyer of the hotel. 'Smithies organised the teams,' she said. 'It's best you stay. We'll need people here to report to. It won't work for us all to go.'

Friedman looked like a caged animal. He'd at least convinced them that staying behind at Riverbank Labs with Fabyan, Tandi and Kitty, who were still searching for clues about the Suppressors, wasn't an option. But now he'd been relegated to the team staying behind at Burford's Tavern and it was obvious he liked this idea even less. 'You want me to just wait for news. Is that it?' he whispered dejectedly to Smithies. 'Haven't I done enough waiting?'

'It'll be a trek, Robbie. We can't all go.'

'Let him go,' said Sicknote quietly.

'But . . .'

Sicknote steered Smithies forward, out of Friedman and Brodie's earshot and out into the porch. 'He's not well. Not fully recovered. Slightly damaged by life. But who of us isn't? I'll stay here and wait for news. Those two should be together,' he said. '"Homo Sum the adventurer" and all that.'

Smithies obviously didn't know what he was talking about.

'The words on Lawrence's grave at Westminster Abbey . . . *I know what it is to be human*. Adventuring together's important.'

Smithies shrugged. 'OK, Robbie,' he said loudly enough for Friedman to hear. 'I guess you're with us.'

Sicknote's eyes twitched into something resembling a wink in Brodie's direction before he turned away and took two rather hefty gulps on his asthma inhaler. She suddenly wanted to hug the strange man who dressed day and night in pyjamas, but instead she went and stood next to her dad.

The car stopped at the top of the hill. The driver reached for his phone and connected to the local server. Two emails from the same address. One he'd read a few hours ago. One was new. It was the confirmation he'd been waiting for.

He forwarded the new email as he'd been asked to. The teams were all set to go.

Then he turned the key in the ignition and pulled the car away from the kerb.

'It's just like when we were in Chepstow,' moaned Hunter.

'It better not be,' said Brodie, remembering, with a

chilly shiver, how the search at the River Wye nearly cost her and Hunter their lives.

As much as she didn't want to admit it though, in many ways, things were the same as they'd been that day. They'd laden themselves down with spades, hammers, torches and blankets. And they were armed with the most basic of maps and a belief that the combination of all the clues and the messages along the way would take them to the treasure.

'Blackhorse Gap, Peaks of Otter, Bear Wallow Gap. Who thinks of these names?' called Tusia, as she strode ahead of the line.

'The very first people who lived here,' Brodie said, and the thought made her excited and she wasn't entirely sure why. And then it came to her as they traipsed their way across the bracken-covered earth and past trees stretching so high she could barely see the top branches. The red fox story. The tale of the coyote. All the clues and the pictures and the stories and the signs had been linked to that one idea. How a fire thief had had the bravery and the determination to steal power from the gods. She remembered the story her mother had told her, of how the coyote had taken the flame from the fire beings and passed it on from animal to animal. And everything connected in her mind like pearls on a string. They were about to find the fire. The fire of Avalon. Its stolen treasure. And as she strode forward through the forest, with her dad walking beside her, and her friends behind, she was excited and scared at the same time.

The sky was as dark as coal, the moon a single spark in a starless sky.

And there was a distant rumble of thunder as if the fire beings were angry at the thought of the theft to come.

'How much longer?'

Brodie rolled her eyes in answer, safe in the knowledge that in the beam of the torch and the waning light of the moon, Hunter couldn't see her face clearly enough to know how annoyed she was. They'd been walking for hours. Her feet were sore, the pack she carried on her shoulders growing heavier with each step. And it was raining.

It had all begun so well. They'd followed the north fork down to Goose Creek and then they'd walked alongside the stream towards the source of the creek at Bear Wallow Gap. But the ground was uneven and covered with brambles and branches. The mud slid under their feet and the stones skittered and skidded where they walked. It was windy and branches scratched their faces as they passed. Dinner seemed a distant memory and any suggestion they stop for food was dismissed. There was nowhere to shelter. Stopping would just make them wetter and make going on more difficult.

So they pulled themselves across rocks and crevices, splashed through open water as above them owls and kestrels circled looking for prey.

'Tell me again why we're doing this in the dark,' groaned Sheldon.

'So we're in position to look for the treasure when it's light,' retorted Brodie. 'It's going to take hours to get there so we're making good use of the time.'

'And are we "there" yet?' pleaded Sheldon.

Tusia stopped walking. She held the torch up to her face and in the yellow gleam of the artificial light her eyes looked almost wild. '*You*,' she said forcefully, 'are the one with the map.'

'We should check things,' said Friedman, trying to calm the tension, his shoulders pulled up tight around his neck, his bandaged hands plunged deep into his pockets. 'Let's go over what we know.'

'What I *know*, is that I'm wet through to the skin, my feet hurt and I can barely walk another step,' said Hunter.

'Well, you're not carrying a spade *as well* as a backpack and a map,' moaned Sheldon.

'And you haven't had your arms nearly severed by branches as you walk, because someone isn't shining the torch so you can see the path too,' Hunter added caustically.

'Enough!' snapped Brodie, marching to the centre of the group and raising her arms. 'Will you all just listen to yourselves?'

There was an awkward silence, broken only by the sound of the rain.

'We're on the edge of an amazing discovery here and all you're doing is moaning and complaining.'

The sound of the rain grew louder.

'We've managed to solve the Beale Papers, for goodness' sake, and according to the map we're only metres away from where we need to be. And all you can do is go on about being tired. Well, newsflash – we're all tired! But we mustn't turn on each other. Surely all the stories we followed this time have been showing us the coyote who stole the fire passed it on to others. He didn't complain about having to run. He didn't complain about putting himself at risk. He was there to help his friends do what needed to be done.' Brodie wiped a droplet of rain from her eyebrow and pushed her way to the front of the group. 'Now, according to the map, we're really close to the vault! So let's keep looking, shall we? Together. Without complaining.'

And with that she strode on into the thick of the trees and out of sight.

And it would have been a perfect rallying cry to encourage the others if, at that moment, the edge of the world hadn't fallen away below her feet and the earth hadn't eaten her alive.

What Lies Beneath

Being swallowed by the earth wasn't a good feeling.

Brodie was pretty sure she screamed, although the air rushing into her lungs as she fell drowned out any noise she made. Her fingers scrabbled at the side of the opening in the ground, but she couldn't hold on. Dirt whipped at her face, clogging her nostrils and stinging her eyes. Roots of trees poked at her body, causing her to twist and turn as she plummeted. And the end, when it came, was sudden and sickening.

For a moment Brodie didn't move. She wasn't sure she could.

Then there was a surge inside her chest. Her heart, which for seconds had forgotten to beat, was suddenly determined to make up for lost time. It thumped so violently inside her she was scared it'd break her ribs. Her head pulsed and from her side she could feel a warm stickiness.

Brodie was pretty sure she wasn't dead. She didn't feel good. But she was nearly certain she hadn't died.

She flexed her fingers. They were, she was surprised to find, still under her control. She twitched her toes. They responded as they should. Maybe, then, things weren't as bad as she feared. So she tried to sit up. And that's when things went wrong.

Her granddad often complained of a 'head rush' when he stood up too quickly from his chair. Brodie didn't really know what he meant by this. Now she did. Her body moved upwards and her head moved too quickly at first, and then her brain inside it rushed to catch up, thumping against the inside of her skull as she moved. She was sure she was going to throw up. She'd felt this way only once before, when she'd broken her toe after stubbing it against a chair leg at home. The source of the sickness was pain. But she felt so battered and confused she wasn't sure where the pain was coming from. She slid her hand along her leg and against her other arm. Then she put her hand on her side.

And felt the blood.

It seemed dangerous situations were all part of being

in Team Veritas. Searching for answers to riddles and puzzles which were hundreds of years old was obviously not the safest thing to do. For a girl who enjoyed stories as a way of escape, she was certainly getting trapped in her own fair share of tricky situations.

Brodie closed her eyes and felt a tear slide down the mud and dirt caking her face.

She wondered what the adventurers she'd read about would do in this situation. Alice had fallen down a rabbit-hole but, as far as she could remember, Alice wasn't badly injured in the fall. Aladdin had been trapped below the ground but he'd walked openly into the cavern in the first place. And Tom and Geoff, in the story of Aquila, found a flying machine at the bottom of the quarry. What marked them all out, Brodie decided, was that none of these people she'd read about were alone. Alice found the white rabbit, Aladdin the genie and Tom and Geoff had each other. Brodie realised, unlike the heroes she read about, she was totally alone at the bottom of a hole.

Morgan Summerfield looked up as a message pinged on to his computer screen. Excellent news. Things in Virginia were going well. The Director was happy. Kerrith would have been happy, if she was interested. But never mind. Things were moving along nicely.

And the Director had explained there was one last thing to do. To ensure everything was prepared.

He reached for the list of contact details he'd got from the IT department. He'd been having fun already . . . but now he could hot things up a bit.

There was a reason Morgan had been chosen to be Kerrith's assistant. She might have begun to lose her edge, but his was still sharp.

He entered the email address from the list.

The message was brief. He knew it would be effective.

It took about five minutes for Brodie to work out she should choose one of three options.

Her friends were above ground, surely not far away, and so one decision would be to try and make them hear her, or to try and climb back up to them.

She lifted her head and pointed the beam of her torch through the darkness. It didn't break the surface.

Brodie lowered the torch.

A second option was to conserve her energy. Shouting out into the darkness might get her rescued, but the strength to call out would need her to fill her lungs and she wasn't entirely sure the pain in her side would allow her to shout. She wasn't sure either, if her voice would carry up to the opening of the hole. The light from the torch didn't make it that far. Trying to get back up out of the hole was impossible. Sitting still was no good to anybody.

Brodie tightened her grasp on the torch.

There was a third option.

Wherever she'd ended up, it was clear to her now, the hole had taken her down to an underground void. Climbing back up to the surface was impossible but there was a chance, a small chance, the space would open out and cut its way to the surface somewhere else. If she walked on, she might find an exit. A way back to above ground.

Brodie pressed her hand against her side. There was a lot of blood and she was scared.

But she didn't have the time to be afraid. If she was alone at the bottom of a hole, she had to be strong. And she had to do something about the bleeding.

And so, biting her lip to stop herself from crying, she reached forward and unlaced her shoes. She took off her socks and slipped the shoes back over bare feet. Then she took the socks and knotted the ends together making a long bandage she could just about tie round her side. She pulled it tight against the cut. Then, with the material pulled across the wound, she tried to stand.

It took three attempts. She needed to move slowly so the pulsing in her head didn't overwhelm her but with enough momentum to actually lift her from the ground. When she was finally standing, she reached out her hand and steadied herself against the lining of the hole. The earth was wet and gritty.

With her other hand, Brodie pointed the torch into the darkness. She blinked her eyes. Behind her, the sides of the hole were enclosed, but in the light of the torch, she could see in front of her, an opening stretching beyond the reach of the light. She dug her nails into the earth, pushed away from the wall and clutched her hand to her side. Then she began to walk.

The space in front of her extended like a corridor. The roof of the tunnel was low and scraped against her head but the ground under her feet was worn away and smooth as if it had been down trodden over time or washed smooth perhaps by an underground river. The tunnel was straight and unswerving and Brodie was nearly sure the ground was pulling up a little and the tunnel was rising. The torch flickered; the beam of light bounced off the walls and pooled at her feet. The air was moist. Every now and then, water dripped from above her and splashed mud on to her face. And a moth, wings thick and heavy like fabric, brushed against her arm as she walked.

Then, quite suddenly, Brodie felt cold.

There was a surge of air which swelled from in front of her as the tunnel opened out and the ceiling lifted.

And the next step she took brought her into an underground cavern in the middle of the Blue Ridge Mountains.

She'd found Thomas Jefferson Beale's treasure chamber.

In the sweep of the light from the torch, Brodie could see the space was almost circular and the walls were roughly lined with stone. In the centre was a long stone step, fairly tall, about the height of a very young child. And side by side on the step, Brodie could clearly see large iron pots shrouded in dust.

It was exactly as Beale had described it. A vault lined with stone and iron pots on a bed of stone. After all the searching and the hunting and connecting of the pieces, she'd found the place they'd been looking for. Beale's chamber. And if she'd found the chamber she'd found the treasure. And if she'd found the treasure then maybe there was something here that would tell them how to get to Avalon.

But something was wrong.

Brodie narrowed her eyes. She pointed the torch towards the iron pots. She remembered the words of the Beale Papers as they described the treasure. *The above is securely packed in iron pots, with iron covers. The vault is roughly lined with stone and the vessels rest on solid stone.* It was as she saw. Everything as he'd described.

Only one thing was different.

Resting, discarded against the lip of the step, all around the base sections of the pots, were large iron discs. They must be lids.

Brodie lifted her feet one at a time up the stone step and rested her weight against the nearest pot.

Now she understood what she was seeing and the desolation she felt was worse than when she'd first fallen into the hole.

The iron lids had been removed because someone had been here before.

Brodie clung to the rim of the nearest container. She peered into the darkness.

The pot was empty.

Someone had found the vault before them and had taken the treasure away.

She closed her eyes and a single tear leaked from the corner of her eye.

There was a rumbling noise as if the earth was responding to her sadness. The cavern shook. The walls of the chamber shuddered. And then there was a burst of brilliant light.

A voice broke through the silence.

She was no longer alone.

* * *

Kerrith ignored the ringing of the phone. She'd got used to doing that. At first it worried her. Her hand had hovered over the receiver and she'd battled with herself not to answer. Now she barely heard the air cracking with the sound of the ring.

It'd been two days since she'd returned from Site Three. The memory was still raw. Much against the wishes of the junior worker in the control room she'd returned to Hantaywee's room. She hadn't told her why she was there. She hadn't explained that she arrived and left of her own free will. She'd just listened as the woman talked about the years of separation from her family and her friends. And it was this final word which hurt Kerrith most.

She'd known it when she first saw the grainy image of Hantaywee on the monitor in the control room, but seeing her in the flesh, talking and crying about all she'd been through, forced it all to make sense.

Hantaywee was her friend.

It'd been years, decades even, since Kerrith had used that word. Life in Level Five had made it pretty much impossible to have friends. If she wanted success then friends were unnecessary.

But Hantaywee had come from a different time. A different life.

Kerrith had studied hard at school and a place at Oxford or Cambridge had been her dream. But her father wanted his daughter to explore the world. To stretch her wings. As a family, then, they'd decided the University of Virginia was the place for adventure. An exciting university with all the thrill of a home from home was what drew Kerrith there. And it made sense she should make friends with the Native American Sioux student Hantaywee, the first of her family to take up a place at university. The teenagers, so far from home, shared a room and they shared three years of laughter and support. It seemed their friendship would last forever. But a great body of water between England and the States and the need to succeed in her career made Kerrith lazy where friends were concerned. And after the trauma with her father, somehow the memory of a time spent in America at his suggestion seemed too painful to remember. She and Hantaywee lost touch. She hadn't even known her friend had married.

Now she understood the feeling she'd felt as she'd first stared at the screen. Site Three was the pinnacle of all Kerrith wanted to know about. It was the ultimate secret. The basis for all the Suppressors did and would do. For her friend, it was a prison. Since first seeing Hantaywee there, Kerrith hadn't been able to think straight. What Level Five did was right. It was good. It had to be. It was about control and about order. It was . . . She wasn't sure she could finish the sentence in her mind.

Kerrith drew in a deep breath and lifted the lid of a small wooden box she'd brought down from the loft. A tiny misting of dust lifted from it but she didn't wrinkle her nose in disgust. The papers inside the box were old and tatty. Photographs, notes, drawings. And letters. Kerrith's hand started to shake a little. Hantaywee had explained she'd once found a letter which changed everything for her. A letter written to her great-grandfather-in-law asking for help to read some coded papers. The letter had to be connected to MS 408. Kerrith knew it. And what Hantaywee had read in the reply to that letter made her dangerous to all those with power. When she'd told someone what she'd read, they'd reported her. Whatever her great-grandfather-in-law had written in his reply had been so powerful it caused Hantaywee to be taken from her family. Could words really be that strong?

Kerrith rested her hands on the papers in the box. Were there words written here which could be as effective? Something which had drawn her to the box full of memories told her yes.

It took a while until she found it. It was on yellowed

paper stamped with a crest. The crest of a secret society based at Virginia University. Kerrith ran her finger across the raised seal.

The letter was from Hantaywee. It was the reason they'd first found each other and become friends. It was a letter of welcome and support. The Z Society chose each year to write such letters to those on the campus who they felt might need encouragement and help. Kerrith held the letter. And for the first time in years she remembered what it felt like to be alone and in a new place and afraid. She remembered what it felt like to be searching for answers.

After she'd received that letter, everything felt different. Virginia felt like home. She'd felt like she belonged. Someone was looking out for her. It'd been such a simple thing. So simple, the complications of life once she'd got back to England had made her forget. But she remembered now that when she'd needed a friend, Hantaywee had been there.

The air was heavy.

And the phone had finally stopped ringing.

12

The Sword in the Stone

'Thank the frozen chicken nugget you're alive!'

Brodie felt a surge of relief wash over her as if she was being lifted up on a wave. Her voice bubbled in her throat. She wasn't sure what she said or if the words made sense, but she reached through the blazing light and held on to Hunter as if he'd saved her, yet again, from drowning.

His arms locked and for a moment he held her. Then suddenly he pushed her forward, needing to see her more clearly. 'What in the name of all that's full of chocolate did you do? Don't you ever, ever do that again, d'you hear me!'

Brodie tried to explain she'd absolutely no intention of ever falling down a shaft in the ground again, but before the words could leave her lips, more arms were around her. It was Tusia, holding her tight, and then Sheldon, then Smithies. And then Friedman. And with their attempts to hold her came questions. No, she didn't know how far she'd fallen. And no, she wasn't sure how far she'd walked underground. And she was sorry if she'd scared them but she'd been scared too. And yes, her side hurt loads. And it was as she explained about the pain in her side that her legs began to buckle and she sank down to the ground.

'Here.' Smithies offered her some water and then Friedman removed his jumper and tied it around the wound in her side. He said nothing but with each touch of his bandaged hands, Brodie knew he was doing all he could to try and make everything better.

'How d'you find me?' she said at last.

Hunter gestured to the huge stone they'd rolled away from the opening. 'Exactly where the map and code said it'd be. You must have fallen into a shaft that other people used to try and get to the treasure.'

Brodie ached and it had nothing to do with the pain in her side. 'It's gone,' she said quietly.

Hunter moved slowly to his knees and then pushed himself to stand. 'All of it?' he said.

Brodie nodded her head slowly in answer. 'Beale's treasure was here. It isn't any more.'

No one spoke. But Brodie felt another hand slide into her own. She turned her head. Tusia held tightly to her.

All that work and the searching and the solving of the puzzles. It had brought them here. And here was empty.

'Who could have taken it?' Tusia asked.

'Someone from Level Five, perhaps. Someone else who knew about the code,' said Sheldon.

'I really thought we'd find a map here, showing us how to get to Avalon,' said Tusia. 'That hope's gone now too.'

No one answered her.

After a moment, Hunter began to walk. He lifted the discarded iron lids and put each one on the empty iron vessels as if he was trying to make things look better somehow. At the replacement of each lid, the empty iron rang out like a death bell tolling.

Brodie couldn't watch.

But as Hunter approached the final iron container, he hesitated.

The iron lid slid from his grasp and hit the ground. It twisted, round and round, and then it fell flat.

A cloud of dust plumed up into the air.

It was only when the cloud had cleared, Brodie could see what Hunter saw.

'You all right? You look a little peaky.'

Tandi smiled meekly at Fabyan. He was doing his best to try and help her focus but even he had to admit they weren't getting very far. Kitty had given up long ago and left them in the windmill and gone into the main lab building for a rest.

'Cup of hot chocolate. Something stronger? Nickel for your thoughts even,' he said.

Tandi didn't know where to begin. She'd felt unnerved really all the time they'd been in Virginia but she was even more nervous here at Riverbank Labs. She'd told Brodie that following things up was what she cared about. But after the strange email she'd picked up on her phone, she was terrified. Eight words. But enough to shake her world. *Hacking into computers is dangerous for your health.*

'Here,' said Fabyan, taking something from table. 'Jon brought this with us from Station X. Helps us to connect the work we do here with the work we did there. Reminds us about the codes and the secrets and the puzzle of MS 408 always being important.'

On his hand he held a small wooden statue of an elephant. The Jumbo Rush Elephant from Bletchley Park.

'You remember the story?' Fabyan said. 'About how

the elephant sat on the table reminding everyone in the war that the codes they were cracking were important.'

Tandi remembered the story well.

'It helps me to think about that. To see our part in the team, even if we're not hunting for treasure, as being vital. Take it, seeing as you're feeling nervy. It'll help you remember we're all connected.'

Tandi knew that was true. But it didn't stop her being scared.

Brodie stood shoulder to shoulder with the others and tried to make sense of what she saw. If you were looking for treasure and you'd found an underground cavern filled with gold and jewels, why would you walk away before you'd taken the greatest find of all?

'It's beautiful,' breathed Tusia.

The cloud of dust which had hidden Hunter's find began to thin. It wasn't hidden now. It was there in front of them, jutting out of the stone step between two of the empty iron pots. The hilt of a small sword.

Brodie had seen many beautiful things before. She'd never seen anything like this.

The hilt formed a cross, sparkling with the most brilliant gold. Pressed into the gold were gems breaking the light into every colour of the rainbow, and around each gem was lacework of gold which looked as fragile and as delicate as spun sugar. The hilt spread its arms wide as the blade of the sword plunged into the rock.

'A sword in a stone,' said Brodie. 'Like the one Arthur found.'

The air prickled with excitement.

'Do you think this sword's Excalibur, then? Arthur's sword from Avalon?' said Smithies.

'If this is a sword of Avalon and it's been pressed into the stone, then that's why it's still here,' Tusia said quietly.

'Because of the legend of the sword in the stone,' Brodie said. 'Everyone knows the story. King Arthur had two important swords. One was given to him by the Lady of the Lake which had been forged in Avalon. And one he took as the mark of him being the true king. The legends are confusing. Perhaps the two swords were really one or perhaps they were very different. But the one which marked him out as king was stuck in a stone.'

'And you think the people who took the treasure away left the sword behind because . . .' Hunter held his hands out in question.

'Well, the legend says the sword in the stone can only be pulled out by someone who's worthy of being king.'

'Not just anyone, then?' Hunter looked thoughtful

and stepped forward even closer to the stone.

The gems on the hilt glistened in the light like water and oil playing with the spectrum. Colours filled the cave. The blade was pressed tight into the solid stone. It disappeared out of sight, not even a chink of light showing how deep the blade was plunged. There was no give, no movement. The blade was stuck fast.

'I can't believe they left it,' said Sheldon.

'Well, the legend makes it clear. If you're not the true ruler, you can't get the sword.'

Sheldon folded his arms. 'OK. I get that. The legend says the sword's not going anywhere. So it isn't.'

Hunter stood beside him. They looked at the sword almost longingly and then they turned away.

'We should get you back,' said Smithies, changing the subject. 'We need to get your side looked at. You might need stitches.'

Brodie let Friedman put his arm around her. She leant on him to let him take her weight. Hunter picked up the extra bags. There was no moaning this time, but Brodie could feel everyone's disappointment.

She couldn't believe they'd come this far and would be going back empty-handed.

And then something deep inside Brodie began to stir. She lifted her hand from her bloodstained side and she clutched the stone pendant hanging around her neck. All sorts of ideas seemed to be bouncing around in her head.

She remembered the time on the steps at Virginia University and the student Caitlin explaining things to her. How it was important to keep thinking like a child. It had seemed such a silly to say but something about the idea just wouldn't go away.

'I would have tried it,' she blurted.

'Tried what, B?'

'I would have tried to pull the sword from the stone. When I was younger, I mean, I would have just had a go and I think I'd have believed I could free it.'

Everyone was looking at her.

'Adults wouldn't, would they? They'd look stupid if they tried. But for kids it would be OK.'

'You reckon you could get the sword out of the stone, B?'

'I think anyone could, who had a go and believed they could.'

'But what about the legend? You're the one who believes in stories.'

'Maybe that's one version of the story. But there could be others.'

She stepped away from her dad and stood at the edge of the step. Then she locked her hand tightly round the hilt, and pulled.

The air shuddered and the ground shook. And the sword rose freely, out of the stone.

'I need to tell you something.'

Hantaywee lifted her head. Her eyes seemed cloudy as she waited for Kerrith to speak again.

Over the last two weeks, Kerrith had made many visits to Site Three. The Director had been encouraged by her enthusiasm for their work there and took this as the explanation for her frequent absence from the office. She'd spoken to several of the MS 408 detainees and listened to their stories. Mr Willer had told of his anger, Evie had spoken of her fear, Miss Longman only of her despair. But with Hantaywee, Kerrith had talked only of the past and of the stories they shared. They spoke of the late evenings chatting in their dormitory, of the terrible food served to them from the university refectory, of the tutor who dozed through their tutorials. Kerrith hadn't meant to talk about these things. She'd meant to be honest from the beginning, but the stories began to reknit a connection between them. The stories of the past were what gave Hantaywee strength. She'd nothing else left.

Kerrith knew the moment had come. She ran the tip of her finger along the end of her thumbnail. It was jagged but she allowed her finger to run back and forth.

Then she took a deep breath and began to explain. 'I'm not here for the same reasons as you, Hantaywee.'

The other woman narrowed her eyes.

'I wasn't brought here, like you, against my will. If I wanted to leave this place now and never return, then I could.'

Still the other woman didn't move.

'You're a prisoner here and . . .' Kerrith fumbled for the words, '. . . I'm on the other side.'

'Side?'

'I'm part of *them*,' Kerrith said, waving her arms at the hidden cameras she knew lined the walls high above them. 'I'm one of the people who allows this place to exist; who tracks down people to bring here; who works to keep this place maintained.'

The other woman lifted her hand from the desk and rested it awkwardly in her lap. 'Why?'

In the uttering of that one word, Kerrith knew Hantaywee had known all along. She'd known from the beginning Kerrith was on the side of the jailers. She'd not been fooled for a moment. And the only thing she wanted to know, the only question she asked was 'why?'.

Kerrith didn't know how to explain. The words she'd practised in her head didn't sound right but she blurted them out. 'Because it was what I was trained to do. What happens here is part of the world I've joined and I didn't question whether it was right or wrong. I'm good at it. It makes me happy.'

The words sounded ridiculous.

'Taking people away from their families and preventing them from asking questions and finding out truths makes you happy?' Hantaywee said sorrowfully.

'I do what I'm told, to make sure things are under control.'

'Whose control?'

'Those who run the unit where I work. I do what I do because they asked me to. And when I do what I'm asked, it makes me feel good. Like I belong.'

Hantaywee lowered her gaze. 'Whose control?' she said again.

'The control of those in charge.'

'And are those in control *right*?'

'I don't know if they're right. But they're in charge.' Kerrith's voice shook. 'Without them there'd be chaos. Someone has to decide what people should think and what people should know. There has to be a right way to see things.'

'My people build their lives on stories, Kerry,' Hantaywee said slowly. 'Here's a story for you from your own people. Your own history.' She sat herself up straight. 'When the peoples of the earth were few they all spoke with one language. They had understanding of each other and they used this understanding to begin to build a huge tower. The tower of Babel. But the creator looked down and saw that in understanding each other they had immense power. He didn't like this. So he divided the languages of the people so they'd no longer understand each other and this scattered the peoples and the tower was left unfinished. In our understanding of each other we had power. But if we choose not to try and understand the different stories we have, we'll never find again the common ground.'

'I don't understand,' Kerrith mumbled.

Hantaywee leant forward and her eyes seemed suddenly clear and unmisted. 'There are many different stories, Kerry. There's no one right way of seeing the world.' She waited for a moment. 'In the letter I found to my great-grandfather-in-law I understood there are other stories out there which need to be heard, but the people you work for, the people you follow, brought me here to make sure my story was never shared. Can that be right, Kerry?'

Kerrith pressed her hands together. If she agreed with her friend then everything she'd done over the last few years and months, everything she'd tried so hard to achieve would count for nothing. It would have been wrong. Her mind swirled. 'But I did what I did because . . .' She couldn't finish the sentence.

In the silence engulfing her there was one more thing Kerrith needed to know. One more thing she wanted to ask. 'This letter,' she said at last. 'About the encoded documents. Who was it written to? Who was your great-grandfather-in-law?'

'Fabyan,' Hantaywee said quietly. 'Colonel George Fabyan of Riverbank Labs, Illinois.'

For a while they just sat and looked.

A beautiful sword, drawn from a stone, in an abandoned treasure vault in the middle of the Blue Ridge Mountains. Eventually, Sheldon took it. He twisted it over in the light. Its surface was like a mirror reflecting back his wondering eyes.

'D'you think it's a sword from Avalon?' said Friedman.

Brodie wanted it to be.

Sheldon bent his knees and put the sword down on the ground. Dust lifted again like wisps of smoke around the blade and it was as the dust was settling, a grey frosting on the golden blade, Brodie saw letters engraved on the sword.

PIGAFETTA

A series of memories and pictures began to collide in her mind. She was back at the Library of Congress. She was back at the pictures of Prometheus and the theft of fire and the writing written below the scene. And she saw the letters raised and pronounced against the wall surrounded by pictures of branches. Letters which meant nothing then. But which meant everything now.

Not PGITAFETA but PIGAFETTA. The name written on the sword.

'Pigafetta,' she said. 'The name's Pigafetta. The bit in the red fox message about Admiral Cockburn and the letters. We knew that was important. Remember? And then we saw the raised writing on the wall of the Library of Congress. We were supposed to see *this* name. Pigafetta's name. That's what we were meant to see.' She stopped gabbling and waited. 'We need to find out who Pigafetta was.'

'So we've got something to go on, then,' Tusia said. 'We've no other treasure and we've no map. But we've got a name. It might be the most important thing of all.'

And they might have left then and clambered from the vault and made their way through the early morning light and back to the inn, if Hunter hadn't repeated Tusia's words. '*It might be the most important thing of all.*' And pulling up from the depths of his memory fragments which needed to be remembered, his mouth began to bubble with new words. They tumbled from his mouth in a cascade of nonsense and confusion.

'Hunter, please.' Smithies' arms were around his shoulders and he was begging him to calm down.

'The Firebird Code,' Hunter blurted. 'We thought we'd found nothing, only ash. But we'd found everything we needed. The scabbard. It's *always* the scabbard! We knew that before and we've forgotten! When Merlin gave Excalibur to Arthur he said it was the scabbard for the sword which was the most important. *That's* where the power came. The source of true invincibility was hidden. Remember.'

'I remember,' said Brodie. 'But I don't see how that helps us now.'

Sheldon held the sword in his hand. The blade sung in the air.

'The stone's the scabbard. It's the case of the sword.' Hunter drew in a breath. 'The answer's in the stone.'

From behind them, Friedman stepped forward. He took the rucksack from his back and he discarded the torch and the rope and took out instead a hammer with a huge metal head. Then he raised the hammer and thumped it down against the stone. The hammer bounced. He couldn't hold it. So Brodie stepped forward and linked her hand over her father's bandaged ones. Together they lifted the hammer against the stone and it juddered and it cracked. And with the final blow the rock splintered like rotten wood.

'The fire's always still inside,' she said and they all knew the answer was inside the stone waiting to be freed.

Friedman bent down and tried to lift the find from the broken fragments of the rock. His fingers wouldn't do as he wanted and so Brodie knelt down beside him. 'Let me,' she said.

Amongst the crumbled rock and dust was a small, yellowed scroll of paper.

She moved back so everyone could see.

She wanted it to be the thing they'd been looking for since the adventure began. A key to understanding MS 408. Maybe a guide to the words.

Brodie unrolled the scroll.

It was a map!

She ran her finger across a name printed small and neat in the far corner under a picture of a griffin. The name of the cartographer; the maker of the map. Martin de Judicabus. It was a name she recognised from the Knights of Neustria ring.

Maybe he'd been an original Knight of Neustria

connected somehow to Pigafetta, the name on the sword. Maybe they were two of the very first knights. A name marked with a griffin and a name marked with a tree. Maybe they'd worked together to leave clues that would finally lead to Avalon.

The Stone in the Sword

Brodie often thought it odd that travelling back from a place took less time than the journey there. The walk through the woods to reach the vault had taken hours and they'd stumbled along in the dark. It seemed to take them hardly any time at all walking back through the early morning sun.

They took it in turns to carry the sword. Hunter swung it in his hand, Tusia carried it as if it was a holy offering and when it was Sheldon's turn, Brodie was sure he made the blade sing on the wind like an exotic hand-carved instrument.

No one else took turns to carry the map. Brodie held it tightly in the hand not pressed against her side.

Back at the Inn, Mrs Smithies took charge of Brodie's

injury. Somehow that too didn't look so bad in the light. Mrs Smithies washed it and smeared some cream on to the wound. This made it sting and burn so much the relief from when the effect of the cream wore off made Brodie sure her side was much better. Mrs Smithies seemed to glow with the pride of having helped and she sat next to Brodie as they gathered round the table to eat and then talk about all they'd found.

'So someone else got to the treasure, then,' said Granddad, taking a sandwich from the plate Hunter offered in his direction. 'And the iron pots were empty?'

'Totally cleaned out. The whole place had been stripped of everything,' said Tusia. 'Except for the sword.'

Granddad finished his mouthful of sandwich then reached across the table to where the sword lay.

'And you think it's really from Avalon?' The sunlight reflected on the patterned blade.

'It would be so great if it was,' said Brodie. 'And there's the story connection about it being in the stone. That's just like Arthur's sword, Excalibur. And that was made in Avalon. It really *could* be from there, couldn't it?'

There was no answer, as if no one wanted to sound too sure.

Tusia reached out for the hilt of the sword. 'These stones are beautiful. They look like the stones on this ring.' She moved her hand so the Knight of Neustria ring twinkled in the light. 'And they look kind of similar to the stone in your necklace, Brodie.'

Her granddad leant forward. 'Your mother sent that for you to have when she was gone that very last time,' he said quietly.

'D'you think they're connected?' Brodie asked. 'This necklace and the sword and the ring? How could that be?'

'Only if your mother found the necklace when she was finding out about MS 408,' said Friedman. 'Is that possible?'

'She didn't have the necklace when she went away to Belgium. She could have found it there. She found out things about MS 408 she never got to tell us,' said Mr Bray.

Brodie took off the locket and let it swing freely on the chain. The light broke and shattered into pieces, burning white then pink then blue. Brodie held the pendant in the palm of her hand and clicked the locket open. Inside was the picture taken from MS 408 her mother had added to remind her what the search was for. Brodie stared at the intricate drawing. Then she tucked her nail behind the paper, easing it free. Never once had she looked under the picture. But now the picture was free she could see a name engraved on the back of the silver casing for the stone. Brodie squinted, trying to see more clearly. The script was tiny but the letters were clear. Everyone was waiting.

'What does it say, B?'

'Hans Barge of Aachen.'

Friedman let out a sigh. Sicknote leant back from the table and Smithies clapped his hands together.

'Who's he?' said Kitty.

'The man who rescued the copy of *Morte D'Arthur* and kept it safe when Savonarola wanted to burn it. The Firebird Code led us to that book. He was a Knight of Neustria. And maybe, somehow, he's connected to Martin de Judicabus and Pigafetta. Maybe the three of them represent the phoenix and the griffin and the tree.'

'And you had the stone with you all the time,' said Friedman. 'Your mother must've known. Perhaps she'd worked it out.'

The thought made Brodie feel hot inside. 'Just like I'd got the middle name Elizebeth all along and should have worked out the connection with you and your mother and my grandmother's name. I wore Hans's stone all the time and never knew.'

Friedman's eyes sparkled. 'Sometimes the most

wonderful knowledge is there for us to find if we look right in front of us.' His bandaged fingers slipped up to the silver key he wore around his own neck but Brodie knew he was talking about more than answers to codes.

'And so, let me get this right,' said Sheldon. 'These three Knights. These particular Knights of Neustria. We think they may be even more important than all the others?'

'There's definitely something special about Hans and Martin and Pigafetta,' said Brodie. 'Whoever they were.'

'And the sword. We still believe it comes from Avalon?' cut in Kitty.

'Seems likely,' said Hunter. 'Don't you think? Perhaps it came from Avalon and was taken on the *Covadonga*. Then, when the ship was captured, it was taken as part of the treasure to England and then Thomas Jefferson Beale hid it in the vault in the mountains.'

'So you think the sword was taken by Lord Anson when he captured the ship?' asked Sicknote.

Brodie mulled the question over. 'He took the treasure like a pirate. It's a pirate's sword.'

'A pirate's sword forged in Avalon,' whispered Tusia. 'Perfect.'

Brodie felt more heat spread through her body.

Knights of Neustria
Hans Barge of Aachen
Phoenix
Martin de Judicabus
Griffin
Pigafetta
Branches
Power of 3!

'And if we've got a pirate's sword, we've also got a map,' she said.

There was a charge of expectation on the air.

'And can you read the map?' said Granddad.

'Not really,' she said at last. 'It seems to show a huge sea and loads of small islands and until we know exactly where the map's set we'll have trouble finding the location.'

'But you're smiling,' mused Mrs Smithies.

'I'm smiling because that never stopped us before. We've got a map to Avalon and a coded book all about it. And at the moment, we can't make sense of either of them.' She laughed and the pain in her side pulsed. 'But we're the greatest code-cracking team who ever lived. We'll find the answers. That's what we do.'

The plane was coming in to land. The pilot had announced everyone should refasten their seat belts but the Director had little time for such instructions. His belt flapped open against the seat leg.

On the table tray in front of him was a pad of white paper. Clean, uncrumpled pages. Just as he liked them. Yet he'd failed to resist the urge to doodle. The large letter 'K' he'd written again and again across the page was now an irritation to him. And his annoyance intensified.

He traced the letter 'K' once more with the tip of his pen and scowled. What was it about her which annoyed him so? Probably her weakness. He sucked the end of the pen and pressed his teeth against the metal casing. She'd promised so very, very much. Her commitment had been undoubted. She'd made a promise to the cause and he was so totally sure she'd carry through with all he'd given her. The pen rattled against his incisors. But there'd been warnings. The merest seed of doubt. But just enough to destroy her from within. Despite all the effort and the pretence, she'd cared too much. She'd wanted friends. It had been only the tiniest of flaws. One he'd been willing to overlook and one, until now, he was sure she'd kept firmly in check. Because that's what she'd been told to do. To keep things in check. Whatever the cost. She was to do what was needed.

The Director put the pen down on the pad. It rolled back and forth as the plane engine growled. From the window he could see they were banking. The sky lifting and falling as the crew channelled the energy needed to bring the plane down to the ground. The pilot harnessing all the skill of his training to direct the great vessel towards its location.

A ripple of excitement fluttered through the Director's chest. It was good this time to be 'hands on'.

To be fully involved. And after all, there was occasion to celebrate. The news had been good. And this time, at last, the plans might be followed to the letter and all he hoped for might finally come to pass.

He sat back in the chair and leant against the headrest, and the nose of the plane lowered like a dart. The earth rushed past, the ground reached up and in seconds, the wheels were churning on the tarmac and the wings lifted to resist the air funnelling around them.

The Director rubbed his neck then reached into his bag. The number he needed was on speed dial. There was no answer, though. The Director killed the call and the phone light flashed to dark. Kerrith was still unwell. This news made the Director angry. But it didn't change his plans. What needed to be done would still happen. This time he'd do it. The Group had been insistent. The latest scroll from them had made it clear. This time there could be no let-out. No middle ground. It was all or nothing now. The amateurs had to learn.

Tandi had been thrilled to hear the news. She'd finally got news of her own, she explained. Things she needed to tell them as soon as they got back to Riverbank.

They drove through the night in a people carrier

Fabyan had hired for them. It was infinitely more comfortable to travel in than the Matroyska, so Brodie was able to sleep. The pain in her side was just a nagging ache now. Mrs Smithies had made sure the wound was dressed correctly and seemed particularly proud of Brodie's rate of healing. The woman seemed comforted too, as if she was discovering, for perhaps the very first time, things could be damaged and not broken. That repair was sometimes possible.

'It might scar,' said Friedman.

Brodie understood. 'And your hands?'

'They won't ever be as they were. But that's OK.'

'Is it?'

Friedman allowed a smile to flicker across his mouth. 'I gained more that day than I lost, Brodie. Much more.'

They sat next to each other then, in silence. But it was a comfortable silence created by the knowledge that the thing they looked for, the thing which brought them together, was closer than ever before. It was in reach now, tantalisingly close.

'What date is it?' said Hunter, calling from the back.

'You sound like Thomas Jefferson,' said Sheldon.

'Really,' said Hunter. 'How d'you work that one out?'

'Well, today's the fourth of July,' he explained. 'The

day Americans celebrate the signing of the Declaration of Independence. It's also the date Thomas Jefferson died.'

Tusia leant forward to hear more clearly.

'Jefferson died on the fiftieth anniversary of the signing of the Declaration.'

'That's kind of neat and tidy,' said Sicknote, obviously impressed.

'Yeah, well I guess that's what Jefferson thought – apparently his last words were to check he'd made it to the fourth of July before he finally gave up and died.'

'And the fourth is a big deal for Americans, then?' asked Brodie.

Granddad seemed to speak from experience. 'A whole weekend of partying usually. Great food and celebrations.'

'And fireworks?' Sheldon pressed on.

'Yeah, fireworks,' he added.

Sheldon smiled nervously. 'Oh, good.'

'Good, why?'

'Because I thought for a moment I could see fire on the horizon in the direction of Riverbank Labs. And that freaked me out. But if you think it's fireworks then all's good!'

Brodie rubbed a circle with her hand on to the misted window and peered out into the distance.

Despite the heating, she felt a little cold. There *was* fire on the horizon. The sky was orange. But it had to be Independence Day celebrations, surely. She rubbed again at the window. If it wasn't that, then what else could it be?

Life can change in a heartbeat. Brodie knew that. You could be walking along one day and the earth could give way under you just when you least expected it. She knew that too. But there was something particularly chilling about when you're watching something and think you're seeing one thing, when in fact you're seeing something totally different.

Once, when Brodie was very young, she'd seen a man running across the road. He'd run straight towards a woman and pushed her hard to the ground. Brodie had screamed. The man was attacking the woman. Her granddad needed to do something. But then as Brodie watched, a pile of slates and roof tiles stacked on some scaffolding above where the woman stood came crashing to the pavement. If she'd been standing where she had, the woman would have died. The man who'd pushed her out of the way had saved her life. He'd rescued her not harmed her. Once Brodie saw the whole picture she understood, and what she'd seen became rearranged and shuffled in her mind. Her mind was shuffling

307

images now as she pressed her forehead against the window and the vehicle pulled closer to Riverbank Labs.

Brodie had seen fireworks light the sky. An orange glow of celebration and victory of America's greatest day. But the shuffling of images in her head continued. Something about the image wasn't right. The sky wasn't flashing with colour. It wasn't sparking with jolts and bursts of well-managed light. The sky was burning. No longer orange. But blood red.

Something was very wrong.

There was movement in the sky but it wasn't from flashes and sparkles of well-controlled explosives. It was from the constant and unrelenting turning and whipping of flames.

Brodie's mind continued to shuffle. And only one explanation eventually made sense of what she saw.

Riverbank Labs was on fire.

The house and the outbuildings and the gardens were ablaze. And whipping through the air, carving the darkness with blades of flame, were the sails of Fabyan's windmill as it burnt.

The vehicle spluttered to a stop. The doors flung open and everyone tumbled out. Smithies tried to hold them back. Brodie heard a scream. It took her a while to realise it was her who was making the noise.

Smithies held his arms around her but she struggled and pulled against him. The flaming sails of the windmill thrashed at the sky.

And then Smithies could no longer hold her.

Brodie burst free and stumbled forward.

Sicknote and Friedman tried to call her back. Tusia and Hunter hurried forward, Sheldon straining to keep up.

But Brodie was still screaming as a man walked from the fire, his back bowed against the weight of the flames.

His clothes were blackened, his face smeared with soot.

Fabyan was alive. His home was burning. All he owned was being destroyed. But he was alive.

And he was carrying something in his hands. Not something. Someone. A body in his arms. And an arm, circled with silver bangles, hung free and swung loosely in the air.

Fabyan looked up. He shuddered and his knees buckled.

Behind him Riverbank's Tower of the Winds exploded with flame.

And then Brodie could see clearly. And however her mind tried to shuffle what she saw there was only one way to read the image facing her.

Tandi lay in Fabyan's arms. Her body was still, her limbs unmoving and her eyes gazing up unblinking at a blood-red sky which burnt with fire.

Tandi Tandari was dead.

14

In the Eye of the Storm

Tandi's eyes looked up at a sky on fire but she didn't see the flames. She was lying, her arms on the ground, her hair trailing behind her. Her body was still.

Brodie knelt beside her.

The earth was wet under her knees and she crumpled awkwardly so her hand brushed Tandi's arm. Her skin was warm.

Brodie was unsure who knelt beside her until bandaged hands reached out in front of her. Her father reached towards Tandi's face. He smoothed her eyelids closed. Brodie longed to shut her own eyes and block out all she saw, but she knew the image of the broken body would still be there in front of her whether her eyes were open or not.

'She was so brave,' whispered Fabyan. He reached inside her pocket and drew out the small wooden statue of an elephant. The Jumbo Rush Elephant. The symbol of battle which stood on the desk at Bletchley Park Mansion during the Second World War to remind them all they were involved in a struggle which cost them many lives and would cost them more. Brodie took the elephant. It was undamaged. Totally free of the traces of the fire, but it felt burning hot in her hand.

'What happened?' said Smithies.

'I don't know,' Fabyan spluttered. 'The fire came from nowhere. We'd made so much progress and then suddenly I looked up and saw the windmill and the sky was ripped apart with flames.'

'And Tandi?' Smithies pressed gently.

'She was inside. She stood no chance. By the time I got to the windmill the whole estate was ablaze.' He gulped back tears and wiped his face with the back of his hand, smearing soot across his cheek. 'They'd blocked the door. There was no way she could have escaped. By the time I . . .'

Mrs Smithies put her arm around his heaving shoulders.

'I was too late to save her,' he said.

* * *

'I'm so sorry.'

Kitty staggered from the husk of the windmill behind them; her face blackened, her hair flaked with ash like snow.

Brodie stumbled towards her. 'It's OK,' she blurted. 'It's not your fault. It's no one's fault.'

Kitty's body shook and then she crumpled, as if the air had been knocked out of her, and she slumped down to her knees.

'It's not your fault,' Brodie said again.

Kitty's body shook. Then she looked up and her eyes locked with Brodie's. 'I didn't know what they'd do.'

And in that moment, Brodie understood.

Suddenly, it was as if Brodie had been pulled back from the scene in front of her, dragged by her waist and suspended from the air so she could look down and see everything clearly. Like when she'd been a child and her grandfather had cradled her in his arms so she could see the tiles falling from the rooftop as the man pushed the woman to safety. Brodie saw the bigger picture.

A kaleidoscope of images swirled in Brodie's head. Snatches of phone calls; solitary walks; Kitty running her hand along the body of her motorbike; staying behind in New York.

There was a reason they'd been beaten to the treasure in the underground vault.

There was a reason for the fire.

The reason was Kitty.

Kitty pushed herself to stand, her body blocking out what feeble light there was. A shadow large across the sky.

'It was you,' Brodie said. 'You led Level Five to the treasure. You led them here.'

Kitty said nothing.

Tusia ran at her like a dog. Kitty tore through the carcass of the broken building, scuffing ash and soot in billowing clouds as she moved. Tusia's arms caught against the blackened beams and blood splattered on to the debris.

Brodie launched herself forward. She locked her hands around Kitty's shoulders. 'It was you!' she screamed again. 'It was—'

She didn't get to finish.

Hunter's hands were around her own, pulling her towards him. 'Let her go, Brodie! Let her go!'

'But she's one of them!'

Hunter held his arms around her own as Brodie fought to be free. But slowly the strength to struggle drained away.

'I didn't know,' Kitty pleaded. 'I just wanted to be

part of something. They offered me money and they made it sound important and all I'd got to do was keep them up to date with what we did and where we were.'

Brodie turned her head. She couldn't bear to look at her any more.

'I wanted to count for something,' Kitty said again.

'You did!' said Sheldon coldly. 'You counted with us. As a friend.' He was shaking his head as if he wanted to get rid of the memory. 'I persuaded them to let you stay!'

'I didn't know this would happen. I didn't—'

Tusia raised her hand to silence her. Blood trickled to her wrist.

'You should go.' Smithies' voice was totally calm. Brodie hadn't heard him walk through the rubble to join them, but he stood beside Friedman now, shoulder to shoulder in the dark.

'But—'

'We trusted you, Kitty. Made you part of our family here and now we're asking you to leave.'

'But—'

This time Smithies raised his hand.

And so Kitty turned and walked away.

It was dark and the Director could see nothing from the window of the plane. He took the document from his briefcase and put it down on the tray table. A series of photographs. The team from Bletchley. The bane of his life for over a year.

He took a pen from his jacket pocket and unclipped the lid.

He flicked through the pages until he found the photograph he wanted. Tandi Tandari. She'd put up quite a fight. But in the end he'd won. He would always win.

He scored two thick, crossed lines through the photograph, slipped the pen back inside his pocket and slid the document back into his briefcase.

He would try and sleep now. That was if the throbbing pain in his neck would go away.

'I just don't understand it.' Brodie stood inside the blackened carcass of the burnt-out windmill. The charred struts and supports like broken ribs pointing to the sky. The air was clogged with soot.

Smithies stood behind her. 'I know,' he said quietly.

Three days had passed since Tandi's death. Three days of confusion and chaos. Riverbank Labs was a shell of all it had once been, the buildings broken beyond repair. The animals which had escaped were being cared for at a nearby farm, and those who'd died in the fire, waited, like Tandi, to be buried.

'She had a large family, didn't she?' Brodie asked, thinking about how they'd be arriving for the funeral and suddenly ashamed about how little she knew.

'Tandi was adopted when she was very young,' Smithies said. 'Taken in by a wonderful couple. They adopted other children too. Tandi was particularly fond of her younger brother, Adam. That young boy will find her loss particularly hard to bear.' He folded his arms around his chest as if he was literally trying to hold himself together.

Brodie pressed a finger against the blackened strut of the windmill. Charred flakes of wood fell like black snow on to her feet. 'My dad knew we weren't really safe. He was too scared to tell me. Did you know they were watching?'

'Brodie, this is all so much more complicated than any of us ever thought.'

'But did you know?'

'Maybe I didn't want to believe it.'

'But my dad did?'

'He was scared. Being hurt does that to you.'

She didn't answer for a while. 'None of this makes sense,' she said at last.

'Isn't that true of everything we've done so far?'

Brodie turned the small wooden model of the Jumbo Rush Elephant over and over in her hand then plunged it back inside her pocket. Kitty had talked once about there being an elephant in the room. Something which was never discussed. And for three days no one had spoken of her disloyalty to the team. Brodie couldn't wait any longer. 'How could Kitty have done it? Betrayed us, I mean.'

'She did what she felt she had to do.'

'But to lead them to the treasure. To tell Level Five where we were.' Brodie found it hard to say the words. 'How could she have been working for them all along?'

'She was doing what she felt was best.'

'But how could that have been *best*? How could she possibly think she was on the right side?'

'The Suppressors do what they do because they believe they're doing the right thing. Kitty believed it was right to help them. They think that what we're doing, when we fight for answers and won't give up our search for the truth about MS 408, is misguided. That we're wrong not to bow down to the regulations. That we're wrong to want to know more. She believed in what she was doing just like we do. But we believe different things.'

Brodie scuffed the ground with her toes.

'Do you remember the quote carved in the stone above the Jefferson Memorial?'

Brodie wasn't sure she could remember anything

about the past few weeks with any sense of certainty.

'Jefferson said he'd fight against every type of tyranny over the minds of man. That's what suppression is. Tyranny. The Suppressors are trying to control what we think and what we read and they drew Kitty in. She needed to have something to believe in, just like us. But she believed in their message first.'

Brodie stilled her feet.

'We've got to make Tandi's sacrifice count, Brodie, otherwise it was all for nothing.'

'But what type of people could want Riverbank and Tandi to burn?' It still made no sense to her. 'When the Library of Congress burnt, the books were destroyed. When the rotunda at Virginia University burnt, the books were destroyed. What did the Suppressors aim to destroy here?'

'Our hope.'

'D'you think they knew Tandi was in the windmill when they set it on fire?'

'It'd have made no difference if they did.'

Brodie rubbed her hands together, staining her palms with ash. 'On Renata's monument back at Shugborough Hall, we worked so hard to find out what the words meant. '

'And?'

'It meant, *Truth conquers. The truth of Avalon*

suppresses shadow.' But I'm not sure it does any more.'

Smithies said nothing.

'Tandi died. How's that Avalon's truth suppressing shadow?'

'She died as part of a team in a battle, Brodie. Like your mother did. And their sacrifice can't be worthless. We must make sure they didn't give up their lives for no good reason. We've got to make their deaths count.'

'How?'

'By pressing on.'

'But it makes no sense any more. I don't understand how we can have lost Tandi to the fire. When our battle was *for* fire. When we were searching for phoenixes and things that survived the flames, how can this have happened? How can fire have taken her?'

Smithies lifted his palms skyward. 'It's a riddle, Brodie. All part of a puzzle. All part of the enigma and the confusion. How can something which brings good things be responsible for bad? But look at all the four major elements, Earth, Water, Wind and Fire. The earth provides us with crops and security, a place to build a home. But the earth can shift and shake under us. It can quake and in seconds houses and homes can be destroyed. Water too, our most basic need and the thing we can't live without. But look at those who lost their lives on the *Titanic*, all of them taken to a watery grave. And look at how even the air we breathe can be whipped up to form hurricanes and tornadoes which throw up disaster in their path.' He watched her take this thought in. 'It's the same with fire. It destroys and it changes and it burns and it weakens. It turns things to ash and snuffs the life from things. And yet . . . in the devastation of a bushfire, seedlings sprout and burst with life. Without the storing of the fire inside the tree, there can be no spark. Without the fire there can never be a phoenix.'

Brodie looked at the ashen lines marking her hands. Rivers of soot pressed into the life lines like pathways across her palms.

'Prometheus and the coyote stole fire from the gods. The fire gives them power. But it doesn't take away its danger. It doesn't mean there isn't any risk.'

'But the risk's too big?' Brodie sobbed.

'Maybe it is.'

They waited for a moment and Brodie tried to pull herself together. She was sad. She was angry. But she still had so much she wanted to know. 'Tandi told us once,' she said slowly, 'when she was teaching us, that when people first learnt to read, they saw it as magic. A power available only to the special few. So maybe we're just not strong enough for this magic. Maybe we aren't special enough to find Avalon.' She balled her hands into fists and pressed her forehead against the broken supports of the windmill.

'Perhaps,' Smithies said softly. He stepped forward and more ash lifted like clouds around his feet. The he reached into his pocket and pulled out a silver bracelet and held it in the flat of his hand. 'It was Tandi's,' he said. 'One of the many she wore. Take a careful look.'

Brodie didn't want to touch it.

'Please, Brodie,' he said quietly.

She reached out reluctantly. The bracelet was cold. Its surface smooth except where, in places, tiny shapes like letters had been pressed into the metal. She narrowed her eyes to see. 'What does it say?' she said.

'I don't know. Tandi didn't know. But look.'

Brodie peered in closer.

'It's figures and letters from MS 408. Glyphs taken from the book she longed to read.'

Brodie could see now, letter after letter, neatly entwined across the bracelet.

'Reading MS 408 was everything to Tandi. She wanted, more than anything, to understand the spark of magic which would make that possible and to find the place of magic that would lead to. And we're so very, very close now.'

Brodie didn't know what to say.

'I'm sure she'd want you to have it,' he said quietly,

holding the bracelet out to her.

Brodie waited for a moment. Then she closed her hand around the metal band.

'And I know something else.'

Brodie slipped the bracelet over her wrist and then looked up.

'I know she'd want us to go on. To take what she discovered and work with the answers we found in the cavern. But it has to be the team's decision. We need to take Tandi and lay her to rest. Then, as a team, we've got to decide what we do next.'

Epilogue

Tandi's coffin stood in the shadow of the broken windmill. Out of respect and a sense of duty, Fabyan had draped the casket in the American flag. 'She wasn't a US citizen,' he said, 'but she was a friend and the stars and the stripes seem appropriate.' Brodie wasn't sure she understood. The stars made sense to her, because of their connection to the phoenix constellation, but she didn't know about the stripes. 'By your stripes . . .' Fabyan said quietly, but it still made no sense to Brodie.

Very little of the past few days made sense, but it was as if a mist was slowly clearing. A picture coming in to view.

They were close to answers. They'd solved the Beale Papers, found the Pirate's Sword and discovered how three names from all the Knights of Neustria were somehow linked most closely with Avalon. Martin de Judicabus, Pigafetta and Hans of Aachen.

Brodie clasped tightly to her locket. One of three stones which had led them to a map. A map which, if they could only make sense of it, might lead them to Avalon.

Tandi's death had affected them all in different ways. Sheldon's harmonica had been unused, Hunter's appetite somehow checked, Sicknote's reliance on tablets diminished as if he wanted nothing to block out the pain, and even Tusia's tendency to boss them all around had slowed. Friedman spent ages on his own. He seemed afraid to talk, but Mrs Smithies had taken to speaking to everyone, checking they were OK. Maybe she feared one of them would break, Brodie thought, if she didn't use words to keep them bound together. Maybe she just wanted them all to know she cared. Maybe this time, at the loss of a daughter, she needed words to try and make sense of the pain.

Granddad had sat with Brodie all that first night. He'd held her hand. And somewhere, deep inside her memories of long ago, Brodie seemed to recall he'd done this before. Many, many, years ago. 'I'm sorry, Brodie,' he whispered, when he thought she was sleeping. And she guessed this was not just about Tandi.

It was for not telling the truth about Friedman too, and so she held his hand a little tighter.

In the morning, Brodie pressed her finger against the intricate engraving laced around the silver bracelet she wore on her wrist and then she closed her eyes. For the first time in days she didn't see Tandi's broken body in the darkness. Brodie breathed in deeply then she opened her eyes.

The destruction of the fire was all around them.

But above them a bird was soaring high, cutting a line through the clouds.

Brodie remembered the story of Lancelot, the most famous of all King Arthur's Knights of the Round Table. The story of how his home was ravaged by fire, his family destroyed. Abandoned, as a child, he'd been rescued by the Lady of the Lake and taken to a place of safety. There'd been nothing left for him but the secret world of Avalon.

The fire at Riverbank had claimed one of their team and destroyed their trust in another, but instead of making their search impossible, it somehow made the search more important than ever.

All there was left now, for all of those who remained, was Avalon.

AUTHOR'S NOTE

COLLECTORS OF CODES

As *Secret Breakers* continues I've had fun including lots of new codes.
I've also had the chance to develop the idea of code collectors.
Probably the most interesting code collector in history was Colonel
George Fabyan. We've heard about him before in the adventures but in
The Pirate's Sword we get the chance to explore Riverbank Labs where
the real Fabyan lived and worked and kept his collection of codes. It
was at Riverbank that Elizebeth and William Freidman worked on the
Shakespeare codes. And it was to Riverbank that the appeal was sent for
help with the code that underpins this episode in the adventure – the Beale
Papers. In 1924 George Hart asked Fabyan to help him break Beale's code
and find the treasure hidden in the mountains of Virginia. How incredible
that Fabyan and his team of code-crackers, including William and Elizebeth
Freidman, were connected to this American coding puzzle as well as to
Shakespeare's codes and MS 408. It was interest in the code collectors
as people which made me determined to include the Beale Papers in the
Secret Breakers adventure.

Riverbanks Lab, just like Bletchley Park Mansion, seemed like an
extraordinary place to live and work. When I heard that there was a full-size
windmill on the estate I was determined to send my characters there!
An American 'Tower of the Winds' seemed a great link to the *Secret
Breakers* story so far.

SECRET LOCATION

I've explained before that locations become characters in my mind. Like
the scene at the end of *Tower of the Winds*, I knew that *The Pirate's Sword*
would end at another 'Tower of light'. This gave me the chance to build in a

dramatic scene involving fire, an element which is so incredibly important to the whole plot of *Secret Breakers*. As well as fire, the idea of hidden secrets is vital to these stories and so the chance to include a whole secret city was too good an opportunity to miss. Site Three, the location used by the Suppressors in this episode, really exists. It has several names but is often referred to as Burlington. It is located 100 feet below ground in Corsham, Wiltshire, England.

The city was built in the 1950s, designed to keep up to 4,000 government officials safe if the UK suffered a nuclear attack. Britain's Emergency Nuclear War Headquarters would be here. There are over 60 miles of roads, underground hospitals, canteens, offices and laundries. There is even an underground lake. The site was built to be totally self-sufficient and a TV studio was installed so the Prime Minister could broadcast to the country if he needed to. Thankfully, the site never needed to be used for the purpose it was built so in December 2007 the site was officially decommissioned. As far as we know this vast underground city is now abandoned. This made it the perfect location for the underground activities of Level Five!

Check out HLDENNIS.COM for more information on the underground city, including a link to an interactive map!

AMERICAN LOCATIONS

For the first time in the *Secret Breakers* journey I was able to take Team Veritas overseas. Having visited New York and Washington in the USA there were locations I knew I wanted to include. The Wardolf-Astoria hotel made it possible to draw links to the Titanic disaster. John Jacob Astor IV had built the Astoria part of the hotel. He died aboard the Titanic and the investigation into the disaster in 1912 was actually held in the hotel. Tiffany's the jewellers and Ellen's Stardust Diner are also real locations in New York.

Moving the story on to Washington gave me the chance to include one of my favourite buildings: The Library of Congress. Along with the British Library, it is one of the two largest libraries in the world according to shelf space and number of books. The architecture and paintings are filled with hidden messages. The Grand Staircase inside the Great Hall is incredible. Built into its carving are everyday people about their work, e.g. an electrician, a student, a gardener. The staircase tells the story of people in all walks of life and gives value to all sorts of work and stories. I wasn't able to use this image in *The Pirate's Sword* but it influenced my writing of the story.

AMERICAN PRESIDENTS

Washington DC is full of monuments to past presidents. Part of the Library of Congress is housed in the Thomas Jefferson building so I knew he was an important president to include in my story. Jefferson really was nicknamed the Red Fox, he really did invent a new way of numbering books and his collection of books sold on to replace books that were burnt, really is on view behind glass in the Library of Congress. I was shocked to learn about the burning of Washington by the British Army in 1814. Also shocking was the true story that Admiral Cockburn insisted that every type letter 'C' was destroyed after the attack so that the newspaper, *The National Intelligencer*, could not accurately report his name in accounts of the destruction! Book burning is a theme that runs through the *Secret Breakers* adventure, and so is the idea that reporting and stories can be altered and adapted – so the actions of Admiral Cockburn are a perfect example of how difficult he made the truth to report!

EXCITING EVENTS FROM HISTORY

History and stories from the past shape the modern world we live in.

This idea is key to *Secret Breakers*. Many mistakes have been made in the past. And many great things have been attempted. In *The Pirate's Sword* we consider the impact of broken societies but we also get to think about attempts to build new societies. In 1794, the poet Samuel Taylor Coleridge and his friend Robert Southey came up with a plan for how people can live together and be valued and treated equally. The idea was based on the image of Utopia – a perfect, imagined place.

Little is known about Coleridge's plan for his 'Pantisocracy' as so much of what he wrote was kept secret.

Also secret was the Z Society at Virginia University. I love to include secret organisations in my stories and, just like the Cambridge Apostles, the Z Society really existed (and may still exist). Like any secret society it had its own rules, myths and stories. The organisation was founded in 1892 and only outstanding students could join. After graduation, members are allowed to wear Z Society rings. Interestingly, the society used to paint its symbol around the grounds, a bit like coded references to its existence. The letter Z really is painted on the stairs of the rotunda and it is seen as being extremely unlucky to step on it.

THE PERFECT CODE

In trying to make sense of the puzzle facing the Team in *The Pirate's Sword*, I mention Professor Robert Patterson who worked at both the University of Pennsylvania and the University of Virginia. He died in 1854. Patterson was extremely interested in ciphers and he regularly sent coded messages to Thomas Jefferson. One particular cipher he sent wasn't decoded until 2007. Patterson referred to it as the Perfect Cipher and it made use of the Declaration of Independence. Jefferson, of course, was one of the authors of this document and so its use by Patterson makes perfect sense.

Paterson is referred to briefly in *The Pirate's Sword*. However, totally central to the plot of the story is another real code that makes use of

The Declaration of Independence. The Beale Papers is one of the most famous codes in the world and its history as described in *The Pirate's Sword* is true.

Three Papers exist and only one is deciphered. The Papers are said to refer to the location of treasure hidden by Thomas Jefferson Beale in Bedford County, Virginia, USA. As of 2011, the estimated worth of the treasure hidden was said to be $63 million. It's no wonder that people have been battling for decades to try and decipher the other two papers.

The coding system used to decipher the Paper is relatively easy! Number every word in the Declaration of Independence. Then find the first number from the Beale Papers in the now numbered Declaration of Independence. Take the first letter of that word and that's the first letter of the hidden message.

For example, the first number of the Paper is 115 and the 115th word in the Declaration of Independence is 'Instituted'. This would give us then the letter 'I' for our secret message.

Over the page is a section of the Declaration numbered for you. You can have great fun writing secret notes taking numbers from this document. It might be that I've hidden a secret message somewhere in this book for you to find. I know how you like the idea of 'light being knowledge' and seeking answers... so have a good look around just in case there is a coded message hidden especially for you to find!

THE DECLARATION OF INDEPENDENCE

Here is a section of the Declaration of Independence numbered for the deciphering of the second Beale Paper. Why not have a go at writing your own message in code using these numbers.

When[1] in[2] the[3] course[4] of[5] human[6] events[7] it[8] becomes[9] necessary[10] for[11] one[12] people[13] to[14] dissolve[15] the[16] political[17] bands[18] which[19] have[20] connected[21] them[22] with[23] another[24] and[25] to[26] assume[27] among[28] the[29] powers[30] of[31] the[32] earth[33] the[34] separate[35] and[36] equal[37] station[38] to[39] which[40] the[41] laws[42] of[43] nature[44] and[45] of[46] nature's[47] god[48] entitle[49] them[50] a[51] decent[52] respect[53] to[54] the[55] opinions[56] of[57] mankind[58] requires[59] that[60] they[61] should[62] declare[63] the[64] causes[65] which[66] impel[67] them[68] to[69] the[70] separation[71] we[72] hold[73] these[74] truths[75] to[76] be[77] self[78] evident[79] that[80] all[81] men[82] are[83] created[84] equal[85] that[86] they[87] are[88] endowed[89] by[90] their[91] creator[92] with[93] certain[94] unalienable[95] rights[96] that[97] among[98] these[99] are[100] life[101] liberty[102] and[103] the[104] pursuit[105] of[106] happiness[107].

SECRET BREAKERS

Discover the world of the Secret Breakers.

For more information about H. L. Dennis
and the Secret Breakers visit

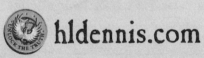 hldennis.com

You'll find competitions, code cracking lessons
and discover lots more secrets!

SECRET BREAKERS

REAL CODES. REAL MYSTERIES. REAL DANGER.

Sign up for the Secret Breakers newsletter and get exclusive news, brand new code cracking activities and lots of behind the scenes information about each book!

hldennis.com/mailing-list

TURN OVER FOR A SNEAK PEEK OF

CIRCLE OF FIRE

THE FINAL SECRET BREAKERS ADVENTURE . . .

The Director of Level Five of the British Black Chamber could still smell fire. This made him happy. He could still hear the blades of the windmill as they whipped the air with flame. The memory made the room spin.

He reached for his drink. The bar seemed far away and it took a while to grip the glass. And the room went on spinning. Odd that.

He loosened his tie and undid his top button. His neck throbbed and when he took his hand away the tips of his fingers were wet with sweat. Yet he felt cold. In fact he was shivering.

'You all right, mate?' The bartender was wiping the counter and the sound was excruciatingly loud. The Director looked up. He could see the bartender through the prism of the glass. There seemed to be lots of him, swirling and dancing, and the noise was getting louder. And the smell of the smoke was overwhelming now.

The Director leant forward. His drink slipped from his grasp.

'Mate, seriously? You don't look right.'

But the Director was always right. It was his job to be right. And he tried hard to concentrate on this thought as he fell from the bar stool and hit the ground. Shards of broken glass cut into his face and the last thing he saw before he closed his eyes was his own blood pooling with his spilt drink on the floor.

Kitty McCloud paid the cab driver then he waved her towards the entrance of a shabby hotel across the road.

The receptionist looked up from her paperwork. She wore a practised smile and pushed the chewing-gum into the side of her mouth. 'Can I help you?'

'A room for the night, please. And I need it to have a phone.'

The receptionist pulled a face, registering Kitty's accent. 'No international calls from the room. There's a pay-phone there.'

Kitty signed the check-in details and took the key she was offered. Once inside the small telephone booth beside the desk she emptied all the coins she had into the change tray. Then she took a folded card from her wallet. She didn't really need to check the number – she'd dialled it so many times before. But things were different now.

The phone rang six times. There was a click as if the call was being transferred to another line. A male voice answered. Not the voice she expected. 'Summerfield here. You have a report?'

Kitty clenched the receiver. She'd no idea what to say.

'McCloud? Is that you?'

Kitty's throat was so tight she could barely speak. 'They know,' she blurted.

There was a shuffle of papers and Summerfield spoke again. 'OK, if you've blown your cover I'm going to explain what we do now. You need to listen very carefully. The team from Station X might have worked out what you've been doing. But you can still be of use to us. We'll bring you home to London.'

It was the use of the word 'team' which made Kitty start to cry.

Brodie Bray was scared.

She held a small, very old book, filled with pictures and writing. But she couldn't read it.

Brodie Bray was good at reading. Most would say she was exceptional. She read all the time. But she couldn't read this, because the book was in code.

For over two years now, Brodie had been part of a team of children and adults trying to work out how to read MS 408, a book which Level Five of the government's Black Chamber had banned people from even looking at. They'd failed. And now things were getting really serious.

Someone had died.

Tandi Tandari had been Brodie's friend. More than that really, she'd been like an older sister. Brodie didn't have any brothers or sisters. She didn't have a mum and, up until several months ago, she hadn't even known her dad. Now her whole world had got mixed up. And she was scared.

When she'd been very young, her granddad, who'd raised her, had taken her to the local leisure centre. There were two pools. One was called the 'Fun Pool' and it was always full of toddlers thrashing about in armbands, teenagers hitting each other with floats and loud tinny music crackling through the sound system. Next door was the 'Diving Pool'. It was silent. Balanced above the unmoving water was a long, narrow blue board. It went nowhere, just stretched out into the cold, thin air. The board was five metres above the surface of the water. There were silver metal steps to the top. There was no handrail.

Brodie wanted to dive from the board. She wanted to plunge into the deep, dark water and curl her back like a mermaid and then burst through the surface and gasp for air.

But she was scared.

Her granddad stood beside the edge of the water. He reached out, as if he could almost catch her. And he talked to her. All the time, he kept talking. She could even remember what he said. Words of a poem she didn't quite understand. Words about being brave. *'Trust your heart if the seas catch fire; live by love though the stars walk backward.'*

Her toes curled around the lip of the board. Her skin looked so white and the water so far below was almost black with depth. If she could turn back from the end of the board she would. But turning would make her fall, she was sure. She wanted to lower herself down on to the board. Press her body flat against the support and cling to the edge, until someone came. But no one could. When you'd gone that far, there was only one way down. Diving. And her granddad's story said she should trust her heart.

So in that moment of fear, she moved herself forward through the air. The tipping point came. There was no changing her mind. And as she fell towards the water, any air she had inside her left her mouth in a scream.

The water wrapped around her. She wasn't sure where the surface was. It was dark. So cold it burned. But even in that moment, when the danger was more real than it had ever been on the top of the diving-board, she was no longer afraid.

It wasn't the water which was the source of fear. It was making the commitment to dive. It was being alone, launching off and letting go.

Now she was in the secret-breaking Team Veritas, Brodie was no longer alone. She had friends: Hunter and Tusia and Sheldon. And adults like Mr and Mrs Smithies and Ingham and Fabyan to help them. And now she had her dad. Friedman.

But they'd lost Tandi.

And that made Brodie feel like she'd done all those years ago on top of the diving-board waiting to dive.

Tandi died in a fire which raged through the grounds of Riverbank Labs and the most terrible thing was, she'd died because they'd been betrayed. They thought Kitty was on their side, but she'd let Suppressors working for the British government know where Team Veritas was. The Suppressors started a fire. Flames took Tandi and destroyed the estate. Only ash remained.

They buried Miss Tandari beside a tree in the

grounds. A small wooden cross marked the place. Brodie wanted them to build a large stone monument like the ones they'd seen in Westminster Abbey. This would take time, Fabyan said. Time to do things properly. So for the moment, two pieces of wood tacked together with a rusty nail were all that marked the place where Tandi fell.

Brodie came to the grave each morning and sat with the book and she tried to make sense of the pictures and words and all that had happened.

And she couldn't.